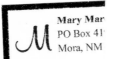

THE SONG OF JONAH

The Song of
JONAH

GENE GUERIN

UNIVERSITY OF NEW MEXICO PRESS ✛ ALBUQUERQUE

14   13   12   11   10   09   08   1   2   3   4   5   6   7

LIBRARY OF CONGRESS CATALOGING-IN-PUBLICATION DATA

Guerin, Gene, 1938–
The song of Jonah / Gene Guerin.
p. cm.
ISBN 978-0-8263-4336-9 (PBK. : ALK. PAPER)
1. Catholic Church—Clergy—Fiction.
2. Self-perception—Fiction
3. New Mexico—Fiction.
I. Title.
PS3607.U46S67 2008
813'.6—dc22

2008014743

Book and jacket design and type composition: Kathleen Sparkes
Jacket art: Mary Sundstrom
This book was designed and typeset using
Palatino OTF 10.5/14.5, 26P.
Display faces are Voluta and Engravers.

FOR RITA

Te quiero mucho.

Author's Note

There is no village called Nueve Niños on the northeastern New Mexican plateau. Neither is there a great caldera with its litter of nine stunted lava mounds. But there could be. Simply climb to the crater rim of the Capulin Volcano National Monument and look south across the Raton-Clayton volcanic field. There you will see an irregular necklace of conical hills that stretch far beyond the eye, reminders of a land that once shook and belched fire.

Chapter One

The word of Yahweh was addressed to Jonah son of Amittal:
"Up!" he said. "Go to Nineveh."

— The Book of Jonah 1:1

Among the clergy of the Archdiocese of Santa Fe, the reputation, both literal and in a manner of speaking, of
the remote parish of Nueve Niños was as a graveyard
for priests.

To begin with, a full dozen priests had died while in varying degrees of service to the people of Nueve Niños. The front yard
of the small church, dedicated to San Eusebio, contained the grave-
stones of five of these clerics. Relatives had claimed the bodies of the
other seven and interred them in family plots from Albuquerque to
Boston. Of those resting in the shadow of the church, one had succumbed to old age, two to heart attacks, one to a diabetic coma, and
one in a fire that burned the original rectory to the ground.

As for those who had been buried there in a manner of speaking—
the alcoholics, the pedophiles, the womanizers, the thieves, the eccen-
trics, and the unlucky—they survived Nueve Niños only to perish
elsewhere, for the most part in quiet and dignified disgrace. Their
markers in the San Eusebio graveyard were invisible but a presence
nonetheless.

In all, forty-one priests had stepped up into the pulpit of San
Eusebio from its establishment in 1877 to the early 1960s. At first

blush, the number should not startle. An average two-year term in an outpost parish was fairly typical for the archdiocese. However, when one considers that the founding pastor lived there for twenty-seven of those years and that the times when no priest was in residence totaled eleven more years, forty priests in forty-five years reflected an unsettling frequency of clerical attrition.

Nueve Niños sits in sullen isolation fifty miles from the Oklahoma border in the northeast corner of New Mexico. Here the Great Plains are at their most forbidding, six thousand square miles of clumping grasses, low mesas, and round hillocks leveling off into pure flatness to the east.

The town's only feature of note is its location by a crater lake some two miles across. In prehistoric times the lake had been the site of a gigantic magma chamber, churning and heaving like a woman in labor while it patiently built up its gasses for that instant when it would erupt into a full-fledged volcano. In the meantime it sent out stringers, nine narrow pipes of lava that broke to the surface in a cluster of parasitic cones. However, before their mother could rise to join them, her ceiling caved in and exposed her innards to the elements. Thus she died, as did her issue of nine open-mouthed brats. The caldera formed by the collapse of her dome eventually filled with water from a seeping aquifer, torrential rains, and renegade rivers and streams. The bodies of her children suffered eons of erosion from wind, water, and shifting landscape finally to form a nonuple of stunted, basalt-studded mounds. These were posthumously baptized "Los Nueve Niños" by a band of dislocated conquistadores. The ranchers and farmers who followed dropped the definite article but kept the rest of the name for the settlement they built there.

Father Jean Baptiste L'Cote, the first priest who came to the people of Nueve Niños, was French. He was born in a small village on the Plateau of Brittany by the Gulf of St. Malo from where his father and uncles plied the seas for fish. Fifteen years after he took the cloth, Father L'Cote was overcome with missionary zeal and volunteered to be a fisher of men in New Mexico. As his wagon train rumbled south on the upper branch of the Santa Fe Trail, the priest immediately fell into despair at the aridness of the place. He was sure that one day he would dry up into a pile of dust and blow away. To his delight, when he arrived for his assignment in Nueve Niños, he found a body of water to walk along, to sail around, and to fish. As an added dividend, he was in a place so isolated that he had the guarantee of autonomy. No bishop, no vicar-general, no chancellor, not even a fellow priest would be dropping in on him unexpectedly to nose into his affairs or those of his parish.

His first order of business was to build a church. He lived in the back storeroom of the general store until the church was finished and then moved into its sacristy until a proper rectory was raised alongside.

He soon came to appreciate that dirt farmers and cattle ranchers were no different from fishermen. What a stranger might take for brusqueness bordering on inapproachability in the citizens of Nueve Niños, he recognized from his own family of seafarers as a perpetual state of wary contemplation. Silence and reserve were necessities for those trying to read the mood swings of nature, she who held their livelihood and their very lives in a tight, unsentimental fist. In their turn the people grew to accept the priest, calling him Padre Juan. They determined that he was like them, a castaway on a landlocked island with no hope of rescue. What they never would understand was why he was always so happy there.

Aside from his priestly ministrations he added value to his presence in practical ways. He weaved his own nets from baling twine and built a flat-bottom, squared-prow boat to trawl the shallows along the shoreline. He gave of his catch to his parishioners—trout fresh from his boat as he came off the lake, and afterward salted and dried from a heavy wooden sea chest in his *dispensa*. And like the good steward he was, he even penned up the waters of a small cove to breed more fish so he could regularly restock the lake. So, although he multiplied no loaves for his flock, his bottomless chest of fish was enough to make him their miracle man.

When he died after twenty-seven years, he was mourned and buried next to the church he had built.

Six months later it occurred to someone in the village that perhaps they had better notify the bishop's office that they were now without a priest.

It was another six months before a replacement showed up. Like his predecessor he was French. Unlike his predecessor he was a city man, born and bred in Lyon. He had no understanding of the people of Nueve Niños. His only concern was that they do his bidding without hesitation. He harangued them from the pulpit. He accosted them in the town's only real street, where he publicly chastised them for their lack of interest in the sacraments and Holy Mass. Both from the altar and out and about he never missed the opportunity to badger them for financial support.

"*Tengo nada*," he constantly reminded them in his nasally Spanish, "and having nothing, I must depend on you for everything."

Soon after the new pastor's arrival, a widow, her larder close to bare, sent one of her sons to see if the priest, in the spirit of his predecessor, could spare a few dried fish.

"*Por favor, Padrecito*," the boy politely informed the curate now blocking the entire front doorway to the rectory, ready to repulse the little invader, "but my mother has sent me for some fish."

"Fish?" the priest barked. "Do I look like a fishmonger?"

Not knowing what a fishmonger was nor what this unpleasant man in the black dress was looking for by way of response, the boy first shook his head then nodded, satisfied that he had covered all the possibilities.

"Does your mother think I was sent here by the bishop just to feed her and her little *mocositos*?" the priest persisted.

These were questions much more difficult than any the boy had ever encountered in the catechism. He did not know of bishops, so this time he merely shrugged his shoulders, but not before swiping his sleeve across his nose to wipe off any offending *mocos* that may have led the priest to call him a snot nose.

"Take this fish to her," the priest bellowed and slapped the boy across one ear. "And if that isn't enough, have another one." Thus he finished the business with a cuff on the boy's other ear.

Since the widow had no champions in Nueve Niños, her husband having died owing money to everyone of importance, no one stepped up to defend her family's honor. However, the priest's bad conduct was duly noted by his parishioners.

"This priest is no Padre Juan," everyone agreed and resolved themselves to wariness whenever they dealt with him.

The priest, misreading reticence for intimidation, would have happily continued his bullying ways had he not soon after overstepped his bounds. It happened in the confessional on a hot Saturday afternoon in August. He was suffering through his usual bout of indigestion, the mean fare available to him in Nueve Niños, mostly beans with salt pork, always disagreeable to his Lyonnaise palate and delicate stomach. And now he was forced to sit in the stifling heat of the narrow confession cabinet, his belly distended and throbbing dully. His discomfort made him even less tolerant than usual of the litanies of peccadilloes that passed for sins among the old women and the children who importuned him from the other side of the partition.

"I gossiped."

"I lied."

"I argued with my neighbor."

"I fought with my brother."

"I stole a piece of bread from the kitchen."

"I disobeyed."

His black mood caused the priest to lash out and rail at the defenseless penitents for their evil ways, promising them eternal damnation if they did not repent. As a final venting of his ill humor, he inflicted penances on one and all that hardly befitted their crimes. He ordered the recitation of rosaries. He imposed physical punishments such as kneeling on pebbles for a half hour or eating a spoonful of salt and then abstaining from water until sundown.

So it was that by the time Benita Valdez entered the box, the priest was primed to hand down justice wholly untempered by mercy.

"Bless me, Father, for I have sinned," she began.

He belched and wiped his mouth with a gray handkerchief. "Yes, yes. Go on!"

Unnerved by this interruption of the formula she had memorized as a child, the girl hesitated then began again.

"Bless me, Father, for I have sinned."

"How long since your last confession, cretin!"

"One week, Father."

"Well then say so and get on with it."

"It's been one week since my last confession," she obediently repeated.

He started to say something but a sudden pain to his midsection allowed him only an irritable grunt.

"I talked back to my mother," she continued. "I was mean to my little sister. And . . ." Here Benita stopped, unsure how and whether to proceed.

"*Allez, allez.*" The priest reverted to French in his exasperation.

"And," she blurted out, "I let a boy kiss me."

She heard the rustling of cloth and the scraping of a chair from the priest's side of the confessional. When next he spoke, his voice was much closer to her and she sensed that he was leaning forward so that his mouth was practically touching the screen between them.

"How old are you?" he demanded.

"Fifteen."

"How many times did he kiss you?"

"Ten," she answered, choosing a nice round number in the panic of the moment.

"And did you let him touch you?" he hissed.

"Yes."

"Where?"

How can I put this, she thought, already on the verge of tears.

"Tell me! Where did he touch you!"

"*En mis chiches,*" she whispered, now beyond panic and in the grip of utter despair.

"Get out!" he screamed at her. "Get out of this confessional! Get out of this church!"

She was too petrified to move. Then she felt the confessional rock and an instant later the curtain to her cubicle flew open and the priest was on her, reaching in to grab her savagely by the arm.

"I said, get out!" he screamed again as he pulled her from the box.

He dragged her down the aisle past other waiting penitents who clicked their beads faster and faster and dared look only straight ahead to the statue of the Mother of Sorrows with the flaming dagger stuck in her exposed heart. When he reached the back of the church, he flung open the door and roughly deposited the young woman on the dirt beyond the steps.

"Never have I known such a wicked girl as you. *Maldita hija del demonio.* Go back to your lover and let him touch your tits until you both go to hell. God does not want you here."

With that he slammed the door of the church and left her sprawled and sobbing hysterically in the dust, now hot and scratchy from the three o'clock sun.

Unlike the poor widow who had wanted nothing more than a dried fish or two for her family, Benita Valdez had champions.

That evening as the priest sat down to his supper, a soothing bowl of scalded milk over ragged chunks of bread, there was a knock. Grumbling but secretly relishing the opportunity to abuse yet another soul, he stomped from the table, his napkin flapping from where he had tucked a corner of it into his Roman collar. When he yanked open the door, his screed died in his open mouth together with a piece of bread still unchewed. There, shoulder to shoulder, were three young men.

"Benita Valdez is our sister," was all that one of them offered by way of explanation before they wrapped a bullwhip around the priest to secure his arms to his body. He choked on his protest as one of the men stuffed the napkin into his mouth. Then they pushed him ahead of them down the lane toward the lake. As they passed each home along the way, doors were discreetly closed and window shades were purposefully pulled down. The people of Nueve Niños had passed their judgment.

At the edge of the lake one of the men jerked at the whip so violently that it sent the priest spinning like a top until he fell sitting down in the water. He rose and tried to stumble back on dry land but the whip hissed and cracked menacingly over his head and he had to back away. Twice more he tried to get to shore, once to the left and once to the right of the trio of his abductors, but again he was met with the whir and rifle shot of the whip.

The man wielding the lash now stepped forward until the water slapped at his booted ankles. Sweeping the whip in a high arc, he began to crack it ever closer to the priest who had no recourse but to retreat farther and farther out into the lake, first up to his thighs, then to his waist, and finally until only his shoulders and head were exposed to the darkening sky.

"Let me be!" he screamed at them. "I am your priest. This is sacrilege." But soon his tone became more conciliatory. "We can discuss this matter like civilized men," he wheedled. Finally, his voice convulsed into sobs. "Please," he begged, "let me be. For pity's sake, let me be."

The men spoke neither to him nor among themselves as they hunkered down, rolled cigarettes, and smoked in silence. Soon he could no longer see his tormentors as the moonless night turned to pitch. However, each time he tried to slosh back to shore he was greeted with the now familiar hiss and crack. Finally, in a last desperate rush, he propelled himself toward dry land, stumbling, gasping for air, and sputtering, "Kill me then. Be done with it. I can stay here no longer."

This time there was no response from the whip and he found himself prostrate, face down on firm ground, quite exhausted and quite alone.

Before sunup the priest was gone from Nueve Niños with all his belongings thrown quickly into his portmanteau. Despite his haste, however, he remembered to take the parish cash box with him.

It took another six months before someone decided they had better inform the bishop that they were once again in need of a priest. It was a full three months after that before they got one.

The new priest lasted barely a week. When he did not show up for the early Mass on his first Sunday in the parish, the mayordomo of the church went to the rectory to rouse him. He found him slumped over the kitchen table dead from a heart attack. They buried him in the churchyard next to Padre Juan.

This time, the people of Nueve Niños decided to immediately report their loss to the bishop. Their prompt action seemed to make little difference in that they still had to bide their time for the next priest to arrive four months later. He was hardly worth the wait, seeing as how he showed up drunk. This, as it turned out, was the usual state of the man.

Aside from running up a substantial bill for whiskey at the general store, this priest had little impact on the community of Nueve Niños. He said Mass and heard confessions when he was able. He baptized, married, and buried people when he was asked, usually on one of his twice-a-week trips to the store for more liquor since he seldom opened his door to callers.

His final legacy to the parish, for all his inert ministry, was a spectacular exit.

Early one morning, as was his custom in good weather or bad, don Antonio Garduño rose, slipped on his overalls over his long johns, stepped into his unlaced high-tops, and walked out his back door to urinate. Bypassing the privy, he headed directly for the lake, not thirty yards from his back door. He groped for his member through his unbuttoned fly, spread his legs wide, and began to piss in a high arc into the lake. This was a tradition he had carried on from a time long before when as a small boy he had first joined his father for the ritual.

"Why waste the water," his father had joked. "Besides, it helps keep the lake quiet so the Niños won't spit fire again."

After he finished his business, the old man reestablished his modesty and then spat into the water and chuckled.

"For good measure, Papa."

Then he looked up to greet the sun. The sky ran from yellow on the horizon, through rose, to red, to violet, and, directly above his head, a dark blue curtain still sagging with stars.

No rain today, he thought, but maybe a little wind.

Then he noticed a brightening to the west, something he had never seen in seven-plus decades of coming to deposit his offering in the lake. He locked his eyes on the unfamiliar glow and walked around his house to the front. There, in the direction of the church with the nine extinct volcanoes directly behind it, he saw an unholy flicker of red and orange just as a gigantic puff of smoke and sparks shot upward. Reflexively, he crossed himself and watched in awe and growing terror.

"One of the Niños is finally awake."

But then he realized that the fire was too close to be coming from the cones.

"*Por Dios*," he whispered and began to run. "*Es la iglesia*."

"The church is burning, the church is burning!" he hollered and banged on door after door on his way to the fire. When he arrived, he saw that it was not the church but the rectory next to it that was in flames.

The villagers were unable to do anything but stand around and watch as the parish house lost its roof and flames gutted its interior. All that stood when the fire finally subsided were the blackened adobe walls. They found what remained of the priest and buried him alongside the other two pastors in the churchyard.

"He must have tipped over a lamp," some said.

"No, he smoked too many cigars and his bedsheets caught fire," argued another school of thought.

But there was no dispute about the fact that he had perished because he had been too drunk to save himself.

When they informed the bishop's office that they had lost yet another priest, the response, this time, was almost immediate.

Within two weeks the chancellor arrived in Nueve Niños to assess the damage to diocesan property and to bless the priest's grave.

"We cannot send you another priest," he said, "until you rebuild the rectory."

"But Padre Juan lived in the sacristy of the church until he had a house," the mayordomo, speaking for the men of the parish, pointed out.

"Padre Juan has been dead for many years," the chancellor countered. "When the rectory is built, let the bishop know. Then we shall see what we shall see." With that last bit of wisdom imparted and after a hasty visit to the graveyard to mumble a prayer and to sprinkle some holy water, the chancellor took his leave.

The rebuilding of the rectory was not a top priority for the people of Nueve Niños. There were farmlands to tend to, cattle to fatten for market. Also, it had to be admitted quite frankly, they could see little difference in their lives with or without a priest. And who knew who or what they would get once they were ready for one.

Finally, however, the men of the parish succumbed to the pressures mounting around them. The women wailed and railed that they needed things blessed, babies baptized, daughters wed. The men also began to feel the sting of loose talk from surrounding communities. When they went to Maxwell, Springer, Wagon Mound, and Raton, the conversation, once it was learned that they were from Nueve Niños, always came around to talk about their inability to keep a priest.

"What kind of people are you?" they were asked. "Who has such bad luck with priests? The place must be cursed. There can be no other explanation."

They were not cursed, they insisted. They were good people, they explained. They were just unlucky in the kind of priests the bishop insisted on sending them. But they knew that no one was listening. They knew that everyone was clucking disapprovingly behind their backs.

Communal pride finally won the day, and after eighteen months of "sede vacante" the men relented. They repaired the walls of the old rectory, laid in a new floor, partitioned the interior space into rooms, and raised a roof.

"We have rebuilt the priest's house," declared a delegation from their number in a meeting with the bishop in Santa Fe.

"I will send you a priest next month," the Excellency responded, "but not as a permanent pastor. Let us call him a parish administrator. Once he tells me that the rectory is adequate and that the people of Nueve Niños are ready to treat their priests with respect, well then,"—he paused for effect—"we shall see."

So began the parade of priests into and out of Nueve Niños. Some died. Some were transferred. Some ran away. Some were driven away. And one poor cleric was literally laughed out of town.

His tenure started smoothly enough. Although by no means gracious, this burly, red-faced Irishman performed his duties adequately and with dispatch. He did not look for acceptance nor was any tendered him. "Live and let live," became the principle by which he and his congregation coexisted. He was better than most, the people concluded, and that was good enough.

But then the pope had to up and die.

Eight years into his reign, which had begun in 1914, Pope Benedict XV was loosed from his earthly coils. The priest, on his twice-a-month trip to Clayton to shop and go to confession, was informed by the local pastor of the pontiff's demise. On his way back to Nueve Niños, the pastor debated on how best to break the horrific news to his flock. Certainly it was too unseemly simply to drop the news on one or two people like a piece of trivial gossip to be spread willy-nilly throughout the parish. It had to be done grandly. Sunday, being only two days off, gave him his answer. Sunday at Mass presented the only sufficiently dignified forum for such a momentous announcement.

So it was at Sunday Mass that the priest, taking the measure of the moment, strode solemnly to the pulpit, read the gospel for the day, kissed the book, closed it, placed it on the lectern, and paused to look over the upturned faces of his congregation.

"Yo tengo noticias muy malas," he intoned in halting Spanish.

Timing a pause for best effect, he then proclaimed, *"Murió la papa."*

For what seemed like an eternity, the congregation stared at him in stunned silence.

Then an old man, hard of hearing, leaned over to his daughter and whispered lustily, *"¿Qué dijo?"*

With a look of puzzlement on her face, she answered loudly enough for him and half the church to hear, "He said that the potato is dead."

Someone sniggered. Someone else chortled. Then someone began to guffaw thunderously, heartily, and unremittingly. This was all the rest of them needed. They all began to laugh.

With the innocent misuse of a definite article, the priest had irrevocably lost whatever hold he had on his congregation.

The mayordomo, seated in the front pew, was finally able to

collect himself enough to approach the dumbfounded priest in the sanctuary.

"*El papa*," he managed to explain through stifled giggles. "Not *la papa*. *La papa* means the potato. *El papa* means the pope."

From that moment on, laughter followed the priest wherever he went. People would see him on the street and begin to laugh. It became impossible for them to conduct parish business with him. The simplest of acts such as buying a candle or arranging for a Mass became daunting tests of their self-restraint. At funerals even bereaved widows tittered while the priest read the fearful words of final disposition over their husbands.

At last the priest could take it no longer. Long ago he had been taught that if his parishioners did not love him, they should at least respect him. But it was too late for that now. Unannounced, he made his escape from Nueve Niños by night.

Perhaps they *were* cursed, the people began to think. What other parish had so much trouble holding on to a priest? Even Mora, where some malcontents had murdered the pastor with poisoned sacramental wine, did not have such a miserable record for keeping clerics.

And what about the neighboring communities? Were they laughing at the people of Nueve Niños just as they themselves had laughed at "Father Potato"? This they could not tolerate. They had no interest in being loved, but they certainly were unwilling to be ridiculed. Their only choice was to be feared.

It was then that Nueve Niños underwent a revision of its history that was radical enough to make a Bolshevik's head spin.

As the people now began to remember it, the priest who had been driven into the lake had not escaped but had actually been swept away and drowned. In fact his spirit now mingled with the mist that hung low to the water in the early morning. It was this same ghost-priest who had entered the rectory to cause his successor to die of a heart attack. He had also somehow consummated an unholy marriage with the mother of the caldera to send a ball of fire from the bottom of the lake to crash directly into the rectory and incinerate the other priest.

In effect, the citizens of Nueve Niños reasoned, they were responsible for the demise of not *one* priest, as were those pikers from Mora, but of *three*!

So perhaps it was not a curse, but that they were just downright mean, they reasoned. And even if they were cursed, it was, after all, by their own doing. Their ancestors had acquiesced to the seminal evil by closing their doors to the plight of the priest being driven into the lake. And it was this very act that had spawned the woes that befell the next two priests.

Unsure how to lift the curse or whether this was even possible or desirable, they resigned themselves to living with it. If they were a mean lot, so be it. If this was how others chose to think of them, let these people beware. If bad was expected of them, they would oblige.

Almost overnight the young men of Nueve Niños began to swagger. The young women grew shrill and contentious. People no longer talked to each other; they barked. And woe betide any outsiders coming to the town. They were made immediately to feel most unwelcome, indeed unsafe. The visitors never stayed around long enough to find out what might happen to them if they remained. Merchants in other towns learned to walk softly when dealing with these cantankerous people. To short change or short order a citizen of Nueve Niños was surely to risk damage to person or property. And you never, ever picked a bar fight with one of them, not if you valued your life.

"*'Mano, soy de Nueve,*" when uttered by one of them was more a threat than an introduction, a warning to the other patrons in the saloon to leave them alone. Or else.

No one ever thought to challenge the men from Nueve Niños, so their reputation was lodged in legend without their ever having to justify it. It was enough for them to say that they went through priests like grasshoppers through a field of sweet alfalfa.

This explains, finally, why so many priests went in and out of Nueve Niños and why, by the 1960s, no priest in the diocese wanted to be sent there.

"It's a dead-end parish," went the common wisdom among the clergy.

✢

Every June when the letters of assignment went out of the chancery office, priests held the envelopes in trembling hands for many minutes before opening them. They knew that the post in Nueve Niños was empty again, and they were fearful that their names had finally risen to the top of the list of those fated to go there.

Of course, not all the priests lived under this Sword of Damocles. Certainly not those who were in good stead with the bishop. Only those on the fringes feared the coming of those June letters, those who had done something or not done something and in the doing or the not doing had tarnished their worth and jeopardized their chances for a good parish.

They knew that the bishop used Nueve Niños as a punishment, a sentence for crimes against his Excellency's sensibilities. When they opened their letters and shook even more, this time with relief, when they realized that they had been spared, they vowed to toe the line, to be the best priests they could be. For some of them, this reprieve led to actual rehabilitation and reformation.

The bishop knew all too well the leverage that Nueve Niños gave him with his priests and he was secretly grateful to its people.

So came to pass a letter dated June 3, 1965, under the coat of arms of the Archdiocese of Santa Fe and over the signature of James J. Duggan, Archbishop. The letter was addressed to Fr. Jonathan M. Armitage and read:

> Dear Fr. Armitage,
> It is our pleasure to assign you to the parish of San
> Eusebio in Nueve Niños as administrator pro tem
> effective June 13, 1965.

The sword of Nueve Niños had fallen squarely on the neck of Father Jon.

Chapter Two

Fr. Jon Marcel Armitage, Golden Boy.

It was that way when he was appointed to the North American College in Rome for his seminary training. It continued on his return four years later, an ordained priest with a licentiate degree in sacred theology, to take up ministry to the people of the Diocese of Fall River in Massachusetts. It was so when he was assigned to the bishop's staff and afterward when he was sent to the Catholic University in Washington, D.C., for a degree in canon law. And it was so when he returned home to run the diocesan marriage tribunal.

Then things fell apart.

The problem was that Fr. Jon loved being a priest. Not so much the ministry to sinners, to the sick, the confused, the poor, the prisoners, the elderly. Not even so much the saying of Mass or the preaching, although he saw their value as a venue for the marketing of his always engaging persona. Rather, the priesthood he enjoyed had to do with the privilege, the respect, the adulation, and the acceptance that it afforded him. He enjoyed socializing with the upper tier of Fall River society. He enjoyed the elegant dinners, the twenty-four-year-old scotch, the fine cigars and brandy in the dark-paneled, leather-bound retreats of the wealthy and influential. Oh, how he loved this part of his priesthood.

Fr. Jon worked very hard for every pat on the back that came to him from the movers and shakers of Fall River. He was in every way a man's man, able to discuss politics and sports with equal ease. He golfed in the mid-eighties and listened to off-color jokes without blanching and even occasionally topped them with one of his own. He could be serious if the situation warranted. He could even pass for wise and compassionate when his counsel was sought.

What of the women, the wives and daughters of his patrons? They were all madly in love with him. For Fr. Jon was a physically attractive man, not pretty, but tall and robust with the dark good looks and straight nose of his Acadian ancestry. And he was gallant to boot. Many a powder room churned with excitement whenever he was present at a gathering of their set.

"Oh, Father Gorgeous!" the women gushed at each other.

"If he wasn't a priest and I wasn't married . . ." The comment was left hanging in midair along with the speaker's raised eyebrow.

The fact that Fr. Jon was an inveterate flirt helped to encourage the infatuation. He knew how to flatter, how to comment on a new hairdo, a frock, or a perfume. He knew what effect the flashing of his bright smile or the intimacy of a conspiratorial wink had on his female admirers. However, it should be noted that his flirtations were taken by the women in the spirit in which they were proffered. It was all just a little bit naughty, but it was also very innocent and harmless fun.

Or so it was to everyone except Carla Montague. At forty-two, Carla, wife of Arthur, was on the cusp. Her debutante freshness had long since wilted, and her young matron's allure was about to head out the back door. Capillaries had started to feather out across the backs of her knees. Her milky skin was lately showing the leathery effects of too many days on the tennis courts and by the swimming pool of the local country club. She was not yet feeling old, but she was beginning to feel that the oldness was coming fast on her. She had done her duty by her husband, giving him two sons to carry on the mushrooming success of his chain of grocery stores and a daughter who could eventually be married off to create even more business opportunities. Of course, the oldest of the children being a mere sixteen, they were all still too young to be of practical use to the Montague portfolio. But soon, Carla realized, they would be ripe. When they passed over the threshold into adult-hood, Carla knew that she would be dragged along, first as a mother-in-law, then as a grandmother, and finally as one of the desiccated crones who hung around the club bar for hours in short skirts and sleeveless blouses to show off their wrinkles, varicose veins, and puckered thighs. There was still time, she figured, for one last fling, one final moment of dangerous indulgence. Her husband would probably not even notice, so intent had he become in his mid-forties on solidifying the legacy of his grocery empire. A tryst with the tennis pro from the club lasted all of one overnight in Manhattan. The tennis pro had been so nervous about being discovered and losing his job that his attempts in bed were a disappointing string of double faults. Then there had been an embarrassing interlude when she tried to seduce the son of their Portuguese gardener. He never did understand what was happening.

So when Fr. Jon gave her one of his special winks one evening and told her that she looked good enough to eat, she forced herself to believe the attention was sincere, and, more to the point, she convinced herself that a door had been left ajar.

Carla took her time. She arranged to have herself appointed to the diocesan hospital board that Fr. Jon chaired. Her committee work was Herculean and gave her the opportunity to sit with him at many meetings. And she always managed to engage him in discussion long after the other board members had gone home. That summer she also saw to it that the Montagues entertained as never before— teas, dinners, cocktail parties, benefits—affairs to which the priest was always invited.

Finally, she was sure of her ground—they were now on a first-name basis—and made her move.

"Hello, Jon. Carla," she breathed into the phone.

"Carla, how nice. Thanks for dinner last Saturday. As usual everything was perfection. Especially you."

"Thank *you*," she purred. "You simply saved the evening. Arthur's friends can be so dull. And those wives of theirs."

"Calling about the hospital oversight report? Good job, as usual. Thanks for all your work."

"To tell you the truth, Jon, this is somewhat of a personal call."

"Oh?"

Now at the crossroads, she paused. She had dialed with two possible strategies in mind. One was direct: "Let's meet for lunch somewhere. I'd like to get to know you better." The other ploy was oblique.

Fr. Jon's assumption that she was calling on business and his noncommittal "Oh?" when he found out it was something personal was somewhat off-putting. This directed her down the more circumspect path.

"It's Arthur and me. Oh God, did that sound corny or what?"

Jon immediately took on the mantle of Fr. Armitage. "Oh, I'm sorry. A little surprised, too."

"You're the only person I can trust. Could we talk? Face to face, I mean?"

"Sure. You say when. My office is completely private."

"Actually, and I know it's silly of me, I'd prefer some neutral spot. Your collar and all those dusty theology books. It's all so . . . churchy? I was thinking of lunch somewhere. I know this wonderful little café in New Bedford."

"New Bedford? Sort of out of the way, isn't it?"

"Jon, it's not going to be easy for me as it is. At least let me choose the place. They serve a wonderful lobster bisque," she added brightly.

Fr. Jon laughed easily then. "Lobster bisque! How can I resist?"

"Wednesday is your day off, isn't it?" She knew full well that it was.

"Wednesday? I have a foursome, but we should be done by ten thirty or so. I can shower at the club and be in New Bedford by one. Will that work?"

"That will work just fine," she answered a tad too eagerly and quickly modified her tone as she gave him directions to the restaurant.

"Yeah, I think I know the place. Very private."

"So I'll see you at one?"

"One. Wednesday. And I'll leave my collar in the glove compartment."

That Wednesday Jon got to the restaurant by one thirty and found Carla already settled at a small table in a back alcove. She had just poured her second glass of wine from a bottle of Soave Bertani dripping beads of condensation into its silver ice bucket.

"Sorry I'm late. There were some real hackers playing in front of us."

"You won, I presume?" she asked, trying to act interested.

He smiled and sat down. "I can pay for lunch, if that's what you're getting at."

The kitchen was out of the bisque, so Fr. Jon settled for a crab cake sandwich while Carla had the Cobb salad. By the end of the meal and the bottle, they were both feeling flushed and free. He refused a brandy and asked for coffee. She ordered a Black Russian.

"So," he said, once the waiter had cleared the last of the silver and left them alone in the now deserted dining room.

"So," she answered, smiling languidly.

"So which of Arthur's kneecaps do you want me to shatter? I've got a five iron that should do the trick."

"Oh, nothing so drastic." She laughed. "Actually, it's not Arthur's problem. Well, Arthur's just being Arthur, but I've lived with that for years."

"So, what then?"

"Me. Just me."

"And what about you?"

"I don't know. Creeping old age. A sudden sense of inadequacy. I guess that about covers it."

Fr. Jon laughed. "Old? Inadequate? You? Carla Montague, the most beautiful, the most charming, the most fascinating woman in Fall River?"

She pouted—fetchingly, she hoped. "It's not funny."

"No, I suppose not." He immediately put on his best counselor's face.

"The children don't need me anymore, and of course Arthur never has. Not really. What good am I anyway?"

"Well if you're fishing for compliments. . . ." He reached across and patted her arm.

But before he could pull back she had covered his hand with her own and squeezed it.

"Jon, how can I say this? Over the past few months I feel that we've gotten very close. Am I wrong?"

Jon found it difficult to take his eyes off the death grip she held him in. "You've been a real peach to work with."

"And how do you feel about peaches?"

He flinched when he felt her bare foot run teasingly up the inside of his trouser leg.

"Carla, please."

"Jon, we're both adults here. Don't you think I know what's going on?"

"What do you mean, 'going on'?"

"The winks, the smiles, the compliments. A girl can read a lot into these things."

Fr. Armitage tried to smile as he shrugged. "You know me, Carla. Good-time Jonny. It's just a game. A harmless little game."

She smiled and half closed her eyes. "*Golf* is a game, Jon. And I don't like golf."

The priest pushed his chair back so unexpectedly that her foot thumped inelegantly to the tiled floor. "Carla, this is not going to happen. It's just not possible. I'm sorry. I truly am."

And, forgetting his promise to pay for lunch, he left her sitting there.

The next morning, as Carla Montague toweled herself off after her bath, she noticed the slight jiggling of the skin on the backs of her upper arms. The mirror disclosed crow's-feet that had not seemed so deeply etched the day before. She knew that somehow overnight she had taken her first step over the threshold. She needed someone to blame. That evening she spoke to her husband. The next morning Fr. Jon Armitage was summoned to the bishop's office.

"I've had a call, Father Armitage," the bishop said solemnly.

"Yes, Excellency?"

"A call from Arthur Montague. A very disturbing call."

Fr. Jon felt a quivering in his sphincter that quickly traveled down his thighs to settle in the backs of his knees.

"According to Mr. Montague, you have made improper advances toward his wife."

Fr. Jon's eyes widened into comic book disks. "Absolutely not," he sputtered.

"Did you meet with Mrs. Montague for lunch two days ago?"

"At her invitation."

"Was this luncheon meeting in New Bedford?"

"Her suggestion entirely."

"Did you then attempt to hold her hand?"

"It was a pat on her arm and it was nothing more than a comforting gesture. That's all. She said she was feeling down on herself. It was just a little pat of reassurance."

"And did you admit to . . ."—the bishop scrunched up his face in distaste to steel himself against the unepiscopal word he was about to utter—"*flirting* with her?"

"I suppose I did. But I do that with all the women I know. That's me."

"Yes. I've been meaning to talk to you about that. But now it appears I'm too late."

"Too late, Excellency?"

"Did you suggest that you wanted a more personal relationship with Mrs. Montague?"

"No, never. She's the one who called and told me she wanted to discuss some personal problems. She's the one who set up the lunch in New Bedford. She's the one who started talking nonsense once I got there."

"You hold yourself blameless, then?"

"I didn't do anything."

"Do you consider arranging a rendezvous with a married woman to be a prudent thing?"

"I'd hardly characterize my lunch with Mrs. Montague as a rendezvous."

"Did you not have a sense of how such a meeting might be construed?"

Fr. Jon shook his head. "I guess I thought I could handle it."

"Pride, Father. Pride."

"OK, OK. In retrospect it was dumb to do it. But, believe me, Excellency, there was nothing to it. I told her she had put us both in an impossible situation. Then I left her at the restaurant."

"Her story is obviously different from yours."

"You have to believe me, Bishop."

The Excellency made a rat-a-tat by drumming his open hand on the desk. "Actually, I do. In fact, Mr. Montague himself intimated his lack of confidence in his wife's story. Apparently there is a history there. Not that it matters, of course."

"I don't understand."

"Truth is not the issue here. It's all a matter of perception. There's a nasty little scandal hanging in the air right now, Father. Mr. Montague doesn't want it to infect his family's reputation and the diocese certainly doesn't need it."

"I'll do whatever it takes to fix things, Excellency."

"I'm happy to hear you say that, Father. All of us want to put this ridiculous situation behind us. In fact, Mr. Montague has agreed to forget the whole thing."

"Well, that's big of him, considering it's his wife who's created this mess."

"He has set down one condition."

"That being?"

"He insists you leave the diocese."

"What?"

"Mr. Montague does not want you around here anymore. I'm afraid he's adamant on this point."

"He can't be serious."

"Oh, but he is. And I am reluctant to try to persuade him otherwise."

"You mean you're actually going to cave in on this? I think I deserve better."

"Father Jon, you more than anyone should know who Arthur Montague is. The diocese can ill afford to lose his friendship."

Fr. Jon fell back into the chair, stunned by the catastrophic turn his perfect life as a priest had suddenly taken. "You're saying I'm expendable?"

"Why, Father!" The bishop sounded genuinely surprised by the question. "I thought you knew. You always have been."

Chapter Three

As a refugee priest in search of a new diocese, Fr. Jon's options were limited. In those days, just before the changes brought about by Vatican Council II began to take their devastating toll on the clerical ranks, every prominent diocese in the country operated under a glut of priests. So the Philadelphias, the Cinncinnatis, the St. Louises, even the Los Angeleses were out as possible ports in Fr. Jon's storm.

His bishop suggested that Fr. Jon might consider service in some far-flung mission field. "Something to cleanse the soul and reenergize the spirit," was how he put it.

But Fr. Jon could not see himself sweating in some steam bath of a Guatemalan jungle parish nor even in a clapboard church in rural Mississippi.

"How about Santa Fe?" a priest confidant of his suggested. "I hear the climate's wonderful. Very quaint. Even sophisticated. If you go in for that sort of thing. They have no native clergy to speak of. A man with your credentials could do worse."

"Is that even in the United States?" Fr. Jon was not altogether joking.

"How about Fargo then?" his friend pushed on. "Cold but a day's drive from Detroit and Chicago when you need a little R and R."

Santa Fe was starting to sound better by the minute. Even the bishop agreed that it was a good choice when Fr. Jon proposed it to him. "Many a priest has gone there for rehabilitation and come out the better man for it. I'll call Archbishop Duggan. We were in the seminary together."

"Jimmy, how's the West treating you?" the bishop of Fall River barked jovially over the phone lines across the two thousand miles that connected him to James J. Duggan, the archbishop of Santa Fe. "I never thought Puerto Rico was a good fit for you. Too . . . too," he said, struggling for an adjective, "Puerto Rican."

Archbishop Duggan cursed a mighty curse on the other end and proceeded into a harangue at the injustice of his transfer, especially to such a godforsaken place as he now found himself. "Why do they punish me for enforcing Church precepts?" he whined.

"Now, now, Jimmy, settle down. You left a bit of a mess down there, you know. All that business with the Pill. Never get into a fight you can't win. The government wanted those tests. What could you do? Just lay low where you are for now. We'll see about getting you back east in a couple of years."

Duggan mumbled something but the bishop of Fall River was already onto the real reason for his call.

"Listen, Jimmy. I've got someone here I want you to take care of. Father Jonathan Armitage. Good lad. Smart as a whip. Best canon lawyer we've ever had. Got himself in a bit of a jam. Woman. Not even his fault, poor bastard. But the husband wants him out of here and he does carry some clout, if you know what I mean. Can you help us out?"

He could. "But don't forget me, Patrick. Don't let them bury me out here."

After the bishop of Fall River hung up, he stared at the cradled phone for a few seconds before muttering, "But if you ask my honest opinion, Jimmy, you got just what you deserved, you pompous ass."

James J. Duggan, the archbishop of Santa Fe, was a tall, hulking vulgarian. He had an incongruously small melon of a head atop which sat a bishop's cherry-red skullcap. This he constantly readjusted, particularly when he was agitated, which could be at any given moment.

The man was mercurial, his moods unpredictable. He came to Santa Fe from Altoona, Pennsylvania, by way of Puerto Rico. There he had not endeared himself to his flock with his sporadic episodes of episcopal frenzy between long fallow periods of inactivity. He was not a doer. He preferred to react.

In the late 1950s, with the government's blessing, Puerto Rico became a testing ground for the Pill. It was the major issue in the island's 1960 gubernatorial elections.

Duggan stirred the pot. He used his influence to form a new Catholic political party whose only mission was to cast out the incumbent governor, characterized as "Godless, immoral, anti-Christian, and against the Ten Commandments."

The bishop threw himself into the campaign with uncharacteristic vigor. The culmination of his efforts, his crusade brought to climax, occurred at a huge rally the Sunday before the election. In an address that rambled on for over an hour, he stressed again and again the evils of birth control and the wickedness of those who promulgated it under the veil of government sanction. The rousing conclusion of his talk bears repeating.

> My dear people, it is not easy to do good. It is a hard path
> that we ask you to walk with us. If you want the easy way,
> go to the birth control clinics. How easy it is to find them.
> There is one just up the street from us. How easy it is to
> walk in and enroll in that depraved program. How easy
> it is to have them give you the Pill. How easy it is to take
> the Pill. Oh yes, my children, sin is so easy!

The next morning the queues in front of the birth control clinic ran several wide and clear around the block. Many of the women in line said that they had never come before, but now that the good bishop had told them how easy it was, they just had to see for themselves.

The next day the ruling party won in a landslide. Of eight hundred thousand votes, Bishop Duggan's party managed to garner a paltry fifty thousand.

There is a saying in the Archdiocese of Santa Fe that priests and nuns went there from other dioceses for one of two reasons, to save their health or to save their reputations. Two years after his public humiliation in Puerto Rico, a very healthy James J. Duggan came to Santa Fe.

Chapter Four

On the night before he left for Santa Fe, Fr. Jon Armitage jotted a hurried note to his sister, a nun in a cloistered monastery in eastern Kentucky.

Dear Sally—
I won't bore you with the details but I'm leaving Fall River.
I'm off to Santa Fe, *New* Mexico, of all places.
    I got a little cocky (Hard to believe, right?) and the bishop decided to knock me down a peg or two.
    Don't worry. I'm sure it's just temporary.
    I'll be in touch.

Jon

Her return note was forwarded to the chancery office in Santa Fe.

Dear Jonny:
You didn't ask for prayers but since that's what we do here, I'll see if I can slip you in. I guess I could go on about trusting in God's will, but you're the one with the theology degree. A more practical option might be to give you a thump on the noggin like I used to. What are big sisters for? Mom and Dad (RIP) always spoiled you.
    Please take care of yourself. I don't know what else to say.
        I love you.

Sally

Chapter five

And so the deal was struck.

On a hot day in July, the rivets on his Buick Electra fairly popping from the stress of his personal possessions, Fr. Jon Armitage, opting for the southern route, drove north on I-25 from Albuquerque to Santa Fe. From the arid bowl of the lower plain, he climbed the stretch of highway called La Bajada. Over the rim, across a broad plateau, he caught his first glimpse of Santa Fe some twenty miles away.

Por oro, Dios, y gloria. For Gold, God, and Glory.

This was the rallying cry of the conquistadores who had made the same journey some 350 years before.

Both Fr. Jon Armitage's car and mind were on automatic drives. His thoughts were as diffused as the morning mist that still clung to the terrace of blue mountains in the distance. There was certainly no gold where he was going, but he was open to finding both God and glory, not necessarily in that order.

He fiddled with the radio dial and stopped on a newscast. President Johnson had just signed the Civil Rights Act into law. There were plans to beef up the corps of military advisers in Vietnam. A search was still underway in Mississippi for three civil rights workers named Cheney, Schwerner, and Goodwin, missing for over a week.

He twirled the knob again and found the driving rhythms of Petula Clark singing "Downtown." After her came the Beatles and "I Want to Hold Your Hand." One hit wonders, Jon had declared when he first heard the group. Now he was willing to give them until Christmas.

Fifteen minutes later Fr. Jon entered Santa Fe on Cerrillos Road, that garish three-mile stretch of commercialism plunging directly into the heart of Old Santa Fe like a neon stiletto.

Having traveled widely in Europe, Fr. Jon felt that by now he was beyond culture shock. Nothing, however, had prepared him for Santa Fe. He had been told and was expecting a small but quite cosmopolitan city. What greeted him were low-slung mud buildings, commercial and residential, seemingly plunked down willy-nilly so that the streets had no choice but to pick their way around them.

Just as Jon had despaired that he was trapped in an irresolvable maze of brown, he broke out into the stillness of Santa Fe's plaza. It was a small, intimate square, tightly enclosed on all sides by buildings of varying heights and architectural quality. He drove slowly alongside the Palace of the Governors, long ago abandoned as a government house for use as a museum. The building stretched across the entire north side of the plaza, like a tired old *dueña* reclining on her side, the fringes of her shawl hanging down to form support posts along the open portico. Beneath this portal Jon saw Native American purveyors, their wares of pottery and jewelry displayed in neat rows before them. Tourists were wandering by, sometimes stopping to stare at such curiosities. The Indians stared back.

Fr. Jon escaped from the slow, deliberate traffic circling the plaza and made his way a short block east past the venerable La Fonda Hotel. Directly before him loomed the oddly conceived and out of place gothic-Romanesque Cathedral of St. Francis. Obviously the building had been erected long before zoning committees and historical societies had gained the day.

To the right along the street running in front of the cathedral was an adobe structure that housed the offices of the Archdiocese of Santa Fe. Next to it stood a three-story Victorian firetrap that the archbishop called home and where Fr. Armitage would take up residence that very day.

Fr. Lawrence Tapia, the archbishop's secretary, achingly young and intensely eager, opened the front door of the chancery office to Fr. Jon. "Father Armitage. Monsignor Montini will be glad to see you."

If Fr. Jon was the least bit uncomfortable, appearing in the offices of the archbishop as damaged goods, any anxiety quickly dissipated with his reception by Fr. Tapia and then by the chancellor. These people seemed genuinely pleased to see him.

Monsignor Amleto Montini, he of the diminutive surname, was a petite man, almost a scale model of what a full-grown priest should look like. He stood no more than five foot three, and although it was hard to tell, Fr. Armitage noticed immediately the high-gloss, black elevator shoes on which the mini-prelate balanced himself. The monsignor was impeccably dressed in smartly pressed clericals. A good three inches of white French cuff shot out from his coat sleeves. These, his Roman collar, and the purple stud directly beneath it to signify his rank were the only break from the fastidious blackness of his suit.

As Fr. Jon would learn, Montini, like himself, was an émigré. Unlike him, however, the monsignor had left the north of Italy with no known blemish on his record. What was not known was his bribing of the chancellor before leaving his old diocese to make sure the file forwarded to Santa Fe was expunged of any incriminating items, the attempted swindle of a wealthy contessa being the most egregious of these.

Montini had come to America to become rich, such opportunities being sorely lacking in postwar Italy but legendary across the Atlantic. He had chosen Santa Fe because he knew that his chances for immediate advancement were excellent, especially for one so astute in the hoary art of church politics. He quickly rose from outsider to the chancellorship. Local pretenders were no match for his well-honed skills when it came to handling bishops.

Now privy to all information that affected the welfare of the archdiocese, the newly elevated monsignor set about putting into action his plan for making lots of money. As chancellor he sat ex officio on the archdiocesan planning board together with a handful of prominent laymen, mostly business leaders with an insight into the growth patterns of a booming Albuquerque. It was their charge to advise the archbishop of population and building trends. The archdiocese could then purchase land for future churches and schools. The monsignor took careful note of these projections, and on the sly he purchased a few small parcels of prime land for himself. Selling off these holdings at a nice profit, he was able to fund phase two of his get-rich scheme. This involved a return to Italy.

"To visit my family," he said, lying to the archbishop.

Before leaving, the monsignor withdrew, in cash, the money he had made from his investments in real estate.

Once back on his native soil, Montini immediately began to visit schools, hospitals, and orphanages. Everywhere he went he displayed a most solicitous concern for the nuns and their charges.

"You have no refrigerator. Let me buy you one."

"You need bedding for the children. Allow me."

"How can you cook on such an old stove? Permit me to help."

As the monsignor expected, the good nuns were most grateful to their benefactor. So when he off-handedly admired a painting hanging for centuries in a hallway or a refectory, something by one of the lesser Italian masters, the sisters were more than happy to make him a gift of it.

"But I can't . . ." he would protest.

"Please, *monsignore*. Take it," they pressed him. "We have so many paintings just gathering dust. What good are they to us? Take it as a token of our gratitude."

Of course he did take it and several more like it as he made his pilgrimage across the north of Italy, leaving a wash of empty frames in his wake. His plan worked so well that by the end of the month he had in his possession ten small masterpieces undocumented in any official registry of Renaissance art. As he packed for home, he unrolled the canvases and laid them flat between layers of clothing in his oversized suitcase. On his return to the United States the little monsignor did not declare his cache of paintings. And, something he had counted on as a priest, he was gestured through customs with nary a second look.

In New York, Montini visited several galleries, and when he found one that suited his needs, he left the paintings on consignment. In the course of one short month he received by mail several checks in the tens of thousands of dollars. After that the entire procedure settled itself into a seamless routine of bilking nuns, smuggling his contraband past customs, and selling it at a handsome price. He made three or four visits a year to his mother country, each time with a sizable wad of U.S. currency with which he bought used furniture and appliances. These he generously donated to needy church institutions, making sure that his largess was always acknowledged with a small token of appreciation: a *Visit of the Magi* hanging in a dark chapel nave; a *Madonna and Child* in a dank and drafty corridor; a *St. Jerome* or a *Daniel in the Lions' Den* forgotten for generations in a seldom-used library.

Then, on one of his returns from Italy to New York, while delivering his latest acquisitions to an art dealer, Msgr. Montini was surprised to run into a familiar figure. He little suspected at that moment that this chance meeting would allow him to shimmy even higher up the money tree from which he was already gathering fruit by the basketful. There on a pedestal in a front showroom of the gallery stood *Our Lady of Solitude*, a statue from New Mexico carved from cottonwood and painted in vivid colors over gesso in the style of a Taos County *santero*.

"What is she doing here?" Montini demanded from the dealer as if inquiring after a dotty aunt who should have been locked up and forgotten long ago. But here she was, prim lips, soulful almond-shaped black eyes and all, holding court in a chic, uptown Manhattan art gallery.

"Southwestern folk art. It's a growing market. Very collectible. I sell them faster than I can find them."

Montini trembled with excitement. The Archdiocese of Santa Fe was sitting on the mother lode of such santos. He had always thought them crude and of little value, but now he gazed on the lady-statue before him with newfound respect. How many churches and chapels throughout northern New Mexico had rows upon dusty rows of such idols? How many villages, with no access to manufactured statuary in the 1800s, had depended on local, unschooled artisans to make their saints for them? How much money could he make off of them? He became giddy with the thought that his road to riches could become a two-way highway. He could show a profit both going to Italy and returning.

On his flight back to Albuquerque, Montini arranged for a layover in St. Louis. There he visited a wholesale warehouse full to the rafters of assembly-line statuary from Europe. Every saint and every devotion were represented there, all done in plaster or molded marble dust, with rouged faces, hard-cast wavy, brown, or blond hair, and blue glass eyes that followed you around the room. He put in an order for delivery of a dozen of these including four crucifixes, three Immaculate Conceptions, three St. Josephs, and two St. Judes.

When the statues arrived in Santa Fe, he put them in storage. On his next free day, he deposited two of the statues in the trunk of his car and set off for the high country up north. Dressed in his finest clericals so there would be no mistaking his identity as a high-ranking churchman, the monsignor drove into the first village he found with a chapel and sought out the mayordomo.

"The bishop has sent me to inspect all churches of the diocese," Montini explained regarding his sudden appearance in this humble setting. "The first order of business is to supply the faithful with beautiful new saints. They are images you can pray to with pride. And I have one for your chapel, a gift from your archbishop."

Once the plaster statue was carried reverently into the chapel and installed in a place of honor, the monsignor was ready to close the trap. "Doesn't it look beautiful?" he gushed, standing back with the mayordomo to admire their handiwork. "Of course, it would look even better if we could get rid of some of the clutter around it. Those old santos have served their purpose, but it's time they were retired, don't you agree?"

And who would not agree with this kind and generous monsignor, a representative of the bishop himself?

"I suppose they have some historical value," the monsignor continued. "Let me take one or two of the best back to Santa Fe with me and see what I can do with them."

In no time at all, in villages from Española to Taos, Msgr. Montini had disposed of his dozen pieces of St. Louis statuary and collected eighteen santos to carry away for eventual shipment back east. Thus began the highly profitable and low-risk operation of funneling art into New York from two directions, canvases from Italy and santos from New Mexico.

By the time Fr. Jon came on the scene, Msgr. Montini was well on his way to the fortune to which he aspired.

"Welcome, Father Armitage," Monsignor Montini greeted the priest. "We've been looking forward to your arrival. Isn't that right, Father Lawrence."

The young priest smiled and nodded.

"Father Lawrence was trained in Rome just like you, Father Armitage," the monsignor volunteered.

"You were ordained the year before I got there," the young priest added. "But I heard a lot about you."

"Probably lies," Fr. Jon demurred, but not without his famous smile.

The monsignor mixed the air with a rotating motion of his manicured hand. "The three of us must get together to speak Italian. But first things first. The archbishop will want to see you immediately."

"Welcome, Father Armitage." Archbishop Duggan was effusive as he pointed to a chair for the priest. "I think you should be very happy here. If you like to work, that is." His eyes narrowed to better assess the man sitting across from him. "You're a first-class canon lawyer, I understand. As it turns out we have a great need for someone to run our marriage tribunal. Monsignor Montini here is just too swamped by the business of the archdiocese without the added burden of processing annulments. Isn't that right, Monsignor?"

The chancellor, standing to one side of the desk, threw his shoulders up and spread his hands. "I try, Your Excellency."

"Now, Monsignor, it wasn't meant as criticism." The Archbishop tsked. "We all know how much time you've put in at the tribunal."

Actually, Montini's efforts on behalf of the matrimonially wounded was close to nil. Files fat with petitions together with their related correspondence, which he had never bothered to open, were stacked several feet high in his office. The monsignor had decided early in the game that his fortunes did not lie in the minutiae of canon law. He knew that his time was best spent with his art dealings. This was the most direct route to his early retirement to a villa in Tuscany, one that he had recently purchased and started restoring.

"I think that Father Armitage will be a great addition to my staff," he purred.

"Staff." The bishop snorted in delight. "Watch out for these Italians, Father. They never say what they mean. His staff now consists solely of you."

Fr. Armitage smiled politely at what the archbishop obviously considered a great joke. "Anything I can do to help."

"You will also say Mass for the nuns across the street," the bishop continued. "Loretto Academy. All the prominent families send their girls there. And your bishop informs me that you did a good job for him on the hospital board. We can definitely lean on your experience there."

Not once during the entire interview was Fr. Armitage questioned about his recent fall from grace. At no time did Archbishop Duggan proffer any advice or veiled warning as to how the priest should conduct himself in his new diocese. For this Fr. Jon was grateful. His bitterness was already dulling and hardening into indifference on the subject of his expulsion from the Diocese of Fall River.

If Fr. Armitage was initially flattered by the courtesy Duggan was showing him in not raking up his past, he soon found out that the archbishop's standing policy regarding the clerical jetsam and flotsam that drifted his way from other dioceses could be stated thusly: "If they can breathe, we'll take 'em. God knows we need 'em."

Duggan was also aware of the points he was making with the hierarchy back east by taking in all pariahs. Some day soon the archbishop of Santa Fe fully expected to cash in his chips for a ticket back to civilization.

Chapter Six

Just as you can prove with metaphysical certitude by use of a simple mathematical elimination that everyone on this planet has a doppelgänger, so by the same process you could come to the conclusion that there had to be someone in Santa Fe who did not like Fr. Jon Armitage. Even the priest accepted this, although he had yet to run into the proof for this theorem.

Santa Fe was not Fall River. However, in no time at all, Fr. Armitage had picked up exactly where he had left off in his old diocese.

There were more than forty nuns at the Loretto Academy, most of them teachers, plus a handful of elderly ones in retirement. Except for some of the younger sisters who in the newly kindled spirit of change refused on principle to accept a priest solely on the strength of his collar, most of the sisters fell instantly under his thrall. Fr. Armitage had not lost his touch with the opposite sex and beneath wimple and habit the nuns were still women. But their captivation was not the same as that of his camp followers in Fall River. They liked him and they liked being around him simply because he always made them feel so good about themselves.

Any venal interest in the handsome and charming priest was left to the heaving breasts, developed and developing, of the young ladies attending the school. For them he was an Adonis, a movie star, a figure from their adolescent fantasies all rolled into one. They ogled him in the school's corridors. They giggled and hugged their books and binders when he talked to them.

Fr. Jon was not oblivious to the effect he was having on the girls. Actually, he was quietly amused, but he was also very careful. He made sure that he was never alone with any of the students after the religion classes he taught at the school twice a week. He referred all requests for counseling to the nuns in charge of such things. The fiasco in Fall River had taught him a hard lesson. Behind the charm of his smile he had built up an impregnable wall of caution that he manned with a vigilance born of sad experience.

The same rampart held fast and secure against the mothers of the schoolgirls who mooned over him. And it did not take long for the matrons of Loretto to come courting. They began asking Fr. Jon to address their church groups and service organizations. After that it was just a matter of time before he was invited to their homes and social clubs for cocktails and dinners and was introduced to their husbands. And soon he was at it again. This time it was with the wealthy and influential gentlemen of Santa Fe—drinking their scotch and brandy, smoking their cigars, trading off-color jokes, joining foursomes at the local golf course, playing cards, and offering counsel. Within the year the City of Holy Faith was his.

Back at the chancery office Armitage had whittled down the stack of annulment files by more than half after just three months on the job. Many of these cases were no longer active due to the fact that the suing parties had moved to another jurisdiction either by physically leaving the diocese or by spiritually leaving the Church. Couples had even reconciled while they waited for Monsignor Montini to address their petitions for separation. Before long, under Fr. Jon's watch, the tribunal of the archdiocese was churning out a steady stream of annulments. The personal care that Fr. Jon gave to these cases endeared him to their petitioners, some representing old-line Santa Fe and Albuquerque families, never a bad thing.

And so Fr. Jon Armitage began to love being a priest again. He rubbed elbows with the men and flirted oh-so-judiciously with the women and resumed his perfect life once more.

He had no real passion for parish work, and so weekend obligations proved the least interesting of all his duties. He showed up for confessions on Saturdays and for Mass on Sundays as a hired gun. He had no proprietorship, no link to the lives of the parishioners and dispensed his priestly wares with a certain perfunctory charm. His sermons were still stirring, his smile was still winning, but he kept his distance.

The only time he felt an urge remotely bordering on involvement was with certain penitents, always male, in the confessional.

"Bless me, Father, for I have sinned. It has been five [perhaps ten, fifteen, or twenty] years since my last confession."

"And what made you decide to come now?"

"My son is making his First Communion," or "My daughter is getting married," or "My mother just died."

They were seldom there for the pure sake of repentance. Rather their confessions were inconvenient passages to a desired end.

"And what are your sins?"

Out came a stream of misdeeds large and small.

Jon weighed bursts of impatience or impure thoughts on the same scale as adultery, slander, larceny, envy, cruelty, gluttony, and more. He did so with hardly the batting of an eye. It was not that he was losing perspective on evil, he was simply unmoved by the expediency with which the penitents rattled off their failures.

At the end it was always the same: "Be sorry for your sins. Say ten Our Fathers and ten Hail Marys. *Ego te absolvo.* God bless you."

What he sometimes wanted to say was, "I absolve you from your sins, you smarmy, wife-beating, child-abusing, carousing, faithless, spineless, self-pitying son of a bitch. I absolve you because you have asked me to. But I know that your remorse springs not from your sense of sin, of the pain and harm you have caused others, but from some trivial social pressure that you don't have the guts to withstand."

Fr. Jon brought the same wariness toward women to his duties after his appointment to the board of directors of St. Vincent's Hospital. There would be no more Carla Montagues. The memory of her bare foot creeping up underneath his trouser leg still rankled. To avoid a repetition or even a near occasion, he begged off sitting on any committees.

"My work at the chancery wouldn't allow me the time," he explained.

The board met the second Thursday of each month. They listened to reports, voted on issues, and had a very nice lunch. The nuns of St. Vincent's prided themselves on their kitchen. Indeed they had every right to since their food had local renown as the antithesis of typical hospital fare.

It was after one of these meetings that a well-fed Fr. Jon, having listened to reports and dispensed his yeas or nays with equal aplomb, walked down one of the hospital's long corridors. A nurse passed him going the other way and they exchanged a nod and a smile. Five steps farther and he heard her voice behind him.

"Excuse me, Father."

Jon turned to face her.

"I'm sorry to bother you, but I'm wondering if you could help me?"

"I'll certainly do what I can."

"There's a patient in the cancer ward. Fourth floor. He's not doing very well."

"I'm sorry to hear that."

"Here's the thing. He's all alone. Never had a visitor or even a call to ask how he was doing. We have no record of any family. When we ask him if there's someone we can contact, he says no."

"Has he asked to talk with anyone?"

"Not that I know of."

"So you don't know if he wants to see a clergyman."

She shook her head.

"Maybe this is something the chaplain should deal with."

"Yes, Father, but he's out of town."

Fr. Jon looked at his watch and felt immediately ashamed.

"I know you must be busy," she said, "but I don't think he'll last the night. Maybe if you could just drop by for a moment."

The elevator door opened and Jon stepped into the shiny, tiled reception area of the cancer ward. It was a place like no other in the hospital.

To begin with, there was no sense of urgency and very little of the quick-paced efficiency of the other floors. Here nurses and technicians did everything with measured step, from medication to therapies, as if time had ceased to define their duties.

The patients themselves were palpably more serene, less agitated, living in slow motion where the real world was no longer a factor.

On other floors a walk down the corridors was met with the competing noises of radios and TVs pouring from almost every room. Here there was none of that. Few of these patients even bothered to read. Songs of love had no meaning. There were certainly no soap operas more poignant and arresting than their own. And how could they be amused to see contestants jump up and down in front of newly won refrigerators when there was only one prize that mattered to them? There was absolutely nothing outside of this place four stories above the ground that could distract them from their mortality.

Fr. Jon had learned that lesson well from watching his father yellow and bloat and then implode with the cancer that slowly substituted its devil-cells for his body. Many years after his father died, Jon still remembered the routine the family was forced to endure. Cancer had taught them how to focus and wait. Tests and biopsies took time. Diagnoses and prognoses took time. Therapy took time. And through all this there was nothing for it but to wait. And at the end of it, had it all been worthwhile? The pain, the nausea. Remission was a word to savor, but not too much. Hope never extended beyond the next blood test. The only certainty was the cancer itself.

Jon stopped at the nurses' station and presented the small piece of paper on which the room number and name of the man were scribbled.

"Last room past the solarium." The nurse pointed and resumed making notations on a chart.

On his way down the hall Jon was jolted by the sight of children up from the pediatric ward to undergo their therapies. They demonstrated no self-consciousness over the spectacle they made with their hairless heads, swollen, sallow faces, and large sunken eyes ringed with bluish shadows. They wandered in and out of open doors, like a scouting party of tiny aliens from a distant planet. They moved slowly, with the shuffling steps of the aged, dragging dirty blankets and stuffed toys behind them, uninterested in each other, seeming to have lost entirely the instinct for play.

The resident population of the ward was adult.

Jon passed an open door where a middle-aged man sat on the edge of his bed. His jawbone was gone and unsupported chin flesh hung like the waddles on a turkey.

In the solarium another man sat in a chair staring out the window. His shaved head was covered with a crosshatching of purple X's, as if some bored intern had decided to play a game of tic-tac-toe on his skull. The marks were coordinates. His skull was a battle map indicating where the radiation artillery should fall to incinerate the thing in his brain that had taken away his ability to walk and speak.

A young woman not more than twenty napped in a wheelchair. Her thin arms were bruised and bloodied from the countless proddings in search of veins still capable of taking a needle. An IV dripped silently into her to dispense hope one drop at a time. A plastic tube snaked from underneath her gown and into a clear bag that contained an inch or so of pale yellow urine.

He should stop and say something to them, anything. They would appreciate his attentions. But what if they wouldn't let him leave? What if they gripped his sleeves and held him fast? What if they did not care about his ministry, but only coveted what he had? Time. What if they wanted him to sit with them and hold their hands as if their connection to him allowed them to stretch their own time beyond a doctor's most optimistic predictions? They were cowardly and selfish, these concerns of his, but real enough. He could not get himself to stop with them. How could it be that in a religion so centered on death that he, one of its ministers, had so few things to say to the dying?

When Jon reached the last room he hesitated. He double checked the room number on the scrap of paper. He listened for any sound emanating from within. He cursed the serendipitous encounter with the nurse. If he had lingered in the meeting room just a minute more ... What the hell was he doing here? He was trained in theology and canon law. Nothing had prepared him for this.

Finally Jon braced his shoulders and walked in.

The room was in semi-light. The doubled rows of drapes kept out the afternoon sun. A low-wattage light fixture on the wall behind the bed gave little relief from the gloom.

The man lay quietly. Stainless-steel guardrails were raised midway up the sides of the bed, only high enough to prevent his rolling off. He was probably in his mid-forties, but with cancer it was almost impossible to tell a person's age. He had a full head of hair and there were none of the purple markings. He was, however, excruciatingly thin and his skin had a sticky sheen as if it had been brushed with egg white. The pallor accentuated the peppery stubble of whiskers on his sunken cheeks. He, too, wore a catheter attached to a plastic bag. The bag was completely empty and hung flat and useless by a hook on the bottom bed rail. They had either just changed the bag or his body had finally decided that it would piss no more. His arms lay above the covers and straight down his sides. The plastic hospital bracelet encircling his wrist was absurdly slack. If he were to hang his arm over the side, the bracelet would surely slip off and fall to the floor.

The top bar of the railing pressed hard into Jon's chest. "Can I get you anything?"

The man's eyes, thinly coated over with a viscous film, were half closed. He slowly moved his head back and forth just once.

"I am a Catholic priest. Would you like me to sit with you for a while?"

With that same economy of motion, the man nodded.

Jon looked around, saw a straight-backed chair upholstered in vinyl, and dragged it to the side of the bed, cringing at the shrill, scraping noise he was making.

They remained as they were, the patient and the priest, for a long time. Jon did not even pray. He soon became aware of the man's breathing. It was shallow but not labored, and it made the priest conscious of his own breathing. For whatever reason, be it because Jon did not want the man to resent his own obscenely strong and healthy exhalations or simply because he was trying to create some symbiotic rhythm between them, he began to match the man's economically precise inhaling and exhaling, breath for breath.

Then Jon dozed.

He awoke to the sounds of the nurse who had sent him into this hell. She was at the door, hesitant to enter and interrupt.

"Excuse me, Father. I'm just checking to see if he needs anything."

"That's OK. I'd better get going."

Jon rose and leaned over the railing. "I've got to leave. But I'll be back if you want me to."

The man opened his eyes fully then and looked directly into the priest's face. With an effort that was obviously heroic, he moved his lips. Jon tried to catch his words but heard only a hoarse whisper.

"I'm sorry. What was that?"

The man closed his eyes for a long moment, swallowed hard, and then looked at Jon again. He formed his words carefully this time. They were clear and distinct and only the priest could hear them.

"I hate you."

You could count Monsignor Montini as one more among those who had not succumbed to the Armitage magic. The Italian began to resent the priest's growing success as a tribunalist. Not that he cared a wit about the people Fr. Jon was helping, but he sensed that his own standing in the archdiocese was suffering some erosion. And this, although he wasn't sure how, might just have repercussions on his goal of making a million dollars in the next twenty-four months. His discomfort with Fr. Jon escalated dramatically on the day of his latest return from Italy, where he had been summoned, he claimed, to the bedside of a sick uncle.

"Monsignor," Fr. Jon said, intercepting Montini on his way to his office. "Welcome back. Good trip?"

"My uncle." The monsignor sighed. "I fear I have seen him for the last time."

"Oh, I'm so sorry," Fr. Jon responded. "Is this the same uncle you went back to visit a couple of months ago?"

"Yes," the monsignor answered. "We had hopes. But now . . ."

"You must be very close to him." There was a curious lack of empathy in the priest's voice.

Machiavelli could not have been any more adept at spotting a red flag. "We Italians are not like you Americans." Montini had not meant to sound so strident, so defensive, and quickly oiled his delivery. "I mean, our families are everything. Especially the elderly. But you should know. You lived with us."

"Yes, I did." Fr. Jon betrayed nothing with his response. "Anyway, glad you're back. I have three marriage cases I'd like you to sign off on."

"Just leave them on my desk," Montini said. "I'll review them later."

Fr. Jon wanted to smile. To his knowledge Monsignor Montini had never reviewed a single one of his cases since he had taken over the tribunal. Up to this moment, the chancellor had been merely a rubber stamp, anxious to clear his desk to give himself more time for the important things, such as keeping the archbishop ignorant and happy.

"Fine," Fr. Armitage responded, "I'll get them for you. Oh, one more thing. You had some visitors last week. Very strange."

"What do you mean?" The monsignor went clammy. Who could it have been? The Italian authorities? U.S. Customs? Had he slipped up somewhere? He breathed a silent prayer to the Madonna to save him from his larcenous self.

"A delegation from El Torreon," Fr. Armitage continued. "They came for their santo. San Isidro, patron of farmers, I believe. They said they needed him for their annual procession before the spring plantings."

"What would I know about their plantings?" The monsignor reverted to peevishness, trying to hide his relief that the jig was not yet up.

"They said you took the statue away last fall."

"Yes, I gave them a new statue to replace it. The archbishop knows what I've been doing. A small effort to instruct them. Some of those santos are products of superstition. They're even a little blasphemous. Such unhappy saints. Religious images should be more pliable, more approachable, don't you think?" The monsignor simpered, looking very much like one of those plaster statues he was palming off on the faithful of northern New Mexico.

Having absolutely no opinion about such a bizarre subject as the pliability of plaster statuary, Fr. Jon pushed on. "Well, they were insistent that they would not leave without their San Isidro, so I looked around your office, but couldn't find anything."

"You searched my office?" The monsignor's eyes widened as his voice rose.

"Just a quick peek. I remembered seeing a couple of santos on your credenza before you left on your trip. But they're gone now."

"And what did the delegation have to say about that?" Montini reddened even as he tried to regain his calm.

"They left. Very unhappy. They said they'd be back."

"Troublemakers," the monsignor said, sniffing.

"Yes," Fr. Jon said. "They do crop up now and then."

After Fr. Armitage had left, closing the door behind him as requested, Monsignor Montini fell heavily into his chair, as heavily as his 112 pounds would allow, and considered his situation. Slow down, he advised himself. The villa can wait a year or two more. Best to be prudent. And then he shifted his attention to Fr. Armitage and muttered a popular Roman imprecation: *Li mortacci tua.* That Armitage was no fool, although there was no way he could know what was actually going on. Still, he would bear watching.

So carefully had Fr. Jon protected himself from a frontal charge by the new women in his life that he had totally neglected his flanks. It was a dangerous oversight. For now bearing down on one wing was the chancellor. And soon, in full battle array, the archbishop himself would attack his other side.

Chapter Seven

Dear Sally—
Santa Fe ain't too bad. I'd give my soul for some chowder,
but the steaks they serve around here are a pretty good
substitute. As for the chile? Well . . .

I'm doing more or less the same stuff I was doing before
only I'm left on my own a lot more, which I like. The people
are good to me and the climate is great.

Come on down!

Jon

Dear Jonny:
Thanks for your "chatty" note. One of these days why
don't you write me a real letter? At least I have an excuse.
Nothing's changed here since they founded the monastery
in 1873. Oh wait, I take that back. We did get a new milking
machine for the dairy last month. It's all white and chrome
and tubes and doodads. I just adore it.

I'm glad things are working out for you. I always wanted
to visit the West.

Is the sky really as blue as they say?

Keep your nose clean. You don't have your big sister
around to take care of that little chore for you.

The prayers continue.

Sally

Chapter Eight

Archbishop James J. Duggan had three passions. He loved to talk, he adored his feet, and he coveted his leisure time. In a matter of two weeks, Fr. Armitage managed to trample on all three.

As for the talking, the archbishop did not so much converse with others as hold court. Anytime he had an audience, be it formally as from the pulpit or at some diocesan function, or at some casual social gathering, he talked. Never listened. Just talked. It could be argued that the expression "captive audience" had been coined specifically for his listeners. Once ringed in by his stentorian pronouncements, there was no escape.

Eventually his listenership became the wiser. Parishioners at the cathedral avoided his masses whenever they had advance notice that he would be the celebrant. His invitations to dinner parties fell off alarmingly after his first year in Santa Fe. Eventually only his priests, by fiat, and a close circle of businessmen, by dint of needing his patronage, remained to labor under the weight of his many words.

Even some of the priests sought ways to absent themselves or leave early from those functions where he was present—church dedications, school openings, confirmation ceremonies, and clergy meetings. Unfortunately for these freethinkers, the archbishop made note of their absences. This gained them a private audience with His Loquaciousness where he would instruct them at length, he knew no other way, about the importance of fellowship among the clergy. "I am very disturbed, Father," he would go on and on. "When a priest avoids the opportunities to be with other priests, one has to wonder why."

By far the most pitiful of all the wretches who had to sit and listen to him pontificate were the three priests making up the archbishop's household, Monsignor Montini and the Fathers Armitage and Tapia. Mealtimes especially were their purgatory. At least breakfasts were an oasis since they all had daily Mass duties away from the archbishop's table. Lunch began their ordeal, mercifully limited by the need to return to work. Dinners were their black hole. Long after the table was cleared, Duggan, having undone the collar of his soutane, lit up a cigar and launched into his nightly panegyric to his ecclesiastical career. From his start as a crusading pastor in Altoona, to his rise to auxiliary bishop, to his appointment to the See of San Juan in Puerto Rico, no anecdote of his life was too trivial to go untold. He regaled them with the history of his thirty-five years in the priesthood, every what, where, when, why, and who recounted in stultifying detail.

Monsignor Montini alone found ways to escape most evenings, couching his excuses in a flattery that the archbishop could never resist. "I've got a meeting in Albuquerque," he might lie. "They wanted you, Your Excellency, but then so does everybody. Father Tapia can fill me in later if I miss anything. Take good notes, Lawrence," he joked, but only the archbishop laughed.

The archbishop beamed his approval. "Quite right. And thank you for your concern, Monsignor. I'd never have a spare moment if I accepted all the invitations to speak. Now then, where was I?"

After that, the monsignor would go to the movies, which he loved, or to his apartment where he played Italian operas on his hi-fi and went over his ledgers. Or he might actually attend a meeting, always making sure that it was scheduled around the dinner hour.

The other two priests, Jon and Lawrence, were left to their fates. Nodding acknowledgments and stifling yawns, they prayed against all hope that Duggan would not reach into his breast pocket for another cigar. Two-cigar nights were the ultimate agony.

Fr. Jon eventually caught onto Msgr. Montini's game and thereafter arranged for meetings at least once a week that took him from the table even as the archbishop was peeling off the wrapper of his gran panetela. Only poor, young, guileless, and unpracticed Fr. Lawrence was left to bear the full brunt of his prelate's words.

On an evening when Fr. Armitage had nothing scheduled, he took his place at the table and promptly overstepped his bounds.

As usual, Montini was an early defector, off to do the Lord's work, the Lord Archbishop's work that is, or so he claimed. Duggan had read a piece in the *New Yorker* about the future of the Catholic Church in these volatile times, and this was to be the subject of the evening's soliloquy. "The man's probably not even Catholic," he surmised about the author of the article. "Or worse, a renegade. Got an ax to grind, that's for sure."

"Or," Fr. Jon chimed in, "he knows what he's talking about." Why he chose that moment to strike ever so slight a blow for rationality, he could not say. Fatigue? Mental acuity blunted by the cloud of cigar smoke that was beginning to engulf them all?

"What's that you say, Father?" The archbishop, poised somewhere between puzzled and miffed, looked at him. Was he being prompted to further expound his thesis, or, God forbid, was he being challenged?

Fr. Jon did not back down. Having bearded the lion he proceeded to shear off its mane. Diving directly into a monologue of his own, Armitage spoke of the new spirit in the Church. He reminded Duggan of the windows that Pope John XXIII had flung open to air out centuries of complacency. He actually mentioned something about scraping off the barnacles from the Bark of Peter. He spoke of movements currently sweeping the Church, many of which he had firsthand knowledge of from his days studying canon law at the Catholic University in Washington. He wasn't even sure whether he actually subscribed to half of what he said. All he knew was that as long as he talked, the archbishop couldn't. And stopping the man from talking for even five minutes was an accomplishment.

Fr. Tapia could only sit in awe of such raw and rash courage.

Thus it was that Fr. Armitage stomped all over James J. Duggan's first passion, talking. The archbishop did not much like it. He harrumphed and said something about radicals and the wisdom that only time and experience can bring. Then he flicked ashes into his coffee cup, rose, and said he had some letters to write and left the table. For the first time in recent memory dinner was over before even the first cigar was finished.

Shortly thereafter, Fr. Jon had occasion to trivialize the archbishop's second passion, his feet.

"Take care of your feet. Soak them nightly. Rub them briskly with a towel. Work some good lotion into them, the heels, the soles, between the toes. Take care of your feet and they'll take care of you." Duggan delivered this dissertation just as they were being served their dinners. Unappetizing in the best of times, the topic of feet was even more revulsive to Fr. Jon as he stared at his plate holding a broiled chicken breast covered with cream gravy.

It happened several evenings later that Fr. Jon needed clarification on a point of diocesan policy before he met with some hospital administrators the next day. Duggan had just retired for the night and the priest reluctantly knocked on his door, needing but a simple yes or no, but knowing the archbishop's answer would come somewhere during a half hour's worth of episcopal elocution.

"Come in," boomed Duggan from the other side of the door.

Fr. Jon entered and followed the voice and the sound of running water into the archbishop's bathroom where the prelate was taking his own advice. He sat on the edge of the tub in his boxer shorts and undershirt, his ponderous feet playing with the steaming water that poured from the tap.

"Ah, Father Armitage," he said as he sprinkled a generous amount of Epsom salts over the water. "Best time of day, let me tell you. Many a problem I've solved here just thinking and watching the dead skin slough off. Take that callus now," he said, roughly jabbing at a horny encrustation on his left heel. "I think I need new golf shoes. But give me fifteen minutes and that skin there will be soft as a virgin's rump. Here, just see how hard that is now." He poked at the callus again.

Fr. Armitage was not sure how serious the invitation was and he was not about to find out. He pointedly looked away, suddenly finding the pattern of tiles on the bathroom wall particularly fascinating. "I can see how you relish these times of solitude, Excellency. What I have can wait until tomorrow."

Before Duggan could reply, Fr. Jon was out the door, in the corridor, and back in his own room. His imagination went wild on the what-might-have-been. "Would you mind toweling my feet, Father? Jesus did it for the apostles. And while you're at it, rub them with a little lotion."

For his part, the archbishop was left to slosh around and ponder what had just transpired. Being paranoid by nature, he took Fr. Jon's actions quite personally. "Damned uppity New Englander." The thought caused him to snort. "Needs to be brought down a peg or two."

Duggan might have found it in his heart of forgive Fr. Jon's rudeness at the dinner table or his finickiness in the matter of the foot bath, but when the priest completely disemboweled the prelate's third passion, his leisure time, it was too much.

One fine day in the middle of May, the archbishop was informed that his golf foursome was being disbanded.

"Too many schedule conflicts," the caller, a prominent Santa Fe lawyer, informed him. "Maybe we can work something out by the fall."

Without the golf there was no drinking and poker afterward. No more chances to talk, to cheat, to renege on bets.

Then word got back to him that the foursome had been reconstituted. Fr. Armitage, it seemed, was now in, but the archbishop was still out.

"Monsignor, what do you make of our Father Armitage?"

The question came after the archbishop had sequestered his chancellor in his office with the door closed.

"How do you mean, Excellency?" Whenever possible, Montini answered the archbishop's questions with his own.

"Do you think he's fitting in?"

"In what way?"

"Well, being from back east and all. How well does he know our part of the country?"

"Which part would that be, Excellency?"

"I think he could use a little seasoning, don't you? Some time away from here. Give him a chance to get to know our good and humble flock."

"You have something in mind, Excellency?"

"Nueve Niños is still vacant, isn't it?"

Montini was finally forced to utter a declarative. "Yes, Excellency."

"Yes," echoed the archbishop. "So I gathered."

Chapter Nine

When the going gets tough, the tough get going.

That is why Archbishop James J. Duggan made sure he was gone when the June assignment letters were mailed to his priests.

"Some pressing business back east," he told his chancellor. "I leave the archdiocese in your capable hands."

It was the only two weeks of the entire year that Monsignor Amleto Montini earned his purple piping. His primary duty was to remain in Santa Fe to field all inquiries about the new assignments—from parish councils protesting over the removal of a popular pastor, to parish councils protesting that an unpopular pastor had not been removed, and from priests who sought reprieves for reasons ranging from health to holiness. In each case Montini listened with a sympathetic ear before he used his considerable powers of deflection to champion the status quo.

"The archbishop is responsible for the entire archdiocese, not just a single parish."

"The archbishop is aware of your particular situation, which is exactly why he made [did *not* make] the move."

"Believe me, the archbishop shares your concerns, but there is always the greater good to consider."

❖

Fr. Jon Armitage was in no mood for such bromides. "Why, Monsignor? Just tell me that. I thought I was doing a pretty good job around here."

"You are, Jon, you are. And don't think that I didn't point out that very thing to His Excellency." Montini raised his scale-model shoulders to hide his earlobes while he thrust his jaw forward and covered his upper lip with his lower—the quintessential gesture of all Italian bureaucrats. "What can be done?" his entire body asked.

"I deserve some explanation."

"And don't I wish the bishop were here to give it to you, Father." The monsignor's eyes went owl-like. "He did mention something . . ."

"Yes?"

Montini spread out his hands on the desk and studied them as if they were a bill of indictment. "He's not quite sure how you're fitting in. He feels that a taste of parish life would do you some good. Get a feel for the archdiocese. It's nothing like back east, you know."

"But I'm not a parish priest. I'm a canon lawyer."

"Perhaps in a larger diocese, Father. But here? We must all bear the heat of the day in the Lord's vineyard."

Unsaid but understood was the fact that Jon Armitage had already screwed up once, that he was now a persona non grata in his home diocese, that he had come to Santa Fe at the pleasure of the archbishop, and that he'd better keep his mouth shut and do as he was told.

"Besides," Montini continued, "it's merely a temporary assignment. The letter makes that quite clear. You'll be back here in no time, no worse for the experience, I would imagine. Perhaps even a little wiser as to the ways of our people."

Fr. Armitage felt the air whistle out of his body and he sat down heavily. "Nueve Niños. I don't even know where that is."

"I have an excellent map of the state. You are welcome to use it if you like."

"I make it twenty bucks."

Fr. Armitage peeled off two bills and handed them over to the speaker.

"I'm going to frame these. Who would believe it? Father Jon finally loses." The doctor turned from the priest and held out a hand, palm up, to the lawyer. "That's twenty from you, too."

Jon's golf partner for the day reached for his wallet but only after a baleful look at the priest. "Magic putter, my Aunt Fanny."

Jon shrugged. "Sorry."

A doctor, a lawyer, a banker, and the priest. It was the regular Thursday foursome, the one from which Archbishop Duggan had been unceremoniously dumped. They would soon be looking for another player to take Fr. Armitage's place.

The doctor placed an arm around Fr. Jon's neck and tugged at it playfully. "You've got a lot on your mind. Next time will be better."

The priest shook the doctor off. "No excuses. And there won't be a next time."

"C'mon, Jon. You'll be back taking our money before you know it. And, actually, Nueve Niños isn't that bad. A little out of the way maybe. I've got a cabin on the lake. The town is directly across. You can see it from my front porch on a good day. Quiet. Pretty nice—unless the wind blows."

Over the next two hours, lubricated with many beers, the three laymen sat in the lounge of the Santa Fe Country Club and consoled the priest. Nothing seemed to work until the doctor came up with his idea.

"So you're due up there a week from Sunday?"

Fr. Jon tossed a wrinkled ten-dollar bill on the table and made to rise. "A week from Sunday. The thirteenth."

"Now, don't be running off. How's this sound? A cooler full of steaks and beer, a couple of bottles of bourbon, and a weekend at my cabin. We can go up on Friday, do some fishing, play some cards, tell some lies, and get drunk. Then you say Mass for us on Sunday and all's forgiven."

It took some persuasion from the other three, but on Friday evening Fr. Armitage found himself standing on the edge of the caldera looking across to the far shore, a good two miles away. He could make out the eponymous nine cones. In front of them sat Nueve Niños like a brown toad, a squatting cluster of buildings that he could just make out through the rising mist. A Guatemalan jungle parish or a Mississippi clapboard church suddenly seemed most appealing.

The weekend of fun became a test of wills and friendships.

The cabin had been broken into, and what the vandals had not taken or trashed had been savaged by the elements and the entire catalogue of local critters.

When the men walked through the door, field mice scurried across the floor and into the woodwork. They heard some larger thing scampering up the fireplace chimney.

It took them two hours to clean up the mess. The gas generator had been stolen, so they had no power for the lights, the stove, the refrigerator, or the well pump. They had to build a fire in the grate to cook their meat and to boil water brought up from the lake. A Coleman lantern was their only source of illumination.

"Well, at least they can't steal the fish," said the doctor. "A day on the lake with some beer and a rod and reel will make up for all of this. You'll see."

Beginning with that Saturday's dawn, the winds came at them off the water.

Any thought of spending the day fishing went swooshing away in a barrage of relentless gusts. The lake churned up malevolent white caps and taunted the men to shove off in their puny aluminum boat. Casting from shore was futile. They might as well try to launch their lines and lures against the side of the cabin.

All that was left to them was cards and liquor. But the wind found a way to sabotage even that. Wanton zephyrs worked their way down the chimney, under the door, through chinks in the walls, and through broken windowpanes that the men had not been able to adequately seal off. Playing cards and poker chips flew willy-nilly from the table at the most inopportune times. The room was in a constant swirl of smoke, ash, and dirt. They tried valiantly to filter their drinks through clenched teeth, but could not avoid ingesting the dustings that coated their whiskey with a fine film.

By evening the four could no longer be considered a group. It was every man for himself. The doctor, lawyer, and banker fed on the edginess brought on by their confinement and openly attacked each other at the slightest provocation. Alliances were made and just as quickly broken as each took a turn being the butt of jokes and barbs. Only Fr. Jon, by dint of clerical privilege and his melancholy, was spared.

They went to bed early and tossed fitfully in their sleeping bags to the harsh lullaby of the wind that tore at the roof and sent grit against windows and walls.

Sunday morning they awoke to find themselves and everything around them covered with a gray patina. But, for all that, it was a glorious day outside, almost as if the lake had decided to reward them for their perseverance.

"See? What did I tell you?" their host, the doctor, asked. "How about a little breakfast before we hit the lake?"

An inventory of their stores revealed the unmitigated perversity of this alien place. Except for two cans of beans, the rest of the food was permeated with fine sand. The mice had taken care of a dozen eggs and the communion wafers that Fr. Jon had brought for Mass.

"Well, that does it for me," the banker said. "I'm all for getting back to Santa Fe as soon as we can load the car."

"We're here to have a good time and to help Father Jon out. It's a gorgeous morning. Why leave now?" the doctor argued.

But the banker was not assuaged, having already disclosed his true character the day before. He was an accomplished complainer. "But we gotta eat."

The doctor took a swig directly out of a whiskey bottle and passed it on. "Clayton's only forty miles away. We can pick up some supplies and be back by noon at the latest. We'll have the whole afternoon on the lake and still make Santa Fe by midnight. What about it?"

The lawyer agreed. The banker shrugged.

"Go without me," Fr. Jon said. "I'll pick things up around here. And I can get some praying in. It is Sunday, after all."

By midmorning, Fr. Jon had swept out the one-room cabin, wiped off as many exposed surfaces as he could reach, and boxed all the ruined food for disposal. It was done with nary a prayer, and he still had an hour and a half more to himself.

Fr. Jon headed outdoors for the lakeshore. The sun lased into the water with such force that even when he shielded his eyes against the glare, he could not see Nueve Niños on the other side. Perhaps it had blown away in yesterday's gale. Wouldn't that be a fine joke on the bishop and Montini? But no, he could not allow himself to indulge in such frivolous irony. The reality of his situation was too stark for any compromise.

Skipping stones across the water involved him for but a few moments. His muscles still ached from a night on a wooden pallet with nothing but the thin sleeping bag to cushion him. He windmilled his arms to loosen up his shoulders and kicked his knees high against his chest as he ran briskly in place. He knew, however, that calisthenics could only occupy him for so long. Maybe he should pray. Had he even remembered to pack his breviary? An hour with the psalms might alter his mood—self-pity was finally becoming a tiresome mistress with overweening demands on his energies.

His examination of conscience shorted out when he spotted the boat. The evening before, he had helped drag it inland where they turned it upside down and shored its sides with large pieces of shale to keep it from blowing away. The prospect of a turn on the lake dredged up happy memories. Growing up in Fall River, profligate in its waterways, Fr. Jon had been a dedicated rower for most of his life. It seemed such a long time ago.

He righted the aluminum shell and pushed it down to the waterline. With a final shove he launched her, hopped in, took a position on the rear cross seat, and clamped in the oars. One stroke and he was ten feet out. After a few runs back and forth along the shore he felt confident enough to strike out into deeper water. Two miles across. He could do that in his sleep, particularly in the ideal conditions with which the day now presented him. Head for Nueve Niños and have a look. Maybe even walk around the village, unknown, like a king in pauper's rags among his subjects. Maybe get a bite to eat, presuming they had a restaurant. It was something to do.

He fixed his eyes on the cabin, lined it up with one of the distant cones on the other side, and began his backward voyage across the lake.

Half an hour later, by his estimation, he had barely reached the middle. There seemed to be a subtle but strong undercurrent grabbing at the hull like watery hands intent on neutralizing the efficacy of each oar stroke.

The sun was now high and his sweat was beginning to react to the grit that had worked its way into the folds and crevices of his body under his clothes. He was growing more and more uncomfortable from the constant chaffing. Maybe he'd better turn back. His companions would be returning soon. But first he must deal with his discomfort.

Fr. Jon stripped and vigorously shook and slapped each piece of clothing against the side of the boat. Then he stood up, spread his legs for balance, and swiped at his upper body with his hands. In his complete nakedness he was Leonardo da Vinci's Vitruvian man, bold, sinewy, and standing astride. He was the absolute fantasy incarnate of every woman who had ever carried lust in her heart for him. And he knew it.

From a crouch he rolled over the side into the water. It was cold but certainly nowhere near as cold as the Atlantic around Buzzards Bay. He held on to the stern until he became acclimated, then pushed off with smooth, strong strokes. It was glorious. The bracing chill of the water. The warm sun. The solitude. He had not felt so free since his days in Italy.

How much time went by while he swam he could not tell, but he was suddenly made aware of his surroundings. The air turned chilly. The water grew choppy. The boat began to bob listlessly. And then the winds came. There was no panic in the priest, but he knew from experience that a rapid change of weather over water was seldom a good thing. By the time he reached the boat, the wind was howling. He made several efforts to lift himself over the side, but it was like trying to mount a wild mustang. There seemed nothing he could do to stabilize the bucking. And he was starting to get very tired. It was then that he could feel the panic grabbing hold. With one last pull he tilted the boat toward himself and tried to swing a leg up and over. His clumsy maneuver, aided by a gust of wind that roared by like a freight train at that exact moment, proved the small craft's undoing. It rose high in the water, hesitated but for a moment, and flipped over on top of Fr. Jon.

An edge struck the priest's head. He saw stars and then he saw darkness. It was as if he had been swallowed up whole by some giant sea creature. Now what? His years of canoeing had not prepared him for this. And even if he could think of something, he was too exhausted and stunned to do anything about it, especially since the boat continued to lurch and bounce. So he wrapped an arm over the span that had until recently served as his seat and let himself dangle in the darkness like a bobbin on a line.

Time became nothing. How much of it had gone by? One, two, three hours? He had no idea. It was as if he were trapped in a sensory deprivation chamber, except he could feel that the crook of his arm was rubbing raw from its half-nelson hold on the sharp edges of the metal seat.

At last he understood from the gentler movement of the boat that the wind had subsided. It was now or never. He held his breath, relaxed his hold on the seat, and let himself sink into the water. Then, with one ferocious kick, he came to the surface like a breaching dolphin and threw his arms across the ribbed hull. Inch by inch, careful not to upset the balance of his tiny universe, he pulled his body onto the aluminum shell and managed to straddle the tapered bow. He had finally tamed his bronco.

However long he had been in the belly of the beast, it was now almost dark. Above him, stars were beginning to wink on, but since he was no navigator, they did him little good. Then he saw twinklings on the horizon. The cabin? Too many lights and too scattered. It could only be Nueve Niños. Apparently, while he was trapped underneath it, the boat had drifted almost completely across the lake.

While he rested, Fr. Jon Armitage now considered his options. He could stay with the craft until morning, when someone would surely be around to search for him. But there was a mean chill in the air now, sure to get colder. How long before hypothermia set in? He could try to paddle, but since he could only stretch his arm down one side of the boat at a time, he would end up going in circles. Perhaps he could hold on to the stern and kick his way to shore. He doubted he had the strength, particularly because he had had nothing to eat since the evening before. The bump to his head was beginning to throb. His only real choice was to try to swim to land. It didn't seem that far, and if the drop-off near shore was gradual enough, he might even be able to walk in part of the way.

What a sight he'd be. Not a king in pauper's rags. More like Boticelli's Venus. There he would stand, the water lapping at his ankles, his hands strategically placed to hide his nakedness. He'd have no secrets from the people of Nueve Niños after that.

Fr. Jon slipped back into the water, much colder now with no sun to heat its surface. Slow and steady. That was his plan. And every twenty-five strokes he would roll over on his back and float while he rested.

As he pushed away from the canoe he immediately began to regret it. He could feel the undercurrent, not overwhelming but damnably persistent. Perhaps his plan was not such a good one. However, he did not have the strength to fight the boat again, so he began to swim. Keep an eye on the lights, always the lights. He saw that his more developed right shoulder kept pulling him off course so he constantly had to make adjustments. He swam. He turned on his back and floated. His mind drifted. Then the lights were gone. He must have closed his eyes for a fatal moment. Frantically, he treaded water and slowly rotated his body until he caught sight of the lights again. How long had he been swimming away from them? How much distance had he lost? Had he dozed? Was he starting to hallucinate? Concentrate. Concentrate. He swallowed water and convulsed with coughing. Come on. Come on. It can't be that much farther. He could almost reach out and touch the lights. Yes, that's right. Do it. Reach out and touch the lights. But his arms would no longer respond.

Chapter Ten

"¿*Quién es?*"

"¿*Quién sabe?*"

"¡*Míralo! Bien empeloto.*"

Fr. Jon heard the voices and his eyelids fluttered and opened.

He was lying on his back, not on water nor land, but on some delicious softness. And that was not the sky above him nor the sun searing his eyeballs. It was a single bare light bulb hanging from a strand of wire that ran into the ceiling. There were four walls. The softness was a bed. The voices belonged to a man and a woman.

They were so engaged in conversation that they had not noticed him stir.

"Where am I?" That's what Fr. Jon wanted to say, but the sound from his throat came out a weak rasp.

The woman immediately knelt by the bed and patted his brow. "*Calma.*"

"*Es gringo,*" the man said. "*No entiende nada.*"

"We found you by the *laguna,*" the woman said to Jon. "How do you feel?"

Jon tried to focus on her face, failed, and closed his eyes. "Where am I?" he finally managed.

"My house. I have some tea on the stove. I'll be right back."

The man followed the woman out the door with his eyes, said something under his breath, and walked over to the foot of the bed.

"How come you don't got no clothes? *Mírate.*" The man pinched the collar of his shirt and jiggled it. "*No tienes ropa.* No clothes."

Jon worked a hand under the cover and discovered for himself what the man had been declaiming for the last five minutes. "My boat," he said. "I had a problem."

"*¿Problema?* You don't got no clothes."

"I was swimming and the wind came up. I lost everything when the boat capsized."

"You swim like that?" The man was curiously fixated on the nakedness.

"I didn't think anyone would see me."

The man grinned and exposed a gap of three missing front teeth. "We saw you. We saw you. *Todo toditito.*" His laugh was hardly pleasant.

The woman returned, holding a steaming cup in both hands. "*Déjalo,*" she hissed at the man.

"I ain't doing nothing to him."

"Just go away."

"Why? So you can be alone *con este chingado empeloto? Los mato a los dos.*"

The woman took a step toward the man. "You ain't killing nobody."

This sort of face off was obviously a common occurrence between them. And, just as obviously, the man was never up to the challenge. He threw his middle finger and a curse in the direction of the woman and stomped out of the room and out of the house with a slam of the front door.

The woman wiped a strand of hair from her face and turned to the bed. "You can drink?"

Jon nodded and, with some effort, propped himself up on his elbows.

The woman handed him the cup. "Drink. It will help."

The steam from the cup assailed Jon's nostrils and informed him that he was not about to take a sip of Earl Grey or orange pekoe. Whatever it was, it burned going down and its aftertaste was reminiscent of scrapings from a stable floor. Its color, bile green, helped to reinforce this impression. Fr. Jon was positive that to drink this brew on an empty stomach was courting disaster.

"What is this?"

"No talk. Drink it all. It's good."

The taste of the tea notwithstanding, Jon began to feel a pleasant tingling in his body. It took him so by surprise that he almost giggled. He closed his eyes and took his medicine to the dregs. Exhausted with the effort, he fell back on the bed.

The woman took the cup and stood looking down on him. "Good?"

"Yes, thank you. How did I get here?"

"We found you by the lake. We thought you were dead. *Muy suertudo*. You are very lucky."

Jon suddenly remembered and tried to sit up again. "My friends. They'll be looking for me."

The woman put the flat of her hand on the priest's chest and pushed him back onto the bed. "Later. Now you sleep. The tea will help."

The glare from the light bulb hurt his eyes and he had to close them. Then he found that he couldn't open them. He slept.

In his dream he was in a coffin half filled with water. He banged on its sides and top and was rewarded with the reverberating noise of fist against tinny metal. He also could hear the wind but could not feel it. What he could feel—and here he could not tell whether this was part of the dream or not—was a warm, soft hand rubbing his brow. Then it moved to his chest, to his abdomen, and up and down one thigh. The touch was not prurient, just gentle and achingly curious.

Never had there been a Monday morning such as this. Never had Nueve Niños known such an armada of water-worthy craft. Speed boats, cabin cruisers, outboards. The din they made brought half the population of the town down to the lake. Dogs ran up to the water's edge, snarled, barked, and retreated behind their masters. Words were shouted back and forth above the noise of the idling motors.

"We're looking for a rowboat. There was a man in it."

"No boat here."

"The man might have washed ashore along here someplace."

"No man here."

"Well, if you see anything."

"*Sí, sí.* If we see anything."

Just as the lead boat started to pull away, a woman stepped from the crowd. "Wait, *señores. Espérense. Está en mi casa.*" She pointed to a house down the shoreline, separated from its closest neighbor by at least a hundred yards.

The villagers began chattering to each other. How much more excitement to their day could they bear? Not only was the man here, but he was at Cósima's house. There would be enough gossip to go around for the entire week.

Two of the launches moored and disgorged their passengers, a captain of the state police, a sheriff, two deputies, and the doctor, lawyer, and banker. They gathered in a tight knot on the shore while they confabbed. Satisfied with their conclusions, they formed a loose phalanx to part the crowd and followed the woman to her house. The villagers fell in behind.

Fifteen minutes later Fr. Jon appeared at the door, draped in the coverlet from the woman's bed.

As he was led through the assemblage, which had by now doubled in size, old women fell to their knees and pulled children down with them. Some people reached out to touch him. Others wept shamelessly. Many in the crowd, men included, crossed themselves. After all, they had just been privy to a miracle. And not just a man's survival out of the caldera. Nothing so prosaic. They had learned from the lawyer that this man was a priest. But more than that, he was *their* priest, assigned to them by the archbishop himself.

And the miracle?

This priest had walked up from the same waters into which their forbearers had cast the wicked pastor so many years before. Apparently the lake was now disposed to give back what it had taken away, the hope of redemption.

The word spread through Nueve Niños with gale swiftness. Perhaps the curse was about to be lifted from Nueve Niños.

They watched silently as Fr. Jon was helped into a waiting patrol car to be driven away.

After a day of recuperation in Santa Fe, Fr. Jon was back in the chancellor's office.

Montini hopped down from his chair, opened his arms wide, and rushed at Fr. Jon. *"Che gioia. Grazie a Dio."*

Fr. Jon stiffened at the embrace and could only be grateful that he was so tall and the monsignor so short as to make a kiss on the cheek next to impossible.

"Come stai, come stai, Father Jon? We were worried sick. The archbishop was ready to shorten his trip, but then we decided that there was nothing to be done."

"I hope he realizes that Nueve Niños is now out of the question."

"That never came up. Why would you think so?"

"The whole thing. It's too ridiculous. The notoriety. The embarrassment. The entire situation. Surely you must agree. I didn't even have any clothes on, for God's sake."

"Yes, I heard. I immediately thought of Michelangelo's *David.* Magnificent. The statue, of course."

Unsure what to do with this curious remark, Fr. Jon let it pass. "I simply can't go to Nueve Niños now."

"I couldn't disagree with you more, Father. And I spoke with the archbishop by phone this morning and he concurs wholeheartedly. Don't you know what's happened here? You, Father Jon, have become a legend overnight. Not just in Nueve Niños, but throughout the archdiocese. The phone calls. The telegrams. The letters. The TV. There's never been anything like it."

"But it's all bullshit. I made a stupid mistake, that's all. And I almost killed myself. I'm no goddamn legend. I'm a bloody sideshow."

Montini smiled beatifically. "God works in mysterious ways, Father. Your people await your return."

Monsignor Montini was not alone in his assessment of the situation. Over the next few days, at parties to celebrate his rescue, on the street, at restaurants and places where he went to clear up his affairs before departing, people approached Fr. Jon with one thing in mind—to have contact with the miracle priest. To think that God had saved and delivered him to the very place that the archbishop had intended for him all along. Nueve Niños was blessed indeed to have such a man of destiny to minister to them.

That next Saturday, a still embittered Fr. Jon Armitage loaded up his car and headed up the highway to his new assignment.

Archbishop Duggan, on his return, was apprised by his chancellor of how things had turned out.

"Well, well," the archbishop responded upon hearing Montini's report, "it appears that our loss is Nueve Niños's gain. We may never get him out of there."

And for one of the few times in his life the archbishop did not elaborate.

Chapter Eleven

Dear Sally—

I guess I've gone and done it again. When will I ever learn? This time I really might have messed it up. I've been appointed to a small, godforsaken parish on the far side of the moon. It's some sort of punishment, although I don't know why. Honest!

I'll go of course. I have no choice. But I'm just a little bit bitter and angry and, entre nous, just a wee bit frightened. Is this what it's all coming to? Thank God Mom and Dad aren't around.

On to more serious things, did you ever get the bikini I sent you?

Jon

Dear Jonny:

There's only one thing worse than your cockiness and that's your whining. I don't want to hear it. Whatever you did, wherever you go, know that I love you. You also have to know that I will not listen to any complaining. Is that God I hear talking to you? Sometimes He works that way. Maybe you don't know as much theology as I thought.

If you were to send a bikini, I know I'd hate the color, and besides you never get my size right.

Sally

Chapter Twelve

It was all very new to the members of the parish of San Eusebio. For the first time in memory they welcomed a new priest not with suspicion bordering on antagonism, but with childlike anticipation.

For his part, Fr. Jon Armitage was equally discombobulated. His modus operandi for most of his life had been to ingratiate himself. But now he must develop a new set of skills. He must learn how to be disliked. As quickly as possible, he must disabuse these people of the notion that he was some sort of beatus. To do this he must be blunt, almost brutally so. He must discourage any effort at adulation. He must show these people who he really was. Certainly not of their kind. The sooner they rejected him, the sooner he could shake the dust of Nueve Niños from his Florsheims.

His assault on the sensibilities of his new congregation began almost immediately. On the Saturday afternoon of his arrival, he was greeted on the front stoop of the rectory by San Eusebio's mayordomo and his wife. They were a matched pair, short, no-necked, round-faced, and beaming, the only difference being that she was somewhat darker complected.

"*Buenas tardes, Padre. Yo soy Esteban, el mayordomo. Esta es mi mujer, Dorotea.*"

"Hello." Fr. Jon made his voice sound as flat and neutral as he possibly could and added to the subtext by responding in English.

Esteban held up a key ring and jingled it merrily. "We have the keys for your house and for the church."

Jon stretched out his hand. "Yes. I'll take those."

The mayordomo began to work a key off the ring.

"I'll take them all."

"But I will need to have a key for the church."

"Does anyone else have one?"

"Sí, Padre. *El sacristano.*"

"Well, you share one. I'll keep the rest."

When Esteban reached out to hand the priest the entire ring of keys, it was as if he were turning over a chunk of his heart. What was a mayordomo without keys? What would he tell the town council? When they had put him in charge of the church for this year, they had made quite a solemn ritual of presenting him the symbols of his office. Now he had nothing.

Esteban had planned to offer his and his wife's services to help unpack the new pastor's car. But now he was too deflated, too disgraced. And the worst of it was that he had put up no resistance at all, the priest's ambush had been so swift. "*Buenas tardes*, Padre," is all he could think to say before he took Dorotea by the arm and walked away.

The little church was standing room only for Fr. Jon's first Sunday Mass, and not just with the regulars, which consisted mainly of old ladies and women with children, but with a fair number of new faces, some who hadn't seen the inside of this or any church for many years.

In the sacristy before Mass, Fr. Jon nodded stiffly to Tobías Rincón, the sacristan, and donned his vestments with cold, silent calculation. The Mass would be respectful but perfunctory. The sermon would be in English rather than Spanish, a sure crowd displeaser. He was actually quite facile with the romance languages. He had grown up speaking French to his grandparents. He had picked up Italian quickly during his Rome studies, and he had spent a summer in Madrid. His Spanish was not perfect, but it was more than serviceable. But not one word of it would he utter from the San Eusebio pulpit.

The sermon itself was anything but a congenial salutatory, something that might be expected of a newly arrived priest eager to make a good first impression. Fr. Jon had never preached a fire and brimstone sermon before, and it surprised even him how naturally it all flowed.

He spoke of the evils of superstition, of the dangers of following false prophets, of the tendency to rely on miracles when hard work was the answer. He told his congregation that they were a wicked lot whose path, up to now, was leading them straight to perdition. He called on them to repent before it was too late. By the time he was done with his tongue-lashing there was little skin left on the hapless parishioners looking up at him from the pews.

Unfortunately for Fr. Jon, the sermon had the exact opposite effect of what he had intended. Those who understood English nodded their heads in appreciation for the truth, albeit bitter, that he had laid on them. Those who did not understand did not seem to mind either. It was as if he were speaking in glossolalia, directly inspired by the Holy Ghost. They humbly accepted the fact that they were not worthy to appreciate the words. They were satisfied merely to allow the cadence of the priest's voice to wash over them with its healing powers.

It was a great Sunday for the people of Nueve Niños. It was not so great for their pastor, even though the collection netted more than sixty dollars, an unheard of amount during the tenures of any of his predecessors.

After Mass, Fr. Jon received the first hint that his strategy of disaffection was flawed.

"*Muy bien dicho, Padrecito.* Your predication was very good."

"My what?" The priest removed his chasuble and handed it to the sacristan.

A squat, dewy, and doughy Tobías carefully folded the vestment and slipped it into a long shallow drawer in the vesting case. "Your predication." His eyes looked heavenward for help. "*La predicación— el sermón.*"

"Oh, you mean the sermon."

"Sí. The predication."

Fr. Jon tossed the remaining vestments on the countertop. "We'll see how wonderful the people think it is."

"Maybe not doña Clotilde, but she doesn't like anything. They say that her husband died just to get out of the house even though she kept the coffin in the *sala de recibir* for almost a week." Tobías reached for the long-handled candlesnuffer and headed for the entrance into the sanctuary. "But the rest, they liked it. I know."

The cloyingness of his smile along with the smell of his aftershave hung heavy in the air of the sacristy after he left.

Fr. Jon rammed the chalice and paten into their black storage case. Damn sycophant. What did he know? He'd probably been giving that same line of malarkey to priests for years. To Fr. Jon's mind, sacristans—and he had encountered his share from Europe to New England to New Mexico—were all the same. They all had the souls of court eunuchs, too eager to please, too fawning in their attentions. Well, Tobías could save his mewlings for the next pastor of Nueve Niños. Fr. Jon wanted no allies. And if the sacristan wasn't careful, he just might get his chubby little ass kicked out the sacristy door.

The crowd at the next morning's 6:30 Mass was not as large but still impressive.

Tobías was there to greet him. "*Buenos días, Padrecito.* Many peoples in church. They love their new priest. *También yo.*"

Fr. Jon was tempted to can him on the spot. But then he remembered that the church bell had tolled at 6:00 that morning to rouse the town. Someone had to do it, and until that someone else came along, perhaps it was best that he temper his distaste for Tobías.

When Fr. Jon returned to the rectory, there was already a long line of people formed outside the front door.

"Go home," he told them. "The office doesn't open until ten o'clock."

Everyone smiled but no one moved.

The archbishop's rationale for sending Fr. Jon to Nueve Niños for a year was so he could get in touch with the people. The priest felt that he had already squeezed the entire 365 days into forty-eight interminable hours.

The calls at the rectory were incessant. There were candles and rosaries to purchase and statues to bless. There were masses and baptisms to arrange. There were marriages to validate. Part of the rush was because Nueve Niños had not had a priest since just after Christmas. The people of San Eusebio had run the previous pastor off when they discovered that he had turned over the carved statue of their patron saint to someone from the archbishop's office. But by far the main reason so many came to the rectory was to make personal contact with the miracle priest.

He scarcely dared to leave the rectory. For the time being at least, he was a walking shrine. On the streets men doffed their hats and stepped aside when he passed. The women gaped and gazed, not with the lust of the women of Fall River and Santa Fe, but with pious intent. The apostles who witnessed Christ's transfiguration on the mountain could not have been more reverential.

How could Fr. Jon hope to counter something that was beginning to take on the trappings of downright idolatry?

By the third day, Fr. Jon had enough. "Come back tomorrow," he told the throng gathered in the front yard of the rectory. "There are no more blessings left today."

Fr. Jon waited until nightfall, when he hoped that everyone would be in their houses having supper and getting ready for bed.

He put on a sweat suit and laced up his Adidas. Through a slit in the curtain of the front window he checked the small square in front of the church for any straggler still out and about. It wouldn't surprise him if Tobías was crouched behind a gravestone just to keep an eye on him. He leaned out the front door to make sure that the road that ran past the rectory was empty in both directions. Finally, to make doubly sure that no one spotted him, he sneaked out the back. At the lake he made a right turn and followed the gentle curve of the shoreline. He ran full tilt for more than a mile and did not stop until he was gasping for air and had to bend over to massage a stitch in his side.

"It's the altitude. You have to learn how to pace yourself."

The voice, cultured and in perfect English, came from the carcass of a rusted pickup truck half buried in a small sand dune.

"Or better yet. Don't run at all."

Fr. Jon walked over to the derelict. A man sat halfway in the truck's cab on a bench seat that was in the process of losing the last of its stuffing. He was dressed completely in the shabbiest of denims. His hair was pulled back from his skull into a ponytail. His beard was gathered at the end by a common rubber band. Around his neck hung a strand of odd-sized and unpolished turquoise nuggets strung together with a rawhide thong. On one wrist he wore a wide bracelet of beads. His bare feet were callused and horny, the nails irregular and curled inward. His odd appearance notwithstanding, Fr. Jon was most taken by the fact that the man was Anglo. The priest had thought that he was the only non-Hispanic in town.

"Didn't mean to startle you." The man took a swig from a half-empty bottle of wine and held it out. "Pardon my manners."

Fr. Jon waved off the offer.

"You must be the new priest."

"Yes. Jon Armitage." He started to hold out his hand but realized that the man was looking elsewhere.

"So what do you think of our little community?" the man asked when he finally returned his attention to the priest.

Fr. Jon shrugged.

"Don't worry. You'll soon learn to hate it."

The man struggled to stand, flailed his arms for balance, and in the process lost some of the wine across the front of his shirt. "The Kiowas used to camp around here. My house is just over that mound over there. Drop in sometime. Maybe we can discuss philosophy."

He walked away, leaving the priest alone.

On his return jog to the village, Fr. Jon took a more leisurely pace. His eyes swept inland. Finally he spotted it. The house where he had been taken in, naked and near drowned.

The woman answered his knock. "Ah, Padre."

The other Fr. Jon, the one he was purposefully denying to his flock, the ingratiating Fr. Jon, smiled. "I didn't get a chance for a proper thank-you the other day."

"Padre, you didn't have to come just for that."

"Of course I did. You saved my life."

The woman now returned his smile, her teeth were as white as native quartz, her eyes sparkling black basalt. She was not beautiful by Fall River standards but there was something about her . . .

"*De nada*," she said.

The silence that now settled between them quickly threatened to turn awkward.

"Well, I won't keep you," Fr. Jon finally said. "I just didn't want you to think that I was ungrateful. I wanted to come sooner."

"The people have kept you very busy."

"Very. It's good to be out of the house."

Sensing that the moment was about to grow clumsy again, the woman stepped back into the doorway. "Would you like something to drink?"

Fr. Jon remembered her last offering. "Uh, no. That's all right."

Her laugh was easy. "Not the tea. I'll save that for the next time you fall in the lake. Maybe some coffee? My name is Cósima."

The house was as Fr. Jon remembered it. Clean if sparse in its furnishings.

The woman was somewhere between thirty-five and fifty; he could not tell. Her skin was smooth, Mediterranean. Her dark hair was pulled back into a single braid that hung down her back to the waist. She was not large, but she had substance. The way she stood in the middle of the room, her bare feet planted slightly apart, was as if she were rooted to the earth beneath the scrubbed planking of the floor. Fr. Jon had seen plenty of hardy peasant women in Italy and Spain. She would have stood out even there.

They drank their coffee and they talked. It had always been easy for Fr. Jon to talk with women. It was the same now, but it was also different. He did not feel the need to perform. There was no artifice, no coyness, no meaningless banter.

They talked about his rescue. They laughed about the tea. He promised to replace the coverlet he had worn like a toga to be transported away in the sheriff's car. They talked about Nueve Niños.

Finally, he asked about her. "And just who is Cósima?"

"*Nadie. No cuento por nada.* I am nobody that you should bother with."

"Now you're being foolish."

"I know what I say." Her eyes bore into him. "You must not come here again."

"And now you've hurt my feelings." For the first time that evening Fr. Jon reverted to facile flirtation and immediately regretted it.

"No, no," she said, "*estoy seria.* I am not a good woman."

"I'd say you're a wonderful woman."

"*Soy una soltera.* I do not even have a man."

"What about the one who was with you when you found me?"

Cósima released a guttural sound from deep in her throat. "He is not my man. He wants to be, but he isn't. He pays like all the rest."

"Say again?"

The woman blushed and looked down at the table that separated them. "I told you already. I am not a good woman."

"Stop saying that."

The woman stood, took the cup from Fr. Jon's hand, and walked to the sink. "*Yo vendo mis favores*, Padre. It is that simple."

"I don't understand."

"Men pay money to be with me."

It was Fr. Jon's turn to blush. "Surely you can find something else to do for a living." This came after a long pause.

"There is nothing wrong with what I do. The men need me. The women need me even more. When their husbands are with me, they know that they will have them back in time to feed and to climb into bed with them. They don't worry that some other woman will steal them away."

Fr. Jon was not at all sure how to respond. As a priest he supposed he should urge her to recognize the error of her ways. But she was no Mary Magdalen, and he certainly was no Christ. As a canon lawyer he couldn't help but wonder how many marriages she had saved. Apparently more than he ever would. And as man? He would not allow his thoughts to roam in that direction.

"Cozy arrangement. For them. But what about you?"

"It is who I am."

After Mass the next morning there were no smiles from Tobías. Instead, as he took a vestment from Fr. Jon, he leaned forward much closer than the priest would have preferred and whispered, "Be careful where you go in Nueve Niños, Padrecito. *La gente sabe todo.* And they talk." Then he was out to the sanctuary with the candlesnuffer.

Chapter Thirteen

If Nueve Niños had ever enjoyed a heyday, there was no evidence of it by the summer of 1965. Even the swagger was gone. The once feared citizens of Nueve Niños had long ago diminished until they were eventually nothing more than a caricature of themselves. However, the three hundred or so villagers still went through all the right motions of simulating a vibrant community. They celebrated the parish feast day every August fourteenth. They dutifully held elections for town council every two years, and that body chose an alcalde to be their titular leader. Because there were no village taxes, there was no infrastructure, and because there was no infrastructure, there was no reason to collect taxes. Besides, who to collect from? A good half of the population was on the government dole. One retail establishment carried the essentials, particularly liquor, but most of the community saved its serious shopping for trips into Raton, Clayton, Tucumcari, and even, on occasion, across the border to Amarillo, Texas, 170 miles away. No new building had been raised since the rectory had been rebuilt a half century earlier. The state had paved a highway to its outskirts, but inside Nueve Niños the roads were still of dirt, muddy during wet times and dusty during dry. A few people continued to farm and ranch, but the rest now commuted to one of the surrounding larger towns for work. The deadliest indication of the town's stagnation was the steady decline in the number of its young. The elementary school had a single room with a single teacher who never had more than a dozen students at any one time. A child wishing to attend high school depended on relatives to provide room and board elsewhere. Nueve Niños did boast of a number of college graduates, but none of them ever returned to ply their skills among their own.

As with all such things, first fervor for their pastor began to wane— the people of San Eusebio had to get back to living their lives. Fr. Jon felt a glimmer of hope that he was making some progress in disengaging himself from their attentions. He knew from Tobías, for instance, that Esteban, the mayordomo without keys—*Sin Llaves*, as he was now called by many—was out and about trying to spread mischief about the priest: *"Es gringo."* "He does not understand our ways." "He is full of himself." However, there were no serious takers aside from the few usual contrarians found in any group.

It soon fell to the priest's ill fortune to be credited by the people of Nueve Niños with yet another miracle.

He had been asked to bless a child who seemed in the last throes of some mysterious malady. What no one knew was that the crisis was not a harbinger of death but of recovery. The little girl was just about to round the corner of her illness, and she would soon be on the mend. Fr. Jon prayed over her and twenty-four hours later she was sitting up in bed and drinking atole.

So it started all over again.

Fr. Jon was the miracle man, all right, and it seemed that nothing he could do would persuade his congregation otherwise.

He was strict.

"See how zealous he is for our souls," people said.

He was dour.

"Es un hombre serio," they said, "and he does the Lord's serious work."

He was unapproachable.

"How much he must have on his mind," they reasoned.

And Tobías, el sacristano, glowed like a chubby debutante in the reflected glory of his Padrecito.

Fr. Jon's consternation was compounded by the fact that he was beset with ghosts. They were not the chain-rattling, wall-rapping kind—something he could deal with. His ghosts were of the nettling kind, the kind that worked their way into his sub- and not so subconscious like termites boring into wood. They were the ghosts of his predecessors and he couldn't escape them. The five grave markers in the churchyard reminded him that many more priests than these had not survived this place. The church reeked of their presence, insinuated between the stale smell of beeswax and incense. He felt them when he climbed the pulpit steps and put his hand on the railing that countless consecrated hands had already worn smooth. He sensed them each time he donned the same threadbare vestments they had worn. He almost cringed each time he bent down to kiss the altar stone during Mass, aware of the many lips that had touched that exact spot before.

The rectory was the worst. The bed he slept in, the cup he drank from, the chair he sat in, the window he looked out of—they seemed to drip with the failure and frustration that had brought down his predecessors. He could taste the lonely days and the even lonelier nights that bound him to them in a brotherhood of futility.

One relic left by a pastor of some time past seemed particularly poignant to Fr. Jon. It was in a hole in the ground just outside the kitchen door. Now covered with a piece of corrugated tin held down by stones, the excavation was at the base of the foundation. Someone had obviously started to dig a cellar. When he lifted one corner of the tin sheet, Fr. Jon saw a rusted shovel, its blade half buried in the earth. It was as if the digger had been plucked away by some unseen hand just as he was about to gouge out yet another pitifully small scoop of hard, adobe soil.

The hole had indeed been intended as a cellar. But not just any cellar. It was to be a bomb shelter, Tobías solemnly informed him. "*Los comunistas*," he added. "Like the ones I fought in Korea."

On September 23, 1949, after a hastily called cabinet meeting, President Harry S. Truman made an announcement to the American people.

Life in the fifties had begun. Russia had the Bomb.

A well-known political cartoonist put the perfect spin on this instant deflation of the national psyche. The single panel shows a bomb-shaped thug labeled "Atom Bum," an American flag tattooed on his arm. Atom Bum is dressed as Robinson Crusoe with ragged pants, a thatched hat, and a frond umbrella. He is kneeling on the sand of a deserted beach inspecting a very fresh looking footprint. Atom Bum is having a humbling epiphany. On this island Earth he is no longer the solitary Super Power.

The Bomb touched on every part of America's life.

The Bomb begat the Fear of the Bomb. Fear of the Bomb begat What To Do About the Bomb. What To Do About the Bomb begat a spirited debate among philosophers and theologians.

The debate around the morality of the Bomb spawned discussion about bomb shelters. Should we build them? If we did, could we keep the less provident among us from using them when the bombs came? Could we ignore their needs? Could we repel them? If need be, could we kill them?

One person who had no patience with this kind of theorizing was Fr. Oskar Kolbitz.

Fr. Kolbitz, a recent émigré from Hungary, had little reason to trust the Russian Bear. He came to New Mexico directly from a Soviet concentration camp, the only member of his family left alive. After a short stint as an associate pastor in the house of his sponsor, another Hungarian refugee-priest, he received a letter of assignment to Nueve Niños. There he was expected to do little more than baptize, marry, and bury people; say Mass on Sunday; and stay out of people's way.

One evening, while he practiced his still rudimentary English by paging through an old issue of *Time* magazine, Fr. Kolbitz came across an article about A-Bomb attacks. His English was not good enough to get him through the thornier issues of the Cold War propounded by columnists, politicians, military experts, and social scientists. However, there was one thing that caught his eye and that he understood immediately.

It was a bar graph that showed the relative nuclear strengths of the United States and the USSR. Instead of bars, however, the artist had used drawings of bombs. The American bombs sported Uncle Sam hats. The Russian bombs wore fur Cossack caps. From the graph, it was clear to Fr. Kolbitz who was winning the arms race.

A side box told the story of an Iowa dentist who had built the quintessential fallout shelter in his basement. It was an open space with ample room for the doctor, his wife, and their five children. Shelves groaned with bottles of water and tightly sealed foodstuffs. The doctor's staple provisions were beans, case upon case of them. He had done meticulous research, he said, and decided that beans were the perfect survivalist fare because they provided both bulk and protein.

The dentist sank a three-hundred-gallon gas tank in his backyard and connected it to two generators, a main one and a backup, which would supply him and his family with their light and power needs. He designed a complex filter system to recirculate the air in the shelter, very important it would seem, if seven people were to rely on a steady diet of beans.

The picture that went along with the story showed the dentist and his family. They smiled as they huddled together on a bunk bed. Belying their open, friendly faces, the doctor cradled a scoped hunting rifle in his arms. A full gun rack was also visible against a wall. The caption read: "In Iowa, ready for anything."

Fr. Kolbitz was so taken by the story that he sliced it out of the magazine with one of the old razor blades he was so reluctant to throw away. (His habits from the camp in Hungary would never completely leave him.)

He attached the clipping to his bathroom mirror and studied it intently every time he used the basin. From this came a determination that he would never again allow the Russians to brutalize him or anyone in his charge. This resolve germinated into a plan. Set up a shelter in the basement of his rectory, and his parishioners would help him build it.

With renewed purpose, Fr. Kolbitz learned more English and Spanish in the next month than he had learned over the course of the past two years. To be an effective prophet he must be able to communicate; he must be able to motivate; he must proclaim the Gospel of the Bomb as if touched on the tongue by the same type of red-hot ember that had given the prophet Isaiah his eloquence.

"*Munda cor meum.* Cleanse my heart and my lips, almighty God, who did cleanse the lips of the prophet Isaiah with a burning coal: through Thy gracious mercy be pleased to cleanse me that I may worthily proclaim Thy holy Gospel."

He had said this prayer during Mass for the last sixteen years, save the two years of his internment. Never before had the words carried such meaning for him.

Once he felt comfortable enough to put pen to paper, Fr. Kolbitz tackled his first letter in English. It was addressed to Jim Leiderman, The *Time* Magazine Dentist, Keokuk, Iowa, and asked for information on how to build a fallout shelter.

Three weeks later, Fr. Kolbitz received a fat manila envelope in the mail. When he opened it and spilled out its contents, he was amazed by the assortment of flyers and brochures. In the main they were advertisements printed on cheap paper for products that "no shelter should be without." There was a three-page, single-spaced bibliography of survivalist books. The publications bore such titles as *How to Live through a Nuclear Attack, What They Don't Want You to Know, The Jews and the International Conspiracy,* and *How to Read and Understand the Book of Revelation.* There were also a few pamphlets that got down to the practical issues. They cited the reasons for refitting a basement and lectured about the importance of maintaining a safe and plentiful water supply. But they were only come-ons that urged the priest to order the books that would deliver the actual goods.

At the bottom of the heap was a letter signed by Dr. Jim B. Leiderman, DDS. It thanked the priest for his interest and requested ten dollars to defray the cost of handling and shipping these "lifesaving" documents to him.

Fr. Kolbitz was a very poor man in a very poor parish. The archdiocese paid his monthly stipend of $85. Sunday offerings barely covered the electric bills for the church and rectory and the sacramental wine and communion wafers for Mass. There was little money left for food or to pay for the gasoline to fuel Fr. Kolbitz's secondhand

Hudson. He relied on the kindness of the women of the parish for an occasional hot meal. For the rest he subsisted on cans of soup and boxes of soda crackers.

In spite of his true poverty, Fr. Kolbitz managed somehow to reimburse the dentist for his troubles and then set aside money each week to send for those books that "every right-thinking American must read."

❖

On a bright Sunday morning in early April, the priest from Hungary mounted his pulpit and declared his intentions.

"I will build an atom bomb shelter in the basement beneath the rectory. And I expect you to help me."

His congregation blanched. Help him? In April? In the middle of planting and branding?

"There will be only enough room," the priest continued, "for ten people. The only fair way to decide who will come into the shelter is to hold a lottery. I will draw the names. The more hours you spend helping me, the more times your name will be entered. Of course, I encourage you all to build your own shelters. *Los rusos son diablos.* We must be ready."

The people of Nueve Niños were perplexed. Why were they suddenly receiving threats from the Russians? Surely news of their pugnaciousness had not reached beyond the ocean. Up to now, no one had paid much attention to them. The state was still dragging its feet on its promise of paved roads, the closest hospital was forty miles of hard driving away, and even the bishop had sent them a priest who had alien ways, seldom bathed, and until recently could not even carry on a meaningful conversation with them. They had grown used to counting for so little that they had begun to depend on it. Why would the Russians now single them out for nuclear annihilation?

To Fr. Kolbitz, the question was categorically beside the point.

Volunteers did not swarm to the priest's side. From one of the ranchers, Fr. Kolbitz cadged an old gas-driven generator that no longer worked. For this the priest offered the man twenty-five entries into the lottery. A woman brought him four jars of canned peaches, which netted her two entries. And so it went. Two broken cots, several lengths of pipe, some battered pots and pans, a spool of electrical wire. The priest scrupulously kept a ledger. Alongside each entry he wrote a number that represented the donor's chances for salvation from the Bomb.

The holy writ on which the priest now almost exclusively relied were the pamphlets and newsletters that he sent for and many more that he could not remember ordering. Each asked for his generosity "to defray the cost . . ." and in no case did he disappoint the correspondent.

His house soon overflowed with the printed word, survivalist style. He read these materials everywhere and whenever. Many of them were do-it-yourself manuals with instructions on such subjects as caulking and sealing to keep out deadly rays. One dealt with the mathematics of pounds per square inch of usable air per occupant. There were calorie intake tables to help "shelterites" ration foodstuffs. One brochure dwelt on the disposal of human waste. The author offered a chemical powder at $19.50 a can that would turn human feces "into a substance more valuable than gold, when you rise to the surface to reconstitute the wasteland that was once your country."

A tract from a nondenominational theologian in Minnesota defended the morality of shelters. In it were set forth all the arguments supporting the duty to survive and the divine right to protect one's resources, whatever it took.

The booklet was fine as far as it went, considering a Protestant had written it. But it did not have that Catholic flavor that would give it doctrinal validity. The only remedy was for Fr. Kolbitz to write his own manifesto where he could toss in words like "mortal sin," as in: "To neglect one's safety and the safety of one's family in time of crisis is a mortal sin." He was even able to make a circumstantial case for excommunication by a judicious and oblique use of biblical quotations and selected excerpts from the writings of the Fathers of the Church, Augustine, Jerome, Ambrose.

After he had finished his manuscript in arduous longhand, he packed his small suitcase, torn and battered and held together with cord. He placed a notice on the church door that he would be away for a week and drove to Albuquerque to the home of his compatriot priest-friend.

He recruited a high school girl from his friend's parish who had acceptable typing skills and proceeded with the transcription of his notes to spirit master carbons. He used the parish printing machine to churn out as many pages as he could until the ink from the masters yielded nothing more than faint purplish hieroglyphics on the copy paper.

When he was finally done with the printing, he felt light-headed, as much from the strong and constant acetone fumes wafting up from the printer as from satisfaction for a job accomplished.

The next morning he packed everything up and bid his friend good-bye. He left by way of the church, where he deposited three copies of the monograph in the back pew. On the way back to his own parish he stopped in fourteen more churches and left his tocsin call: The Russians Are Coming. The Russians Are Coming.

A parishioner from one of those churches found a copy of Fr. Kolbitz's work and brought it to the attention of the pastor. That priest telephoned the chancery office.

"Does he have permission?" he asked the chancellor.

"Permission for what?"

"Permission to threaten my congregation with excommunication unless they build bomb shelters."

No, he did not have permission, and would the Father be so kind as to mail the document to the chancery as soon as possible, where it would receive the immediate attention of the archbishop.

Fr. Kolbitz had been back in his parish for a week, time he devoted almost exclusively to digging his shelter, when an envelope bearing the address and coat of arms of the archdiocese arrived.

> Dear Father Kolbitz:
> It has been brought to our attention that you, or someone using your name, is circulating a document that espouses

certain principles that run contrary to Christian thought and to the will of Holy Mother Church.

Please make yourself available for a meeting at our office at 2:30 p.m. on the afternoon of Thursday, May 19, to discuss these matters in full detail.

Your brother in Christ,

⊹ Edward Edwin Byers

Archbishop of Santa Fe

Fr. Kolbitz had never seen something at once so beautiful and so terrible.

The snow white paper, heavy, watermarked, and of a fine linen bond, was dazzling in its purity. At the top, the bishop's coat of arms, embossed and printed in emerald green, sat strong and triumphant. Each character that made up the text of the letter was boldly incised, black and uncompromising. An artist could not have arranged the layout with better balance and composition. Each colon, comma, and period was well struck and lustrous in its economy. At the bottom, the archbishop's signature was a large, free-flowing creation, a perfect counterpoint to the printing.

Fr. Kolbitz was so moved by the format that he almost resented the distraction of the message. He read it several times and didn't understand it, so he put it away only to take it out time after time for further analysis. Each time he unfolded the letter as if spreading out a starched square of linen over the altar stone in preparation for Mass. He ran his hand over it to smooth it down, his fingers electric from the feel of the embossing and the grain of the paper. Then, barely breathing and moving his lips as in prayer, he tried to dissect the epistle line by line.

What was he to think?

Of course. It was his manuscript. His spirits soared. The archbishop had read it and apparently had some problems with it. No matter. He could clear that up. What was important here was that he finally had the ear of the hierarchy.

Really now, what could he do by himself in this place so far from everywhere? But if the bishop took up the cause, such good they could do together.

Father Kolbitz left his parish on the evening of May eighteenth and stopped for the night with his friend in Albuquerque. He did not bring up the letter during dinner or while they sat, smoked, and reminisced. The mission to the bishop was too delicate.

His friend did not ask any questions, although the gossip around the archdiocese had been rampant for weeks. Everyone knew about the monograph and everyone knew, since the bishop's secretary could not hold his scotch or his tongue, that the chancery office was about to reel in one Fr. Oskar Kolbitz.

That evening the two friends maintained the pleasantries, drank inferior domestic Tokay, talked about Budapest in autumn, wept together, and went to their separate beds.

The next day, although it was only an hour and a half drive to Santa Fe, Fr. Kolbitz volunteered to say the 6:30 Mass and was on the road shortly after seven.

He arrived in Santa Fe by midmorning and spent his time on a bench in the plaza, where he read from his breviary and watched as pigeons alit on the ground around him and pecked at his shoe tips. He did not like pigeons. He remembered a man in the concentration camp killing another man over just such a bird.

At noon he had a cup of coffee and a cheese sandwich at the lunch counter at Woolworth's. His waitress, a good Catholic girl, managed to salvage a slice of peach pie that had only been nibbled on by a previous customer, trimmed off the ragged tip, and offered it to him "on the house."

He was unfamiliar with the term but brightened when informed of its meaning.

When he tried to leave a ten-cent tip, she gave it back to him.

"Pray for me instead."

Afterward he walked the two blocks to the street fronting the chancery office and paced the sidewalk until two o'clock. By then, the wait had grown unbearable, so he entered the long, single-story, pueblo-style building and announced himself.

The bishop's secretary looked pointedly at his watch. "Oh yes, Father Kolbitz. It's still a little early. Have a seat. I'll let His Excellency know you're here."

The waiting room was dark and musky with shelves full of dusty tomes of theology and canon law. Fr. Kolbitz found an uncomfortably soft and overyielding chair and sat down. Before long, the secretary was back. Fr. Kolbitz flailed for balance against the arms of the chair and managed to wobble to his feet.

"No, Father. Not yet."

The young cleric then turned and addressed someone in the hallway. "If you'll just have a seat, Father Medina."

The secretary glided back through the entrance and revealed another priest, one whom Fr. Kolbitz vaguely remembered from some clerical function or other.

"Hello, Father," said the Hungarian and offered his hand.

"Hello, Father." The other took the hand perfunctorily and headed for a chair.

The two priests sat silently while the loud ticking of a wall clock mocked the awkward silence between them. Finally, Fr. Medina spoke. "And how are you?"

"Fine. And you?"

"Not too good."

"Oh?"

Fr. Medina patted his chest gently. "Asthma."

This was not a familiar word to Fr. Kolbitz. "Please?"

"Asthma," the other priest repeated, this time loudly as if to a deaf person.

Fr. Kolbitz shook his head.

Fr. Medina bent forward and shouted in Fr. Kolbitz's face with a mighty gust of his lungs. "I can't breathe. My basement. I have problems with my basement."

"Me too," Fr. Kolbitz shouted back and smiled broadly.

In his office Edward Edwin Byers, Archbishop of Santa Fe, was putting his signature to the last of a stack of papers that his secretary had deposited on his desk earlier that morning.

"Well, Charles, can we call it a day?"

"Not quite, Your Excellency. Fathers Medina and Kolbitz are here for their appointments."

"Together?"

"No, Archbishop. Separate matters. Father Medina has a flooded basement in his rectory. It's affecting his health."

"And?"

"And the parish doesn't have the funds to correct the problem."

"He thinks we do?"

The priest shrugged.

"And who else?"

"Father Kolbitz."

"Kolbitz, Kolbitz. Ah, yes, the fellow from Poland."

"I believe Father Kolbitz is from Hungary. The bomb shelter priest."

When Fr. Kolbitz entered his office, Archbishop Byers rose and walked around his desk.

The priest scampered across the room and fell to his knees. The episcopal hand turned just so to exhibit the episcopal ring and Kolbitz swiped his lips across the sharply faceted purple amethyst.

With a firm grip the bishop pulled the priest up and pointed to a chair.

"Well, Father, they tell me you're an expert on basements."

"Excellency?"

"Basements. I understand you like to refurbish them."

"Re-fur-bish?" Kolbitz repeated the unfamiliar word slowly. "I'm sorry, I don't . . ."

"Well, that's just perfect. It happens that the diocese needs someone to fix up one of its leaky basements. Congratulations, you are the new parish administrator of San Acacio in Arroyo Largo."

An upward motion of the bishop's hand had Fr. Kolbitz up and moving his legs as if controlled by strings. With a fatherly arm around the priest's shoulder, the bishop led him to the door.

"Oh, by the way, Father. If you continue to preach, write, or propagandize in any way about bomb shelters, I will suspend you from your priestly duties. Understood? Good. Good-bye then, Father. God bless you. Keep up the good work."

Fr. Kolbitz found himself, he knew not how, in the corridor outside the bishop's office. He was still standing there in confusion when the secretary swept by with a wheezing Fr. Medina in tow.

"Father Medina, what a wonderful surprise I have for you," Archbishop Byers boomed from his office.

The secretary stepped back out into the hallway and softly closed the door.

"If you would just wait back in the study, Father Kolbitz, I'll have your letter of appointment typed up and signed in a flash."

When Fr. Kolbitz read this new letter, it boasted none of the beauty, the mystery, the elegance, the power of his original summons.

> Dear Fr. Kolbitz:
> I am pleased to appoint you to the pastoral administration
> of the church of San Acacio in Arroyo Largo, New Mexico,
> effective May 27, 1955.
> May God bless you in your new ministry.
>   In Christ,
>   ✠ Edward Edwin Byers

Father Kolbitz could see that the letter had been typed in haste. All the text was to the top of the sheet giving it an unpleasing, unbalanced look. There were several erasures that marred the pristine whiteness of the stock. The bishop's signature was hurriedly scrawled and he could see where the pen with its gold tip had snagged the paper and blotted. The resultant splotch was very much like that left by a pigeon on Fr. Kolbitz's shoe that morning when he sat in the sun in the plaza in Santa Fe.

When Fr. Jon inquired from Tobías as to who might be interested in making $10 for filling in the hole, the sacristan immediately offered his services. If only to stop the sacristan from wheedling, the priest eventually gave in.

Later that morning the pair stood at the edge of the hole and assessed the work to be done.

"You're sure you can handle it?"

"Sí, Padrecito. Don't worry. I will take care of it." Then Tobías slowly shook his head and let out a sigh of pity. "He only dug the hole because he was afraid of the Russians. *Pero nunca vinieron.* The people said he was *poco loco.* Can I have the shovel? It's not very good."

"No, I think I'll keep it."

Fr. Jon propped the rusted shovel against a corner of the rectory living area.

What was one more ghost?

Chapter Fourteen

Dear Sally—

It's so isolated out here and that's the last complaint you'll hear from me. For some ridiculous reason (letter to follow. Hah!) the people here regard me as some kind of miracle worker. I've decided to keep my distance until the hysteria winds down. Then we'll see.

There's a large lake by the village that might prove a distraction, but I'm reluctant to make use of it. More of that "miracle man" story when you read the letter.

I know we didn't see each other much after you were cloistered, but at least you were in hollering distance (kinda). Now I feel like you're on another planet. I guess that's my way of saying I miss you.

Jon

Dear Jonny:

So now it's a miracle worker I have to put up with. Saints deliver us!

Don't turn your back on your people. They need you, and who knows, you might even need them.

I miss you too, Jonny. I always have. But I have a perfect picture of you in my mind and perfect memories of how much we enjoyed our time together with the folks. It's enough for me.

Sally

Chapter Fifteen

Fr. Jon soon had reason to regret his relentless gospel of doom and damnation from the pulpit. Penitents were coming at him from all sides. The Saturday confessional lines sneaked down the aisle almost to the vestibule of the church. He was even expected to make house calls.

One morning, Fr. Jon received a group of supplicants. There were five of them: a couple in their early forties, an elderly woman, a teen-aged boy, and a four-year-old with a death grip on a fold of her mother's dress.

The office, actually a corner of the living room, was small with space only for a desk and two chairs opposite. Fr. Jon squeezed in a third chair from the kitchen for the man. The teen seemed satisfied to lean against the wall.

"We heard there was a new priest," the younger woman said.

"Yes. My name is Father Armitage."

She was not in the mood for chitchat. "My father, her *esposo*,"—she indicated the old woman to her left with a tilt of her head—"did not like the other priest. He gave away our santo. He was mean to the people. Nobody liked him."

Fr. Jon put on a stern face, the one he was so practiced in by now. "We're not here to be liked. We're here to do the Lord's work."

"He was mean," she insisted. "We were ready to start a petition to the archbishop to get him out."

"Well, Father José's gone now, so you should be happy."

She sized up Fr. Jon. "Like I said, my father did not like the other priest. Now he has cancer. My father, I mean."

The old woman beside her crossed herself.

"The doctor says he will last only six more months," the daughter continued.

Fr. Jon spread out his hands. "I'm sorry. But what can I do? I'm not a miracle worker, if that's what you're thinking."

"It's his time. *No queremos milagros.*"

"What then?"

"He needs to confess his sins. He hasn't confessed for forty years. He tried once when I got married, but another priest, another mean one, yelled at him and chased him out of the church."

"Has he asked to see a priest?"

"No."

"Does he want to confess?"

The woman looked at her mother and then at her husband. They both turned down their mouths, pleading ignorance. The teenager occupied himself with his fingernails, gnawing at them and spitting out the tiny splinters all over his shirt front. The child was now on an unending trek up and down the mountain of her mother's lap.

"Perhaps you should have asked him before you came to see me."

This time there was no reaction from any of them, not a hint of understanding, not a twitch of an eyebrow or the curl of a lip.

Finally the daughter mustered a response of sorts. "He hasn't been to confession in forty years. The other priests were too mean."

"So you keep saying. Maybe it's your father who's the mean one."

The woman did not argue the point. "You can come to talk to him?"

"As long as he knows I'm coming."

"Now?"

"You must talk to him first."

"He has cancer," the woman reminded the priest, as if they had frittered away the six months her father had been given by the doctor during the five minutes they had been talking about him.

Again the old woman crossed herself.

Fr. Jon saw that the conversation had gone full circle. He must either face a stalemate or capitulate. "What about tomorrow morning. Say ten o'clock?" He suddenly remembered the unexpected visit he had paid to the cancer patient in Santa Fe. "But you must tell him I am coming. I will not stay if he is surprised to see me."

She thought it over and nodded.

Don Plácido Cárdenas.

He was seated smartly in a rocking chair on his front porch with an unobstructed view of the caldera. A light gray, small-brimmed Stetson sat squarely on his head. His white shirt with faded blue stripes was buttoned at the throat and secured by a leather-thong bolo tie gathered in by a large silver medallion with a chunk of turquoise set in its center. He wore a fresh pair of bib coveralls and over this a brown suit coat. His trouser legs rode an inch or two above his tightly laced high-top shoes to reveal a pair of thick calves encased in white cotton long johns.

Don Plácido did not look like he had cancer. He was broad and powerful looking and his eyes were clear of any pain or any sign of drug torpor.

His daughter introduced Fr. Jon and brought out a kitchen chair for the priest. "Papa," she said, "here's the new priest, like I told you. I don't think he's mean like the other ones. He wants to talk to you."

Don Plácido glared at his daughter and waved her off with the back of his hand. She retreated into the house, pausing only to allow the screen door to slap against her rump so it would not slam into its frame.

"You be good," she told her father from behind the protection of the screen.

"*Vaya*," he growled at her.

The old man began to rock back and forth, his gaze fixed on the lake. "*¿Y qué?*" he finally said.

It was the best opening Fr. Jon could hope for. "And so how are you feeling?"

"Where did Padre José go?"

"Down south. Española."

"I liked him. He didn't take *mierda* from nobody."

"No, I don't imagine he did."

Don Plácido gave Fr. Jon the once-over. "Now you're here."

Fr. Jon nodded. "Now I'm here."

"Dicen que haces milagros."

"They say a lot of things, but no, I do not perform miracles."

"Leave the women alone." The old man seemed to be speaking from personal knowledge of the tainted history of the parish and of its uneven line of pastors.

"Yes. I expect to."

"Padre José left the women alone. Not like the priest before him. The Irish one. He ran away with Lázaro Molina's wife." Don Plácido smiled contentedly.

"Well, priests are human too. They can be tempted like everyone else."

"He was too drunk all the time to be tempted. And she was ugly. She made him steal money from the church and they left one night and didn't come back. Only Lazáro was happy and who could blame him? You should have heard the talk. Terrible."

The smirk on don Plácido's face told Fr. Jon that the old man did not really think it was all that terrible.

"We can only pray for him."

"You pray for him."

"So, you liked Father José?"

He grunted.

"What about the others? Your daughter says that one of them kicked you out of church when you tried to go to confession."

The old man winked. "She wanted me to go to communion for her wedding. Don't ask me why. She was the one getting married. I told her the priest chased me away just to shut her up. I haven't been inside a church for thirty years," he added proudly. "Not even for her wedding."

Don Plácido snatched up a flyswatter from his lap and took a sudden swipe at Fr. Jon's knee.

The priest barely felt the blow through the thickness of his cassock, but when he looked down, he saw a fly squashed against the material, blood and white innards in stark contrast to the blackness of the robe.

Expertly, the old man flicked the carcass away with the tip of the swatter. "I didn't want to go to the wedding anyway. I've never liked that pachuco. But he made her pregnant. What could the poor thing do? She's not too pretty . . . or too smart."

"She said you might want to go to confession."

"Why?"

"Because you're sick."

"That's what the doctor says."

Don Plácido watched another fly land on Fr. Jon's shoulder and slowly raised the swatter. Before he could strike, the priest brushed it off.

The old man sighed and dropped his arm. "They're all liars, you know."

"Who's that?"

"*Los doctores, los abogados, los políticos.*" He paused for effect. "*Los padres.*"

"So you don't think you're sick?"

"The cancer? Oh, I have it. Those women in there don't let me forget it."

"Well, at least that's not a lie. You have cancer. According to you daughter, you will probably not live out the year."

Don Plácido's laugh was as dry as the wind that was just starting up from the west. "I don't need my daughter to tell me that."

"Do you believe in God?"

He clicked his tongue. Don Plácido obviously considered this a very stupid question.

"Isn't it time, then, to make your peace with Him?"

The old man tilted his head slightly to one side. "Let me ask you something."

"Anything."

Don Plácido's eyes folded into sly slits. "If you can answer me, you can hear my confession."

"I'll certainly try. But you should not gamble with your soul based on how smart I am."

"It's a church question. How smart do you have to be to answer a church question? How long did you study to be a priest?"

"Eight years."

"Well, there you are."

"What's your question?"

The old man learned forward and beckoned the priest to do the same. There was a twinkle in his eye, a not so amiable twinkle, and this is what he asked in a conspiratorial whisper: "Why is it that when you enter a church, you go in the front, but once you're inside you're in the back?"

Fr. Jon never heard don Plácido's confession. Six days later the daughter came to the rectory to inform him that her father had shot himself with his favorite rifle.

Chapter Sixteen

The rapid knocks on the rectory door were persistent enough to finally pierce through the helmet of Fr. Jon's sleep and into his brain.

2:30 a.m.

His voice was gravel as he spoke through the thickness of the front door. "What do you want?"

"I need to talk to a Father."

The voice was female, heavily accented, and sing-songy in the northern New Mexico way.

Father Jon cracked the door and pushed a side of his face against the opening. What he saw with his one eye was a thin, pinched-faced woman swimming in an oversized man's shirt, a definite counterpoint to the tight-fitting toreador pants that screamed for relief.

"Are you the Father?"

Father Jon opened the door wider.

"I'm Father Armitage."

The woman's eyes widened. Here was a disheveled personage in wrinkled pajamas and barefoot to boot. She had never given much thought to what priests looked like in the privacy of their bedrooms, but this apparition was like none she would have expected, priest or no. "Are you the Father?"

Of course he was the Father. Who the hell did she expect to open the rectory door at two in the morning? "What do you want?"

"My husband has to talk to a Father."

"Why can't he wait until morning?"

"He says he's going to kill himself unless he talks to a Father."

Don Plácido Cárdenas came immediately to mind. Doesn't anyone around here die of natural causes? thought the priest.

"Does he have a gun?"

"Oh, no, no. A can of gas and a cigarette lighter."

Just the day before, Fr. Jon had used his day off to do some shopping in Raton. He dropped in on the pastor of St. Patrick's to go to confession and availed himself of an invitation to dinner. They eschewed conversation for television viewing while they ate.

It was over plates of fried chicken that they watched a Buddhist monk immolate himself on a busy Saigon street.

Jon had some grudging admiration for the dedication but had some serious doubts about the monk's common sense. Now some nut, in his parish of all places, wanted to get into the act.

"Who is your husband?"

"He says that the Father knows him." She looked past Jon into the darkened rectory, still not completely sold on the idea that it was Jon she should be talking with. "*Son amigos. They drank wine at the lake.*"

So it was the drunk Anglo in the abandoned pickup. Amigos? Hardly.

"Where is the gasoline right now?"

"He has it."

"You tell him that I will come over only if he gives you the can. You understand?"

"Yes."

"If he agrees, bring back the can to me, and then we'll see."

Twenty minutes later, time for Fr. Jon to splash his face, run a brush through his hair, gargle, and throw a cassock on over his pajamas, there was another knock. He had hoped to end the matter with his demands, but apparently it was not to be so. When he opened the door this time, the woman was panting from the exertion of running back and forth from her house to the rectory. She held in one hand a dented red gasoline can with a long, articulated goose-neck spout.

"Are you the Father?"

Jon almost answered, then didn't. Surely the woman remembered talking to him face to face not a half hour before. "You have the gas?"

She held up the can and the priest could hear liquid sloshing inside it.

"Does he have any more?"

She shook her head and set the can down on the stoop to massage the fingers that had been curled around the metal handle.

"Leave it. We'll take my car."

The drive took them along the lake, past Cósima's house and through a cluster of small hillocks. Neither spoke.

Finally, when they pulled up next to a weather-weary adobe hut, she turned to the priest. "I don't know why he's so crazy all of a sudden. He got a letter from one of his kids today."

"And a fine model of fatherhood he must be," Fr. Jon muttered as he climbed out of the car.

She opened the door and stood back for him to enter.

"You first," he said firmly.

Inside, she took a sharp left. "*Está en la cocina.*"

The house was dark except for a strange, uneven glow that emanated from somewhere beyond them.

"*Por aquí,*" she whispered.

The pathway to the kitchen was constricted by piles of boxes that funneled them toward an open door, a shimmering rectangle of that same mysterious light.

Fr. Jon entered and the woman stepped aside to stand behind him. The man still wore the same battered pants and denim shirt bearing the wine stains from the night they first met. He sat on a low stool at a small Formica-topped table that could have been the twin of the one in Jon's very own kitchen.

The man sat bolt upright, his hands open, palms down on the table. Before him, set in uneven rows, was a haphazard cluster of votive lights, their delicate flames now disturbed and twisting frenetically from the breeze created by the priest's entrance. Candle wax was flowing sluggishly in lavalike streams onto the tabletop. Directly in front of the man were several religious objects, a rosary, a small plastic crucifix, a dashboard Jesus, and several frayed holy cards. There were also other items, some bits of colored string, a pine cone, some beads, a scrap of dirty lace, and a small clay pot containing something organic, shriveled brown buttons that Fr. Jon did not recognize. Closest to the man, and what riveted the priest's attention, were two butcher knives, their long, slightly curved blades transecting each other to form an X. Their handles nearly touched the fingertips of the man's hands.

He had practiced reaching for these knives. Fr. Jon was sure of it with no proof other than the sudden dryness in his mouth and a spontaneous gurgling in his lower regions.

The man gauged the priest with heavy, red-rimmed eyes. "You came." His voice was the same as before, calm and cultured, certainly not the voice of someone who was threatening to pour gasoline over himself. "I told her you would. A priest always has to come if called. It's expected."

"Well, yes. Ordinarily."

"Do you know who I am?"

"The man I talked to by the lake."

"But do you really know who I am? Of course not. How could you? My name is Fell. Ridley Ashford Fell."

"And I'm Father Armitage. What's going on here?"

The man became intent on moving some of the objects this way and that on the table. "I have a title too. Dr. Fell. I used to be a scientist, an archaeologist. Another life. Another story. Do you know anything about archaeology?"

"Well, I studied in Rome. Lots of ruins in Rome."

"Ruins? Things. Archaeology is not about things. It's about people. How they lived. How they died. But they're not really dead, you know. Not if you can still sit down with them and talk. I talk to them. Do you think that odd, Father?"

The priest shrugged off the question. Why argue with a madman?

Dr. Fell picked up one of the dried brown buttons. "I talk to them with these. They're not happy, you know. Too many changes. Too many people trying to destroy their sacred places. Obliterate their history. The Kiowa summoned me here. They have graves that must be found before they are desecrated. But I failed them. I failed them miserably."

He popped his unholy communion into his mouth, chewed and swallowed, and rolled his eyes back so only the whites were visible, reflecting the dancing glow of the candles. Then he refocused on the tabletop.

"They insist I do something about my failure. Some sign of atonement. If you hadn't come, I was prepared to burn this shithole to the ground. And me. And her. But you did come."

Fr. Jon could feel the woman's shifting weight as she edged toward the doorway to block it. This was a rehearsed move. The man had just given her some kind of cue. The priest's eyes were now glued to where the man's hands rested so achingly close to the handles of the knives. It now occurred to Jon that if he were going to do something, he'd better do it now.

"All right. Enough." The priest's voice was loud, even louder than he had expected. "First we need light." He flicked at the switch by the wall to his right, praying that there was electricity, praying that the bare bulb in the ceiling above the table was good.

God bless Thomas Edison.

The small kitchen was flooded with shocking brightness. The theatrical excess of the votive lights was ruined immediately.

Fr. Jon pointed to the woman. "You. Over there on your knees by your husband. If he is your husband."

It had worked for Jesus when He talked to the Samaritan woman. She had been so blown away by His ability to read her heart that she jumped through hoops for Him. Fr. Jon was hoping for some of the same. Maybe this woman had known some pastor like mean Father

José in her past, one who never allowed his will to be questioned by his parishioners.

She did not disappoint. Like a child who had just been caught doing something naughty, she cast her eyes down and wriggled by Fr. Jon to kneel by her man.

Dr. Fell's eyes were now fully on the priest, burning and moist, but quite focused. Suddenly he was no longer in charge. His mouth opened to protest.

Fr. Jon did not give him an opportunity.

"And you. What makes you think you can pull people out of their beds to come down here and listen to this shit?"

The woman recoiled, probably more in shock at hearing a priest use profanity than from the impact of the words themselves.

The priest made a broad gesture over the man and his table of fetishes. "This, Dr. Fell, is crap. Do you hear me? Crap. And an educated man like yourself should be ashamed. There's absolutely nothing I can do here except give this place a blessing, for all the good it will do."

He reached into his cassock pocket, drew out the bottle of holy water, uncapped it, and swung it in a sweeping arc. The geyser caught the man squarely in the face and a goodly portion of the liquid entered his still open mouth. He began to sputter and cough and the woman jumped to her feet to give him three solid thumps on the back. Another swipe with the bottle across the table and five of the candles hissed and flamed out.

"I think that just about does it," the priest declared. "Amen. Good-bye. Alleluia. God is love. And don't bother me again."

Back in the safety of the rectory, Fr. Jon poured himself a glass of scotch and took it neat, in one swallow. Then he sat at the table and watched his hands twitch. At 6:25 he rose and went to the church to say Mass.

Chapter Seventeen

The phone rang, an unusual sound in the San Eusebio rectory. Few parishioners had telephones and hardly anyone from the outside world had any reason to call Nueve Niños.

"Could I speak to the reverend in charge, please?"

"This is Father Armitage."

"Yessir. Sir, this is Corporal Bryce Turner. I'm with the Marine detachment here at Kirtland Air Force Base in Albuquerque." The voice had a honeyed drawl, polite and languid.

"Yes, Corporal."

"Sir, I'm afraid that we have a sad duty to perform this afternoon. We have just received notification that a Private Daniel García has been killed in combat in Veet-nam."

Vietnam. Were they still fighting that thing? World affairs had become as nothing to Fr. Jon since his arrival in Nueve Niños.

"Terrible. How can I help?" he asked, although he thought he already knew.

"Well, sir, we understand that Private García was Catholic and that his family attends your church."

"Who is the family?"

"His mother, sir, is a Mrs. Anna García. There is no head of household listed. Would you be familiar with the individual, sir?"

"Not offhand, Corporal. But if you'll give me a moment, I'll check our parish records."

"Thank you, sir."

Fr. Jon's fingers fumbled as he flipped through the parish file cards. There were three García families listed on the parish rolls. One was an Anna. And she had a son, Daniel T., born May 3, 1947. He was, or deserved to be at that moment, eighteen years of age. There were three other children listed on the card, all younger. There was no mention of a man of the house. So whether Anna García was widowed, divorced, or abandoned, the burden of the news of her son's death was hers alone to bear.

"Corporal?"

"Yessir."

"I do have a parishioner by that name, and she does have a son, Daniel T."

"That would be T for *Toe*-mas, sir."

Fr. Jon did not know Daniel's middle name, and he felt curiously chastened that a marine from somewhere in Dixie should know more about one of his parishioners than he did. "Are you sure about this? I'd hate to make a mistake."

There was a pause. "Sir, the Marines do not make that kind of mistake."

"No. Of course not."

"Nossir. Lieutenant Pettigrew and myself are on notification duty. It falls to us to inform the family of their loss. Since they attend your church, the lieutenant has asked me to invite you to come along."

It was an invitation tendered with no expectation of refusal.

"It should take us about four hours to get there if we leave now. Two o'clock? Would that be all right?"

"Certainly. Whatever you think. You've got the experience with this type of thing."

For the first time there was a crack in the young man's reserve. "Actually, sir, this will be my first notification."

Fr. Jon took a break from a morning of blessings and arrangements for sacraments and, with some misgivings, sought out the parish yenta.

Tobías was out in back of the rectory worrying a small pile of dirt to death. The filling of the bomb shelter hole had become a daunting task for one so seemingly unaccustomed to manual labor. *"Buenos días*, Padrecito. The work is almost done. A few more days is all."

Fr. Jon took a doubting and distracted look into the less than half-filled cavity. "Yes, yes, that's fine. Tell me about Anna García."

The sacristan took out a handkerchief from his back pocket and wiped away the dampness that had accumulated on his flushed brow and cheeks. "Anna García. Her husband was killed in a bar fight in Raton two years ago. She sits in church by the statue of San José. Always the same place with her three young ones. The oldest son is a marine. *Lo mismo que yo.*"

Fr. Jon tried to imagine Tobías undergoing the rigors of boot camp in a New Jersey swamp and failed. "Is she at home?"

"She works at the hospital in Clayton. Every day she goes with three other women. They wash and iron. Why, Padrecito?"

"I must see her this afternoon."

Tobías crossed himself. *"¿Su hijo?"*

Fr. Jon blinked. Was he that transparent or was there more to the sacristano than he had credited?

"Tobías, listen to me now. This is very important. No one in Nueve Niños must know. Not before the boy's mother does. You understand?"

The sacristan flushed even more deeply and stood as tall as he could manage on the uneven ground. "Padrecito, I am a veteran. I have seen young men die in war."

Four hours later, almost to the minute—four hours more in which Danny García was dead and his mother did not know that she no longer had a son—a gray Ford with government markings on the door pulled up outside the rectory. From it emerged two very tall marines dressed smartly in khaki and blue. They retrieved their white-peaked caps from the backseat and placed them at precise angles on their heads.

Fr. Jon waited for them to knock. Delay the inevitable. Ten more seconds of peace for Anna García . . . and himself.

"I've asked around. Apparently Mrs. García works at the hospital in Clayton. In the laundry. She won't be home now. We'll have to go where she works. I'm afraid you have another forty miles of driving ahead of you."

The lieutenant weighed this piece of information. "Well, that's where we should go then. The hospital."

"Do you want me to ride with you?"

"If you have a vehicle, I suggest you take it. Oftentimes, the bereaved prefer to be left alone with their clergyman."

A sad motorcade of two drove the highway to Clayton. When they arrived at the hospital, Fr. Jon pulled into a reserved space and slapped a "clergy" card on the dashboard. The marines pulled up next to him.

The hospital smelled clean and antiseptic but with a subtle undercurrent of rankness and contagion. The three approached the woman at the reception desk.

"How do we get to the laundry area?" Fr. Jon asked.

The woman had greeted them with a smile, but now she frowned. "It's in the basement, Father. The freight elevator is just around the corner. Press B-1. But I don't know if visitors are allowed down there."

"It's all right," Fr. Jon assured her and turned to follow the marines who were already on their way across the lobby behind the counter.

"Let's take the stairs," the lieutenant said.

He pushed open the steel door by the elevators and walked through. They descended the concrete steps and the sound of their synchronized footfalls ricocheted off the walls of the narrow stairwell. It sounded like the riff of muffled drums. Tap, tap, tippity-tap.

At the bottom, they walked through another door and found themselves in a long cinder-block corridor lit by a succession of bare bulbs recessed into the ceiling and protected by hemispheres of steel mesh. With an uncanny sense of direction, the lieutenant turned right and walked some twenty steps to a set of large double doors. Each had a small rectangular window reinforced with a diamond pattern of embedded wire. On both doors stenciled in black were the words: "Staff Only."

Lieutenant Pettigrew did not even bother to look through the windows. Without hesitation, he pulled at one of the doors and the priest and Corporal Turner followed him through.

It was a spacious room and it smelled of soap, bleach, and the oddly comforting odor of leftover scorch from two idle Mangle irons. There were several rows of long tables for sorting and folding. Beyond them on the far wall ran a set of rectangular interior windows. Behind these squatted a pair of obese, bile-green, front-loading washers.

At a table in the middle of the room stood three women who laughed and talked while they folded a pile of pillow cases. At the sound of the door all three looked up. In that instant there was no mistaking which of the three women was Anna García.

The moment she saw them, two ramrod marines and her pastor, coming toward her, she put out her hands in front of her as if to create a force field that they would be unable to penetrate.

"No," she said. And then she said it louder.

She whirled and began to run down the aisles of tables, toppling some over, pushing others toward the unholy trio that dogged her every footfall. One by one, the marines pushed each of these flimsy barricades aside. Nothing she could do would stop their advance.

Finally, she had no place to run, nothing was left to her to keep them at bay. She collapsed in a corner and covered her head with her arms.

"Danny!" she screamed once. And then again and again. And she screamed long after Fr. Jon reached down to touch her chapped red hands, pitifully inadequate shields against the relentless firestorm that now rained down on her.

From what seemed a great distance, Fr. Jon could hear Lieutenant Pettigrew begin to speak his lines.

"Ma'am, it is my sad duty to inform you that . . ."

Chapter Eighteen

Despite his narcissism, or perhaps because of it, Fr. Jon did not masturbate, at least not according to his rationalizations. On occasion he would lay in bed late at night, his libido rampant, while he tried to distract himself with prayer or with neutral thoughts of movies he had seen or books he had read. His attention, however, would remain riveted on the feel of the bedclothes that pressed down on his torso and created electric irritations that, with the slightest movement, shot up and down every square inch of his skin. He never touched himself but he was unconvincing in his efforts to avoid those movements of thighs and trunk that eventually pushed him over the edge. There was always a shudder of relief, which was quickly followed by a surge of guilt.

He would lie wet and sticky and suddenly cool and wonder what he had done or failed to do that caused this explosion. He would go over and over again the criteria for a mortal sin. Was it a gravely sinful act? Did he perceive it to be a gravely sinful act? Did he give full consent to it? Yes, yes, and a qualified no.

These incidents did not spring from a conscious choice. When they happened he was never engaged in fantasies involving some imaginary bed partner. There was never an intellectual or even an emotional commitment to the act. It was all completely and unabashedly physical. His reason denounced it even while his nature rolled and reveled in it.

He had always managed to reassure himself of his integrity and to distance himself from guilt even while he knew that all too soon those twitchings would recur and leave him defenseless, spent, and defeated in his celibate's bed.

But now there was Cósima. And although he did not evoke her image to solidify the experience, she was always there when the climax came.

Luckily for him, neither Tobías nor the prying eyes of Nueve Niños could see and thus their tongues could not wag.

One afternoon, on his return from a walk along the lake—he was careful to go in the direction opposite from Cósima's house—he spotted the unmistakable shipping-crate shape of a Volkswagen van in front of the rectory. In a county of Ford pickups and well-worn Buicks, this could only mean strangers.

As he moved closer, Fr. Jon speculated that the van had enjoyed better days. Surely sometime in the distant past it had rolled off a spiffy German assembly line, bright and clean and with that new-car smell. But now it was painted in a crude paisley motif that was fast losing the battle to rust from the bottom up. He shuddered to think what had replaced the new-car smell.

There were four bodies taking advantage of the vehicle's shade, two men and two women, all with long, stringy hair and patched up clothing. The less said about their general hygiene the better. One of the males was using long, dirty fingers to choke the life out of the neck of a battered guitar, while the other stroked his Jesus-beard. Both of the women cradled beribboned tambourines in their laps. They all smiled and waved when they saw him.

"Can I help you?"

"Peace be with you, Brother," the bearded one said.

"That's Father," Fr. Jon corrected and made his way around four pairs of dirty, sandaled feet to stand before them. "Are you looking for someone?"

"You, Brother . . ." persisted the one with the beard, the apparent spokesman for the group.

"Father," Fr. Jon insisted.

The man with the beard smiled a compromise. "Brother Father, we're here in the name of Jesus."

Fr. Jon gave out with a most audible *why me?* sigh. "And . . . ?"

"We're here in the name of Jesus," the man repeated.

"Me too."

Then they just sat there with their silly smiles.

Fr. Jon looked to the churchyard beyond them and saw Tobías seated on a gravestone, his short legs swinging free of the ground. Determined not to contribute grist to Nueve Niños's resident gossip mill, and against his better judgment, the priest turned toward the rectory. "It's cooler inside."

Even as they settled themselves into three chairs—the man with the guitar slid down the wall and rested his bony posterior on the floor—Fr. Jon was calculating how he could get rid of them. He sat across from them, behind his desk. "So. You were saying?"

"Jesus is our Savior," the man with the beard said.

"Jesus is our Brother." This from the man with the guitar and no beard but the wisp of a goatee that made him look even seedier than the rest.

"Jesus is our Provider."

Another county heard from, the older of the two women, blowzy and in a voluminous crazy-quilt skirt.

"He was mainly talking about *spi-ri-tu-al* provisions." Fr. Jon was careful to enunciate all four syllables. Not a bad touch, he thought.

"He promises us *everything*." Wide eyed, the younger female joined the conversation.

"Behold the lilies of the field . . ." Beard intoned.

The priest waved off the rest of the recitation. "Yes, yes, I'm familiar with the passage."

They went back to smiling.

"OK. So what do you want?" Fr. Jon was already debating between the five-dollar bill and the single dollar he had tucked away in the desk drawer for exactly this kind of situation. He settled on the five, figuring that it would be worth it if he could just get them out of his house.

Beard tilted his head and stared at Fr. Jon out of one eye, as if assessing his capacity to understand. "Like I already said, we're here to talk to you about Jesus."

"Well, I'm really kind of busy right now . . ."

Suddenly Fr. Jon was witness to a convention acting immediately and purposefully as one. On no perceptible cue, Goatee took up his guitar and strummed a chord. The two women began tapping their tambourines gently against their open palms. Then the four began singing in close harmony:

> Leaning, leaning. Safe and secure from all alarms . . .
> Leaning on the everlasting arms . . .
> What a fellowship, what a joy divine . . .
> Leaning on the everlasting arms . . .

They were actually pretty good. Beard was a passable if nasally tenor. The blowzy one had a thin but clear soprano. The younger woman was a surprisingly strong and confident alto. Only Goatee, with a tubby sounding bass, needed some work.

The singing caught Fr. Jon by surprise, but it did not prepare him for what came next. Beard began to speak while the other three now hummed softly in backup.

"Hummmmmmmm."

"We all want to share this Jesus. We want this Jesus to be the brother of all men. We want the world to be full of Jesus."

"Hummmmmmmmm."

Jesus, Fr. Jon thought, not so much a prayer as an imprecation. He nodded to let them know he was still paying attention but his eyes were no longer his. They darted. They moved to his hands, the telephone, the pointed letter opener within reach of his right hand, the door, and the distance to it.

"Amen," Beard concluded abruptly.

The blowzy one was now crying. The younger girl had thrown her head back and was quivering with pleasure. Goatee, taken off guard, stopped humming a beat or two after the others. Without support of the melodic line his bass voice sounded like a prolonged belch. He quickly bowed his head and began to shake it. Whether it was from embarrassment or rapture, Fr. Jon could not tell.

The priest hinged his fingers in front of him and opened his palms. They glistened with perspiration. He looked to the heavens, then he looked back at the group. "I still don't know what it is you want from me."

"Like I said, we've come to talk to you about Jesus."

"Well, now, I'm really too busy working for the Lord to sit around and talk about Him all day."

Fr. Jon made a mental inventory of what exactly he could do for Jesus during the next hour or so. He supposed he could spend a desultory fifteen minutes looking over the church books. And with a parish heavily subsidized by the archdiocese, any paging through the books was always desultory. Perhaps something more pastoral. A much put-off visit to the bedside of old Mrs. Sandoval? This would mean two hours out of his afternoon just to prove a point to a bunch of hippies.

What the hell can a grown man with four years of postgraduate training and a doctoral degree in canon law do in Nueve Niños at three o'clock on a Tuesday afternoon? Check the boiler in the church? This at least had the appeal of being practical. The problem was that he didn't know how to check boilers. He did know that the one in the church looked and sounded bad, just as Mrs. Sandoval looked and sounded bad. But despite constant complaints, they both continued to function.

Beard pressed on. "Sometimes you have to talk, Father Brother, to get your brain straight, Jesus straight."

Fr. Jon had had just about enough. He pushed himself forward to stand up and fell just as abruptly back as his cassock caught on the under edge of the desk. *Pop.* One of the buttons flew up and hit him on the nose. "My brain is straight enough," he sputtered, whatever the hell that meant.

"You have things, Brother Father. And as long as you have things, you can't have Jesus."

"Sell all you have to the poor . . ." began the younger girl.

"Sell all you have and *give* to the poor, Sister Shirley," corrected Beard.

"Oh, I'm sorry, I was only trying . . ." She blushed and hung her head.

Fr. Jon picked up the cassock button from his lap and tossed it on the desk. "What I own wouldn't bring very much."

"But that's not the point, Father Brother. You do own things." He cast a look around the cramped rectory. "But Jesus didn't. If you want to be Jesus-straight, you can't have things."

"You must interpret these things according to your own condition."

They stared. They hadn't the slightest idea what he was talking about.

"I mean, some people have to have *something* or nobody would have anything."

"Jesus didn't have," Beard responded after some thought.

"But Jesus had others who DID have!" Fr. Jon was getting a headache. "Women. Rich people, poor people, tax collectors, fishermen, whores. They were always giving him stuff."

Beard scowled. Here was a complication.

The other three turned expectant eyes on their leader.

Suddenly his face lit up. "But He kept telling them that they shouldn't have."

Eyes dancing with delight, the two women clapped softly. Goatee still looked lost.

"He didn't mean it like that," Fr. Jon countered.

Beard spread his hands out in front of him daring the priest to refute the irrefutable. "He said it."

"He said lots of things."

"Oh, He did, Father Brother. He did say lots of things. And you haven't been listening very closely, have you? You're just like Brother Troy here, and Sister Shirley and Sister Kate."

And how did Jonathan Marcel Armitage fit in with this piteous lot?

Beard now proceeded to enlighten him. "Brother Father, like you, these poor souls weren't listening to Jesus. They were listening only to themselves. Tell him, Brother Troy."

"I was strung out. On reds, on acid, on jujus. And I was nowhere. Total oblivion."

"And then, Brother Troy?" encouraged Beard.

"And then I met you."

"No, no, Brother Troy, you met Jesus," Beard corrected.

"No, I didn't. I met you. And then I met Jesus."

Beard accepted the clarification. He actually winked at Fr. Jon and his smile was positively beatific. Then he turned to the older of the two women. "Sister Kate?"

Sister Kate took a deep breath in prelude to her testimony.

Fr. Jon stopped her dead. "I think I get the idea."

"It's the same with all of us," Beard said. "We were lost sheep and He found us. And now He's looking for you, Brother Father. You've been trying to hide but He won't give up. He'll pound, and pound, and pound on your door until you open it up to Him. We've been following Jesus, Father Brother. We know. That's why we want you to know. So you can follow Him too. So you can tell the people who come to your church to follow Him. You've got a nice house, food, clothes, a car. He wants you to give it all away and follow Him. Don't you hear Him? Can't you see Him? He's singing with joy and walking through fields of lilies. Follow Him."

"It's the way, it's the way, it's the only fuckin' way," muttered Brother Troy.

Beard was now giving Fr. Jon the fierce look of a headmaster. "Father Brother, Jesus can't come close to you if He has to climb over all the things you own to get to you."

"Would you just let me . . ."

"Give it up, Father Brother. Give it all up. Jesus is knocking at your heart."

The priest rose up, an imposing figure in black, he hoped.

"Let me tell you something. Sometimes Jesus can be a colossal pain in the ass!"

They flinched.

"Yeah, that's right. Jesus can be a royal pain right in the old keester. I work my fanny off for Him and then He says that without Him I'm not worth shit. He gives me the itch for an occasional woman and then tells me I can't scratch that itch. He tells me not to love the things of this world and then gives me an appetite for good scotch, good music, and a good night's sleep."

"You're not talking about Jesus."

Fr. Jon walked to the front window. A pickup drove by, slowed down as it passed the VW, then sped off.

"You're damned right, I'm talking about Jesus," he finally answered. "So you clowns think you've got the whole thing figured out. You think that I should be like you? Buddy, we're not even in the same league. I'm a pro. You're amateurs."

This declaration was as great a revelation to Jon as it was to his audience. Despite his master's degree in sacred theology from the Gregorian University in Rome, his doctorate in canon law from Catholic University, Washington, D.C., his romps through marble halls as a celebrity priest, he had missed the one reality that even the simplest priest in the most remote parish could have told him. The bishop of Fall River had been right. He was expendable, disposable. All priests were. Only the work mattered.

Fr. Jon leaned back heavily against the windowsill and looked at the floor, still struggling to assimilate this newfound wisdom. "You see," he finally said, "Jesus is really the only one who's got it all figured out. For amateurs it's all supposed to be love and joy, so you won't lose interest. For pros like me it's mainly a job. Now let me give you some advice. Get out of Nueve Niños before dark."

He gave them both the five- and the one-dollar bills, a loaf of bread, and three cans of pork and beans, and they left.

Chapter Nineteen

On the morning of August 2, 1965, the caldera wove a gossamer shroud of mist. When the work was done, an impatiently waiting breeze dipped its fingers into the water, pulled up the steaming mantle, and laid it over Nueve Niños and the nine cones.

Precisely at nine o'clock the tolling began from San Eusebio's modest belfry. It was a single, muted note dealt out in a slow, doleful tempo. The same wind that was spreading the fog picked up the ding, ding, ding and carried the sound through the parish, along roads, up front yards, through half-opened windows, and under doorways.

Mothers dressing their children for Mass suddenly clutched at them for reassurance, squeezed them hard, and wept into their freshly washed hair. Not understanding, the children complained and pulled away. The men sat in their kitchens, toyed with cups of cold, sour coffee, fretted about the time taken from work, and felt guilty for their venality.

It was the day of Danny García's funeral.

At precisely ten minutes to the hour, the tolling stopped. A minute later Tobías appeared in the sacristy to assist Fr. Jon with his vestments.

The priest, who seldom gave the sacristan a second look during this daily routine (twice on Sundays), immediately noticed a difference. Atop Tobías's absurdly round head perched a serviceman's overseas cap. His body was stuffed into a suit coat with seams that strained to hold the serge together. Pinned to a lapel was a small American flag. Over the left breast pocket hung a Purple Heart and a Silver Star.

"A Purple Heart? You were wounded?"

"A long time ago, Padrecito."

"And a Silver Star. Isn't that for bravery?"

"Sí, Padrecito. A long time ago."

"You must be very proud."

"It was a long time ago, Padrecito." Tobías took up a staff topped with a crucifix and stood at the door to the sanctuary. "The people are waiting."

Fr. Jon mounted the pulpit and looked over the congregation for this day. The church was full, fuller even than with those oversized crowds that still greeted him every Sunday. In the left front pew sat Anna García and her family. Across from them were six white-gloved, stiff-backed marines. Catholic or not, they would remain seated, eyes front for the entire ceremony. Directly in the middle, up by the communion rail, stretched a flag-draped casket. Off to one side a small table covered with a crocheted doily held a vase of flowers and a picture of Private Daniel Tomás García.

Happily for Nueve Niños, Danny would be the only son it would send off to Vietnam. However, from the barrios of Albuquerque to the villages that dotted the landscape across the Sangre de Cristo range, young men and women at that very moment were still being offered up as their communities' single-most disposable resource. They were, for the most part, skinny, pimpled teenagers with few aspirations and fewer opportunities. To these young people, military service was a way out. Their pictures sat on prominent display in the homes to which they would never return. In framed 8 x 10 memorials, the boys and girls posed smartly in their dress uniforms. Their faces were retouched to remove all blemishes, and their cheeks and lips were rouged. They were ready for their coffins.

Fr. Jon recited the text of his sermon: "Greater love has no man than this, that a man lay down his life for his friends." It was standard and expected, a glowing tribute to all the young men and women who made the ultimate gesture in service to their country.

Halfway through, Fr. Jon paused, oddly disoriented by the upturned faces of his parishioners. He started up again, stumbled over a phrase, backtracked to correct it, and then abruptly stopped speaking altogether.

When he finally broke his silence, it was in Spanish, soft and gentle, a conversation rather than an oration. He talked not of valor and sacrifice, but of children—how they must be loved and cared for, how they must be nurtured and taught, how their childhood must be treasured since it could not be preserved.

After he finished speaking, Fr. Jon's eyes wandered across the pews. Anna García sat stoic. She had no more tears to give. The marines were ever stalwart. Children fussed. Many women were openly weeping. One man honked loudly into his handkerchief while several others cleared their throats or wiped at their eyes with their sleeves. At the very back, standing against the wall, Cósima smiled at him. It was the first time he had ever seen her in church.

Surprisingly, the one person in the entire church who was not listening avidly to Fr. Jon's sermon, English or Spanish, was his single-most devoted disciple, Tobías.

The sacristan stared at the casket and was worlds away.

It was on a dusty, rut-gouged Korean road that Corporal Tobías Rincón sat with the rest of his platoon on side benches in the canvas-canopied rear of a troop transport.

Tobías was looking directly into the face of his sergeant seated across from him when the explosion came. His next recollection was of gravel digging into his right cheek. Next, he was aware of screaming. He lifted himself up from the road and stumbled toward the burning truck. The sergeant was hanging halfway out the back. Tobías pulled him to safety, went back to retrieve two more of his comrades, and was about to make a third run at the vehicle when it disintegrated in a series of ear-blistering blasts. He sat by the side of the road with the others and watched. No one spoke. They only moved when their bodies jerked involuntarily at the noise of cartridges and grenades popping and detonating in the pyre that consumed their friends.

When Tobías placed a hand on his lap he discovered the blood. It was fresh and it was his. The pain came in a rush and persisted until he lost consciousness.

"I couldn't have made a cleaner job of it myself." This was the opinion of a MASH surgeon, one shared with his colleagues over yellow mounds of scrambled powdered eggs in the officers' mess tent.

The "it" was the total castration, by an object unknown, of Corporal Tobías Rincón.

"Maybe shrapnel. My money's on a piece of glass. Swish." The surgeon made a slicing motion with his fork and managed to scatter lumps of egg across the table. "Sharp as a scalpel. All I had to do was clean it up and suture it. Poor bastard. Don't know if I did him any favors. These Mexicans don't have much to live for except knocking up their girlfriends." He sensed that he had stepped over some line and quickly moved on. "The wound to the neck was a lot messier. Made hamburger out of the thyroid. How it missed the carotid artery, I'll never know."

He used to look like that.

Tobías was in the process of putting the church back in order after the funeral. He took Danny García's picture from the table and held it at arm's length. Young, slim, smiling but with fear behind the eyes. So bright and proud in his uniform. Yes, Tobías used to look like that.

When Tobías returned to Nueve Niños (he had nowhere else to go), he moved back into the little house that had been boarded up since his mother's death. He could already feel his body bloating and going soft.

Every time he shaved he thought he detected that his eyes had bulged just a fraction farther out of their sockets and that his cheeks had puffed out a bit more. He was starting to look like a chubby little boy blowing up a balloon. Every time he put on his stockings he noticed that his feet were pudgier, and when he poked at his arms the skin depressed and took its time springing back.

He no longer so much walked as minced, possibly because his thighs were beginning to rub together or because he hated the feel of the soles of his feet as they bore the load of his swollen body.

He knew that people laughed at him behind his back. He sensed the reluctance of the menfolk to be around him, as if they might catch whatever it was that he had. He was relegated to socializing with the women. They made room for him at their kitchen tables for midmorning coffee. They pumped him for information about each other. From them he learned how to gossip, how to cover his mouth when he laughed, how to sit with his legs clamped shut.

Fr. Jon had been more accurate than he could have imagined during his preliminary assessment of Tobías. The sacristan was a eunuch all right, and not just in his soul. But this eunuch had earned both a Purple Heart and a Silver Star. How Tobías won them and how he came to be as he was, he never deigned to share with the good people of Nueve Niños.

Three priests before Fr. Armitage, Tobías assumed the job of sacristan. There was no salary but his disability check covered his modest needs. It was something to do. By the time Fr. Jon arrived, the sacristan was a fixture in the community, a harmless clown of a man who was useful for nothing except to sweep out the church, snuff out candles, make sure that the altar appointments and the Mass vestments were in order, and keep the women of the parish amused.

After the graveside ceremony, after taps had been played, after the echo of the rifle salute dissipated over the caldera, after the marines were gone, after Anna García went home to receive visitors, after the townspeople dispersed to their daily business, the sun finally burned off the mist. And after all that, the gravediggers came to fill up the hole.

Tobías was there to stop them. "*Déjenlo.* I will take care of it."

"But we're being paid to do the job," they protested.

The sacristan handed each of them a five-dollar bill. "*Váyanse.* This is work for a soldier, not *peones.*"

The men walked away with their shovels on their shoulders and wondered about the sacristan who had never been so bold before.

"Maybe he grew some *cojones,*" one of the men suggested, speaking metaphorically since he did not know Tobías's true condition. "*Otro milagro* by the priest."

They laughed at the joke and at their good fortune in having money in their pockets without having to earn it. They were so pleased with their wit that the gravediggers spread the word among their friends that Tobías had developed a set of testicles overnight. "Watch out for him," they teased. "Next thing you know, he'll be after our women."

The work of filling the grave went slowly since Tobías was really not up to it—witness his progress on the hole behind the rectory. But he kept at it through the rest of the afternoon and well into the night.

From his window, Fr. Jon could see his sacristan struggle with the mound of dirt beside the open grave. He momentarily entertained the thought of going out to help but immediately realized that those two war heroes were best left to themselves.

After dark, the priest could only hear the labor—the spasmodic, slicing sound of blade cutting through earth and the muffled thud of clod falling on clod.

Chapter Twenty

Dear Sally—
I said a funeral Mass for a kid today. Just 18. Vietnam.
    I feel so sad.

                  That's about it.
                  Jonny

Dear Jonny:
I've prayed for your young man. I hope his family can
find some peace.

    Sadness can be good. Use it.
                  Sally

Chapter Twenty-one

The six o'clock bell was exactly on time. On his way to Mass, Fr. Jon passed the mound that marked Danny García's fresh grave. Another ghost to deal with. The flowers on the high-peaked pile of dirt were already wilted. Someone had tied two small American flags to the temporary marker. He wondered whether there would ever be a permanent memorial to replace the tin one.

In the sacristy, Tobías was his usual bustling self.

"Ah, Padrecito. You slept well?"

"I did . . . eventually. What time did you finish out there?"

"Who looks at a clock, Padrecito?"

For reasons he could not decipher, Fr. Jon felt an urge to keep the conversation going. He had, however, already experienced firsthand the reticence that overtook the sacristan with regard to his personal life. "Tobías," he finally said, apropos of nothing, "I've noticed that you never receive the Eucharist. Even yesterday, which must have been a very special Mass for you."

"Ah, muchas gracias, Padrecito. No es nada." Tobías started toward the sanctuary and stopped. "Still . . ."

Fr. Jon looked up from tying the cincture around his waist. "Yes?"

"If it is true what they say about la santa comunión, then I am not worthy. Y sí no es la verdad, why bother?" He shrugged.

❖

This was not a day for visitors. Fr. Jon printed up a sign in both English and Spanish and taped it to the door. "THE OFFICE IS CLOSED TODAY."

He drank his coffee, ate his toast, and read from his breviary. Then for the longest time he stared at the boxes stacked against a wall in the living room. From the moment he had arrived in Nueve Niños he had resisted unpacking. It could only mean that he was raising the white flag and accepting his exile. But now? Who was he kidding? There was no one out there interested in offering him a reprieve from this wasteland.

He had no place else to go. The archbishop and his chancellor had already forgotten about him. The marriage files were piling up again, of that he was certain. But someone else would eventually come along and take up the work he had been forced to abandon.

Expendable.

Fr. Jon knelt down among his boxed treasures. They were books for the most part. Canon law, theology, spiritual readings, best-selling novels, biographies, art, history. He sat cross-legged on the floor, opened the cartons, and began to sort the books into piles. The job was mindless until he came upon a gold-edged book in a rich morocco binding. *Ritualis Romana*, the cover read, the Roman Ritual. He consulted the index, found the page, and began to read with care and nostalgia the ancient ordination formulas that had been said over him years ago in a Roman basilica.

Jon was one of sixty-eight candidates that day, Americans all, average age twenty-six, with four years of postgraduate theology under their cinctures. They stood in rows across the wide sanctuary. In their white albs they looked like a host of angels or, better still, innocents who were completely unprepared for the world they would soon enter.

Everything spoke of solemnity—the high altar with its tiered marble backdrop supporting rows of towering brass candlesticks—blazing tapers flickering against the wall of the apse with its Transfiguration mosaic soaring to the stone-ribbed dome high above—and, in the forefront, the ordaining bishop flanked by scores of ecclesiastics in their full regalia.

The archdeacon began to read from a red leather folder the Latin words starting the process that turned men into priests.

"Let those who are to be ordained to the order of priesthood come forward."

One by one and in alphabetical order he announced the young men's names. Jon was the third to be called.

"Ionatan Marcellus Armitage."

He took a step forward and answered, *"Adsum*—I am here."

He could feel the eyes of the congregation boring into the back of his neck. He imagined his parents among them, smiling and proud yet overwhelmed as only a mailman and his wife on their first trip outside of New England could be.

Soon the ranks of Jon's classmates filled in beside him, each proclaiming their presence as well as their willingness to accept this most revered and daunting of callings.

When the roll call was complete, the archdeacon recited the Admonition.

> *The most reverend father and ruler in Christ, His Excellency, by the grace of God and the Apostolic See, Bishop, commands and charges, under pain of excommunication, that no one here present for the purpose of taking orders shall come forward to be ordained under any pretext, if he be irregular, excommunicated by law or by judicial sentence, under interdict or suspension, illegitimate, infamous, or in any other way disqualified . . .*

Fully aware of the drama of the moment, the archdeacon took time for the weight of the words sink in before he turned and addressed the bishop.

> Archdeacon: *Most Reverend Father, our Holy Mother the Catholic Church asks you to ordain these deacons here present to the burden of the Priesthood.*
> Bishop: *Do you know if they are worthy?*

In spite of so many years of scrutiny, self-imposed and by others, Jon sensed in himself a disconcerting twinge of bridegroom's remorse. Was he really worthy? Really? He had been so adjudged by his superiors during eight years of seminary training. Wasn't that good enough? A sudden white-hot blast of panic almost had him bolting from the sanctuary.

> Archdeacon: *As far as human frailty allows one to know,*
> *I am certain and I testify that they are worthy to undertake*
> *the burden of this office.*

Burden. There was that word again. Why had Jon never thought of the priesthood in that context? What did they know that he didn't?

> Bishop: *Deo gratias.*

The bishop then addressed the congregation.

> Bishop: *Be perfectly free, then, to say what you know about the*
> *conduct and character of the candidates and what you think of their*
> *fitness. But let your approval of their elevation to the priesthood be*
> *based more on their merits than on your own affection for them.*
> *Consequently, if anyone has anything against them, let him for*
> *God's honor and in God's name come forward and sincerely speak*
> *his mind. Only let him remember his own state.*

The young men waited in the silence of the cavernous church for the moment to pass. They expected that no one would rise to denounce. But still. After a titillating protracted pause, the bishop once more turned his attention to the *ordinandi*.

> Bishop: *Therefore, my dear sons, chosen as you are by the*
> *judgment of our brethren to be consecrated as our helpers,*
> *keep yourselves blameless in a life of chastity and sanctity.*
> *Be well aware of the sacredness of your duties. Be holy as*
> *you deal with holy things . . .*

Let the fragrance of your lives be the delight of Christ's Church, that by your preaching and example, you help to build up the edifice which is the family of God. May it never come about that we, for promoting you to so great an office, or you, for taking it on yourselves, should deserve the Lord's condemnation; but rather may we merit a reward from Him. So let it be by his grace.

Then, in a defining gesture of obeisance to the church, to the bishop, and to the people of God, Jon joined the other young men as they lay flat, face down, on the cold marble and cradled their heads on their crossed arms.

A choir from high in the nave of the church began the staccato chanting of the Litany of the Saints over the prostrated forms. The entire host of heaven was being called on to witness the commitment of these young men. The choir called out their names one by one—the Archangels Michael, Gabriel, Raphael . . . *Ora pro nobis!*; the holy martyrs, Stephen, Lawrence, Agatha, Agnes . . . *Ora pro nobis!*; the heroes of the church, Benedict, Dominic, Francis . . . *Ora pro nobis!* Wave upon wave of names from the roster of the blessed washed over the young men, an assurance or perhaps a warning that the saints would support them in their work or stand in witness of their failures.

After the Great Litany the young men rose to their feet. It was time to be ordained.

Deacon Armitage knelt before the bishop who placed his hands on Jon's head. There were no words. This simple gesture that took no more than the tick of a clock conferred the power of priesthood.

When the young men were back in their places, the bishop stood and stretched out his hand over them to speak the formal decree.

Bishop: *Almighty Father, we pray that you bestow on these servants of yours the dignity of the priesthood. Renew in their hearts the spirit of holiness, so that they may be steadfast in their priestly office received from you, O God, and by their own lives suggest a rule of life to others.*

May they be prudent fellow workers in our ministry. May they shine in all virtues, so that they will be able to give a good account of the stewardship entrusted to them, and finally attain the reward of everlasting blessedness.

Jonathan Armitage was a priest. *Pray for him.*

The rest of the ceremony was a mere filling in of the details.

The new priests received the insignia of their office, the stole and the chasuble. They were charged as servants to the people of God to say Mass for them and to lead them by the example of their lives. Their hands were anointed with holy oil affirmed their duty to sanctify others by their touch. They accepted the juridical commission to hear confessions and absolve people from their sins. And finally, to seal the contract, they promised their unquestioning obedience forever.

> Bishop: *Do you promise me and my successors reverence and obedience?*
> Ordinati: *We promise.*
> Bishop: *My dear sons, ponder well the order you have taken and the burden laid on your shoulders. Strive to lead a holy and devout life, and to please almighty God, that you may obtain His grace. May He in His kindness deign to bestow it on you.*

It was over.

Jon put down the book. His mouth was dry, his hands trembled. The priesthood he had loved—the golf, the scotch, the adulation, the friends in high places, all dross. Cutting through all the bullshit of what he had thought it meant to be a priest, of what others had led him to expect of his calling, there it was in black and white. His only charge, from the very beginning, had been to serve and to live a life worthy of that service. But hadn't he known that all along?

Was it arrogance that precipitated his failure? For now he knew that his priesthood was indeed a failure. Perhaps his initial presumptions were born of first fervor. How many young doctors, lawyers, teachers has not been cocky enough to think they could be the best ever at their professions, superstars? This was forgivable. What was not forgivable was the arrogance that came later to mask a curious mixture of self-doubts and self-service. By then, the comfort of his life was too grasping a mistress. It made him so self-absorbed that he was unable or unwilling to rip the blinders from his eyes. Why was it so clear now? How had he forgotten that the Church had called him to the priesthood for one reason only? To serve.

Now, there was every possibility that such an exquisite moment of grace was gone, never again to be proffered.

Unless he changed.

But could he change?

Chapter Twenty-two

Late that evening, books still scattered in small piles across the rectory's living room floor, Fr. Jon stood at the lake.

Every synapse of his being was keyed to penetrate the blackness that stretched out before him. Jon went to one knee and let the wavelets lick at his fingertips. He could feel the lake, see it, hear it, smell it, almost taste it, but still he could not grasp it, something he needed most desperately to do.

Here, after all, is where it had all begun. His ridiculous adventure. Here is where he had lost himself in the deep. Here is where the caldera had vomited him up on shore and left him naked to be found and taken in by strangers. Here is where he had become, through none of his doing, the rebuttal to an unfounded curse, a reluctant living miracle. The lake had assumed full control of his life. It owned him.

He pulled off his running shoes, discarded his sweat suit and underclothes, and waded to midcalf. Confetti-sized bits of shale dug into the soles of his feet and worked themselves between his toes. He remembered the water's being cold. It still was. He remembered the undercurrent. It was still there, lapping at his legs and gently but firmly tugging at him.

Come deeper.

He hunkered down until he was submerged to his waist and splashed water over his torso, face, and head. It was a chilling business. His breathing became shallow and his teeth began to chatter.

Unfazed, he extended his arms in front of him, stretched out his body, and began to swim.

His strokes were long and efficient, his kick deliberate and powerful. Jon felt as if he were gliding mere millimeters above the surface, challenging the lake to reach up and take him if it could. He did not stop swimming until he was far from shore. In the absolute stillness, he treaded water and set his eyes on the meager, joyless lights of Nueve Niños. When last he had seen them from that vantage point, they had been a beacon of hope. Now they had shrunk in importance to a mere point of reference.

On the swim back, the undercurrent fought him as before. Then, however, he had been at the end of his resources. Now he slapped it down and kicked it away with a fury that almost had him shouting with the grim exuberance of it.

When his feet touched bottom, he stood and walked onto dry land. Jon deliberately kept his back to the lake, like a prizefighter whose opponent sprawled out on the canvas behind him. He had no need to look upon his foe. This time he had won. He was once more quite naked on the firm ground of Nueve Niños. But this time it was on his own terms.

He dried himself off with his sweats, dressed, and sat on a boulder to put on his shoes. Then he allowed his mind to drift to thoughts of Cósima.

After the lake, she was the next logical rung in the ladder toward his reclamation. She had rescued him. She had offered her house and bed. He had drunk of her potion and slept naked under her blanket. In that room he had dreamt his dream of lying on a watery pad, trapped in a metallic coffin. It was also there, in Cósima's bed, that he felt the touch that ran from his brow to his chest, to his abdomen, to his thigh. This had not been a dream.

Fr. Jon stood at Cósima's front door and knocked. Light from the two flanking windows projected a pair of sharply defined rectangles on the ground to either side of him.

"*¿Quién es?*" Her voice did not try to disguise her consternation.

"It's me. Father Armitage."

Cósima cracked the door wide enough for him to see that she was using both hands to clutch a robe at the neck and waist.

"Is something wrong, Padre?"

"I didn't mean to startle you. I was just walking by and I saw your lights on. I saw you at Danny García's funeral."

There was a crash from somewhere in the house.

"*¡Con cuidado!*" Cósima tossed the words at the door to the same room where Jon had once been confined.

The crash was replaced with a vigorous thumping.

Fr. Jon tilted his head to one side to look in. "Is this a bad time?"

Cósima rolled her eyes. "*Espera*. Let me take care of this."

She padded across the room, opened the door just wide enough to slip in, and closed it quietly behind her.

Fr. Jon could hear muffled voices, another thump or two, and then there was silence.

When Cósima emerged a few minutes later, she was fully dressed. She stepped to one side and addressed the open doorway behind her. "*Ándale, ándale.*"

A figure slowly sidled out of the room. Fr. Jon could see that it was a man. He had draped his shirt, back to front, over his head and clamped the whole thing down with his hat. With his hands feeling for the air in front of him and with Cósima's guidance, the man took shuffling steps across the room and out the front door.

"*Buenas noches*, Padre," he said and touched the brim of his hat before he stumbled into the darkness.

"Buenas noches, Señor Alcalde," Fr. Jon answered, just loud enough so that only Cósima could hear him.

She covered her mouth with one hand, pulled him in the house with the other, and slammed the door shut with her foot. Then she began to laugh. It was a deep, throaty sound that shook her body. She leaned back on the door and slid down until she sat with legs splayed on the floor.

"He tried to go out the window," she finally managed to say between gasps, "but it's nailed shut."

"Oh."

"I'm sorry." Cósima took several deep gulps and wiped her eyes on the hem of her skirt. Then she held out her hands so that Jon could pull her to her feet.

"I'm the one who should apologize," said the priest. "I didn't mean to interrupt anything."

"*No es nada.* It isn't the first time he's been caught. He was lucky it was only you. The last time it was his wife with their five kids."

Fr. Jon had come to Cósima with a purpose, but suddenly he had been brought up short. This was not how he had envisioned his visit. This was impossible. How could either of them recover from the farce, a scene right out of Feydeau, that had just played out before them.

"I should not have dropped in like this. My fault. You made it very clear the last time that I was not to come back."

Cósima cleared the last of the laughter from her throat but kept the smile. "And you came anyway."

"I was swimming on the lake. *Muy, muy frío.* I could sure use a hot cup of coffee."

It felt so damnably natural sitting across the small table from Cósima, his hands wrapped around a steaming mug. How to explain it? The casual flow of their conversation. His growing confidence with the situation. Cósima's obvious ease with him. He could just as easily be sharing cocktails with one of the matrons of Fall River. He struggled to wipe away an image that seemed so unworthy of the moment.

"It was nice to see you in church."

"I like Anna García. She's almost a friend."

"You should come more often."

"Nobody wants to see me there."

"I do. Your smile brightened up the place." The line was vintage Jon Armitage. He realized it but he didn't care.

"Maybe someday, many priests from now. Maybe then."

Jon reached across and rubbed her arm. "You have a problem with the priest you have now?"

Cósima pulled back and nested her hands in her lap. "I have a problem with God."

Her words were not at all what he had expected. Not just because they broke the mood, but because they had a jangling familiarity to them. Hadn't he himself said something like that not long ago? Jon leaned back and took a sip of coffee. Cósima's declaration echoed with more eloquence than his own words to the foursome with the VW van. Jesus can sometimes be a pain in the ass, he had said to them. Now a similar sentiment was being thrown back in his face. For form's sake he struggled for a response. "He can work in strange ways," was the best he could do.

"Tell that to Anna García. Her son is dead and she doesn't know why. Why him? Why there? Killed by strangers? Why any of it?"

"That's not God. It's the politicians."

"Blame who you want. I'll blame God."

It was the age-old Problem of Evil. Don Plácido Cárdenas had eschewed it for a frivolous punch line to avoid a death-bed conversion. What he had really wanted to ask was, Why me? No matter. Fr. Jon was unprepared to answer either the old man with the deadly flyswatter or the woman who had saved his life. Still, he felt he owed Cósima something.

"God never answers the why of anything."

"Then I have a problem with Him."

"I guess we all do. Did you hear about the hippies who came to town the other day?"

Cósima gave him a puzzled look.

"They said they wanted to teach me about Jesus."

"But you are a priest. You already know about Jesus."

"That's what I told them. But I don't, you know. What I thought I knew is garbage. For that I blame myself."

Cósima shook her head. *"No entiendo."*

Fr. Jon drained his coffee and placed the mug on the table with studied deliberateness. "Can I tell you about Father Jon Armitage?"

Cósima crossed her arms. She had heard many stories from many men. "If you like."

Fr. Jon told it all. About the young man with raging ambitions that were way beyond the means of his family to accommodate. His calculating run at the priesthood. The cocksure indiscretions in Fall

River and the exile to Santa Fe. His problems with the archbishop that led to the demotion to Nueve Niños. The oddly self-defining moment with the hippies. The confusion since Danny García's funeral. It flushed out in a self-serving torrent that by the end had Jon weeping with his head buried in his arms.

There was a touch on his neck, gentle but electric. He straightened up, put his arms around Cósima's waist, and crushed his face into her breasts. When he finally looked up into her eyes, they were serious but soft.

She patted him on a cheek, bent down, and kissed him on the lips.

The kiss was as gentle as had been her touch, but with the same electric results. Jon grabbed for her and tried to pull her toward him.

Cósima pried herself loose and stepped away. "*No más.*"

Jon was unprepared for the rebuke and not a little bit angry. "Is this your idea of some stupid game?"

"I don't like games."

"Then why the kiss?"

"That was wrong. I should not have done that."

"But you did it anyway."

"I wasn't thinking."

"And what about the touches. Were you thinking then?"

"Touches? What touches?"

"The night you found me by the lake. Someone touched me while I was asleep."

Her eyes fluttered. "I did not touch you."

"Who then?"

She exhaled in consternation. "No one touched *you*. It was my husband."

"I don't understand. What husband? He touched me?"

Cósima threw up her hands and laughed. "*Ay, Dios mío.*"

Jon's eyes flared. "Now you're making fun of me."

"I would never do that."

"I'm not so sure."

Cósima took the long solitary braid that lay to the front across her shoulder and began to brush its tip against an open palm. "You told me your story. Now I'll tell you mine. I was married once. The last time I saw my husband was when he climbed into his truck one morning and went to work. He drove a bulldozer for the highway department. When they came and told me he was dead, that the bulldozer had flipped over on him, I did not believe them. When they showed me his body at the mortuary, I still did not believe. I didn't believe any of it. That was not my husband in the coffin. That was not my husband that they buried in the ground." She spread her hands wide as if waiting for an explanation. "But I came home and I had no husband."

Fr. Jon exhaled slowly. "I'm sorry. I didn't know. You don't have to go on."

"You asked about the touch. You have a right to know." She sat down on the floor, crossed her legs, and ran an open hand across the depression made by her skirt.

"What I felt the worst about was that I never got to touch him one last time. I would never feel his arms around me, his body next to mine. Sometimes when I am with a man, if he's young, if his smile is just right, with a bit of the devil in it, I close my eyes and I touch. For a moment my husband is back in my arms and it feels so very good." She looked directly at Jon. "Yes, I touched. But it was not you. *¿Entiendes?* I only want to touch him."

The words and the vehemence with which Cósima said them came at Fr. Jon like a dousing with a bucket of icy water. He cleared his throat. "You're right. I should not come here."

"But you are here, Padre. You came because you had a problem with your Jesus and you thought that I could help you forget. *Tú eres él quien hace los milagros.* I have no miracle for you."

Cósima rose and stood by the door to the back room. "If you've come to be with Cósima, that is your business. But I have a business too. Did you bring money? Who knows? It might be good. At least you have clean fingernails."

Jon pushed himself up from the table with such force that the chair went toppling over behind him. "You can't talk to me like that."

"Why not? Because you are a priest? Well then, if that's what you are, be one, and leave me alone."

He once more stood at the water's edge. If the caldera was expecting him to gloat, he would disappoint. He had returned, not in triumph, but with deep shame.

He had had his pout, over two months of it, and what had it gained him? He had treated the people of Nueve Niños as shabbily as possible, and they had responded with respect and devotion. He had tried to hide behind the conceit of his priesthood, but it had been snatched away and torn to shreds by a humble sacristan, the village prostitute, and four hippies.

He dropped to his knees on the lake's edge for the second time that night. But this time he prayed.

The next Sunday and on all the Sundays left to him in Nueve Niños, Fr. Jon preached to his people in Spanish.

Chapter Twenty-three

Before Mass the following Sunday, Fr. Jon broke one of his own cardinal rules. Instead of going around to the side door that led into the sacristy, he entered the church through the front.

He had adopted the practice of not walking through the church for two reasons. The congregation tended to foist infants on him for blessings or to scramble over each other to touch him as he passed, thus provoking a minor riot in the pews. He had also seen it as one more way to reinforce his determination to keep distance between himself and his congregation.

But today he considered none of that. As he strode up the aisle the people were too taken by surprise to do anything but gape and poke each other with their elbows.

Fr. Jon saw what he was looking for in a pew toward the middle of the church—the backs of two round heads that belonged to Esteban, the mayordomo-without-keys, and his wife, Dorotea.

They had contemplated changing parishes and driving to Clayton for Sunday Mass, but the cost and inconvenience resigned them to Sundays in San Eusebio, where they knew that people were pointing at them behind their backs and mouthing the dreaded sobriquet—*Sin Llaves*.

Fr. Jon stopped immediately in front of the couple and motioned them to stand.

What now? What further disgrace did this wicked priest have in mind for them? They stood up, weary and wary, and Dorotea clung to her husband's arm while they both bowed their heads and waited for the blow.

The priest reached into his cassock pocket and pulled out a ring of keys. "Here, Señor Mayordomo," he said, loud enough for everyone in the church to hear. "I believe these belong to you. I had no right. Please accept them with my deepest apologies."

❖

The very next day, the mayordomo and his wife appeared at the rectory with a loaf of homemade bread. *"Por las llaves,"* Esteban explained.

"There is no need," said Fr. Jon. "The thanks go to you for taking back the keys. You are most forgiving. I only wish I could do something more to make up for the pain I caused you."

Dorotea gave Esteban a mighty nudge.

"Lo sé. Lo sé," the mayordomo hissed at his wife and turned to smile at the priest. *"Tal vez hay algo."*

"Anything," Fr. Jon said.

"La madre de mi mujer. She came from the hospital to be with us. She had an operation, but she is not doing too good."

"I'd be happy to see her. Just tell me when."

❖

Lydia Manygoats was Navajo, which explained her daughter's darker complexion and exotic, for Nueve Niños, look. Because Dorotea had married an outsider she had, for all practical purposes, been ostracized by her clan.

"When *mi suegra* got sick, they sent her to the government hospital in Santa Fe," Esteban explained to Fr. Jon as he escorted him into the house. "My *mujer* wanted to bring her here. It is not easy for Dorotea to visit her family in Four Corners. *Usted sabe."*

Fr. Jon entered the sick room and a small, wrinkled, nut-brown face greeted him from the bed. Lydia Manygoats's head was barely large enough to cause an indentation in the white pillow that cradled it. Two thick braids of black hair liberally streaked with gray stuck straight out from either side of her skull. The top sheet was drawn tightly up and under her chin. Her body was faintly outlined as a mere wisp of a presence under the covers. She was quite motionless, that is except for her deep, dark eyes. They grew large as Fr. Jon approached her, took him in for a split second, and flitted off to examine something on the ceiling.

Esteban edged out of the room. "If you need me, Padre . . . ," he said and closed the door behind him.

Fr. Jon walked around the bed and smiled down at the patient. "Lydia, my name is Father Jon."

Her reaction was no reaction. Her eyes pointed resolutely upward.

"How are you doing today?"

No response. Perhaps she was hard of hearing.

Fr. Jon leaned over until his mouth was about five inches from her face. "Hello, Lydia . . ."

Before he could finish she shot straight up and drove her forehead flush into the bridge of his nose. It sent the priest reeling back. He saw stars. Many stars. Manystars from Manygoats. His arms did a backstroke into the amorphous curtain behind him and he plopped unceremoniously into the window well. His eyes watered. His nose throbbed.

"Goddamnb, Lydia, I dink you broge by dose!" Fr. Jon's voice was so loud that Lydia would have heard him had she been not only deaf, but dead as well.

The mayordomo and his wife rushed into the room and retreated just as swiftly when Fr. Jon waved them away.

"Id's duhthig. We're find."

Jon could only hope that it was nothing. How to explain his injury to the ER doctor if he indeed had a broken nose or worse, a fractured orbital bone, and had to make an emergency trip into Clayton or Raton? "I got coldcocked by an eighty-pound Navajo lady."

He wiped his eyes with a sleeve, worked his way back to his feet, and braved another look at his assailant. She lay there as before, except for one braid that was now trapped beneath her head. The covers were remarkably undisturbed. It was with some perverse satisfaction that Fr. Jon noticed that she bore a small, angry knot on her brow, the blunt instrument that had sent him into the window curtains like a floundering actor trying to find his exit.

"You all right?" The question rose from his guilt for a blasphemous outburst and because he might have helped undo a delicate piece of surgery with the bang to her forehead.

Lydia now had something to say. It was guttural, clipped, and concise. It was likely Navajo and she was possibly telling Fr. Jon that she had a splitting headache.

It dawned on to the priest that Lydia probably spoke no English. This very well might not be a deaf Lydia, but merely a Lydia who was off the reservation for the very first time in her life.

He pulled out a small black crucifix with a corpus in molded silver and positioned it somewhere between her eyes and the ceiling. She blinked, refocused, and moved her eyes past him to study a crack running at a diagonal on the wall opposite the bed.

One more try, this time in Spanish. "Would you like to go to confession, Lydia?"

Nada.

What could he do for poor Lydia? How could he yet make things right for Esteban and Dorotea, who had brought him here to do something good for the old lady, not to cause her further pain. In emergencies he could administer the absolution conditionally without having to hear the confession. He felt good about that. He would absolve her of her sins, including her most recent, he thought grimly, an assault on a man of God. Then he would offer her Communion. No words need be exchanged. He was her priest and that was all that mattered between them. And besides, giving her the Sacraments was the least he could do, particularly if she were to lapse into an irreversible coma during the night from a mysterious bleeding of the brain.

Fr. Jon walked around to the other side of the bed and intercepted her line of vision. "Lydia, *ego te absolvo ab omnibus peccatis tuis, in nomine Patris, et Filii, et Spiritus Sancti.*" He parted the air between them with the sign of the cross.

Lydia's hands crept up and out over the top of the covers. A breakthrough. She was going to cross herself. But no. Instead, her bony talons gripped the edge of the sheet and ever so slowly pulled it over her head.

A job is not done until it's finished. Communion Fr. Jon intended to give her and Communion she would have. In his determination to make things right with them, he would not let the mayordomo and his wife down again.

He snapped open the pyx and took out the consecrated bread. With his elbow he hooked an edge of the sheet and pulled it down. There was that enflamed, accusing forehead. There were those eyes, which now looked straight into his.

Her expression told him nothing. He saw no fear, no surprise, no wonder, no recognition of what he was about to offer her. He held the host high and her eyes became fully attentive to that small, stamped circlet of wheat. *"Corpus Domini,"* he said and brought the Communion to her mouth.

Lydia reached out, delicately pinched the wafer between her thumb and forefinger, and took it from him.

Finally, she understands.

Lydia next placed the host between her teeth and took a careful nip, very much like a pirate biting into a doubloon to test its worth. Obviously satisfied that it was something she might want to hold on to, she closed her fingers tightly around the wafer and pulled her hand back under the covers.

Fr. Jon stood there for a very long time.

What to do now? Go after it? Wrestle it from her bony clutches? Was he supposed to fish blindly under the sheet for the very Body and Blood, Soul and Divinity of the Lord and Savior Jesus Christ and risk a very ugly scene? His theology told him yes. His common sense and fear of what might happen were he to plunge under the sheets told him no. Common sense and fear won out. He smiled at Lydia, told her to get well soon, and quietly left the room.

"She's at peace with her God," Fr. Jon declared to the mayordomo and his wife and beat a hasty exit.

The next Sunday Fr. Jon sought out Esteban and Dorotea as they were leaving the church. "How's Lydia?" he asked.

"Oh, she died Friday. Dorotea's brothers came and took her back to the reservation."

Jon swallowed hard. "Died? From what?"

"She was very old, you know. *Era su tiempo.*"

"But you didn't call me to give her the last rites."

"Oh, don't worry, Padre. She wasn't even Catholic."

"But what about my visit?"

Esteban shrugged and smiled. "*Mi mujer.* She thought it couldn't hurt."

Had Esteban set him up? Was that more a smirk than a smile? Was it just a harmless retaliatory act that the mayordomo needed to even the score and reestablish his dignity? This was not beyond the realm of possibility. The sacristan who was a war hero. The whore who was a romantic. Even don Plácido Cárdenas, who had baited him with a foolish question. All setups. Why should he be surprised about another? As deep as were the waters of the caldera, Fr. Jon was discovering that the serendipitous psyche of the people of Nueve Niños ran even deeper.

Fr. Jon absentmindedly reached up and touched the bridge of his nose. It was still sore but otherwise none the worse for the assault. This brought him to thoughts of Lydia.

There she'd be, standing at the entrance to Heaven.

"Got a ticket?" asks St. Peter.

Lydia holds out her small fist, unclenches it, and reveals the Communion wafer.

St. Peter takes it without comment, and as he ushers her through the gate, says, "That's a pretty nasty bump on your forehead. You'd better have somebody look at it."

A few diehards still persisted in calling the mayordomo "*Sin Llaves*"—why waste a perfectly good nickname?—but the general consensus around Nueve Niños was that it had lost its bite.

Chapter Twenty-four

St. Eusebius.
    St. Eusebius.
      St. Eusebius.
       St. Eusebius.

Pick one. There are four of them listed in the Roman Calendar of Saints: one pope, two bishops (of Vercelli and of Samosota), and one priest (of Rome). They were more or less contemporaries, all living or at least dying in the fourth century AD. Three of them opposed the Emperor Constantinus, champion of the heresy of Arianism. Two of the Eusebiuses were imprisoned, and one of these possibly died in chains. (Or maybe not. The hagiographer is vague on the point.) Another died when a woman, a professed Arian, conked him on the head with a roof tile. This was a confirmed kill.

When the alcalde and members of the village council came to their pastor to inform him that, its being August, it was time to celebrate the feast of San Eusebio, Fr. Jon asked them what he considered to be a perfectly logical question.

"Which San Eusebio?"

The council conferred on the spot and gave the only possible answer. "Our San Eusebio."

"But there are several of them."

"Then it must be one of those," the alcalde answered for the group.

"But which one?"

"The one that the santero carved when Padre Juan started the parish."

The men signed themselves at the mention of the venerable founding pastor, Fr. Jean L'Cote, the fisher of fish.

Hoping that the question of which San Eusebio was now put to bed, the alcalde proceeded with the real reason for the council's visit. "The priest before you, Padre José, gave our santo to another priest from the bishop's office. We need it for the procession. Will you go to Santa Fe and bring San Eusebio back to us?"

Fr. Jon rubbed the back of his neck while he framed his answer. "I suppose I could. But perhaps it would be more suitable for a member of the parish to do it."

"But, Padre, you are a member of the parish. *El número uno.*"

"And how will I know your statue? Perhaps I am not the best person for the job."

"It is San Eusebio." The alcalde was unsure how else he could state the obvious and was beginning to wonder why the priest was being so contrary.

"Come back tomorrow," Fr. Jon said. "Let me think about this."

After the councilmen left, Jon dug into his church history books. There were no parish annuls to consult so he had no other way of determining which of the four St. Eusebiuses had graced the parish of Nueve Niños with his patronage. Finally, as a footnote in the missal, he found that August fourteenth, now celebrated as the eve of the feast of the Assumption, was also a day of commemoration of the priest, St. Eusebius of Rome. Close enough.

What was not yet settled was the matter of his return to Santa Fe. He had not been there nor had he spoken to anyone in the chancery since he had packed up his car and motored the 140 miles to his personal Elba. Still, the trip held some intriguing possibilities.

Start with a confrontation with Msgr. Montini. The chancellor had had every opportunity to argue before the archbishop against Fr. Jon's transfer but had declined. Jon thought he knew why. The Italian wanted him out of the way. The only plausible reason was the matter of the santos that disappeared from the chancellor's office at the same time that he took one of his trips to Italy.

Jon remembered that during the monsignor's absence, a delegation from another parish had come to Santa Fe to retrieve their statue. When Jon questioned Montini about it on his return, the little man had bristled and become quite defensive. He had babbled on about the blasphemous depiction of holy people by ignorant local craftsmen who knew nothing about iconography.

The chancellor also cited the archbishop's support for his efforts to replace the santos with a more decorous statuary. He had, however, steered the conversation away from any mention of how he was disposing of the images.

The fatal stroke for Jon had been when he told Montini that he had rummaged through his office in search of the statue. From that day on, Jon noticed a definite downturn in his stock with the chancellor.

So where were these santos so unworthy of display in village churches? Why was Msgr. Montini so sensitive about the subject? More to the point, where was San Eusebio? Was Jon prepared for the ugly scene that such questions would provoke? Why not? What was the worst they could do to him now that Nueve Niños was no longer a threat?

The other reason that a trip into Santa Fe was growing in appeal was the opportunity to go through the archdiocesan archives. What had really happened to the priest who had been driven into the lake? If Fr. Jon were to be a true pastor to his people, a vocation lately assumed, could he do it under false colors? The people of Nueve Niños still regarded him as their miracle priest, his rising from the lake a sign that the curse had been lifted from them. They deserved better. They were good people maligned for almost a century by a piece of distorted folklore that no one had ever questioned. It was time for the truth, whatever that was, and the archives might provide the key.

When the alcalde and the other councilmen returned to the rectory the next day, Fr. Jon was ready for them.

"The patron saint of Nueve Niños," he announced, "is St. Eusebius of Rome. He has a church on the Quirinal that I visited a time or two."

The council fidgeted. What was all this to them? Their patron was San Eusebio. Had they not already settled that with the priest the day before? All the rest was irrelevant detail. They turned to their alcalde to return the overriding issue to the table.

Their leader stepped forward. "Sí, sí, Padre. If you say so. But what about our santo?"

"I will go to Santa Fe as your representative. Tell me about your santo. What am I to look for?"

The voices came at him from all directions. He is this tall. No, taller. No, not so tall. *Es bigotón*. No. The beard is short. Just painted on. He holds a book. No, the commandments like Moses. Fr. Jon theorized but did not vocalize that it might even be a roof tile. The one thing there was no argument about was that the statue had a crack that extended down one side of the face to the neck like a dueling scar. The santero had apparently been an inexperienced carver and had used an uncured piece of wood. The cleft had appeared soon after the statue was installed and widened through years in the dry air of the high plains.

"Very well," Fr. Jon said. "I will do as you ask, but under one condition."

The people of Nueve Niños were used to conditions. No one ever promised them anything—not the county, not the state, not the bishop, not even the priest who had tried to dig a bomb shelter— without attaching some proviso to the offering. The shoulders of the council gave a communal sag.

"Sí, Padre?" the alcalde asked.

"The condition is this. For too long, this parish, this community has waited for things to happen to it. It is time you took your lives into your own hands. I will do this one thing for you if you promise that from this day on you will do things for yourselves. No one is going to step forward to improve the village unless you do. There is no reason for the people of Nueve Niños to hang their heads for anyone, including me."

For Fr. Jon this was a momentous demand he was making. To the council the whole thing seemed singularly unspecific and unthreatening and nothing that they would have to address at any particular time. This made the condition quite acceptable. They were fairly confident that if, sometime, somehow, the need should arrive, they would be up to the challenge.

The alcalde spoke and the group nodded its agreement. "*Lo que usted dice*, Padre. If that is what you want. But you will get San Eusebio back in time for the fiesta?"

Fr. Jon purposely arrived in Santa Fe unannounced. Where once he might have sought out his friends and allowed himself to be feted, he considered his trip a pilgrimage of sorts, and like any good pilgrim he felt the need to shun worldly distractions. On a practical, much less spiritual level, he wanted to spring his visit on Msgr. Montini with no advance warning.

On the three-hour drive, U.S. Highway 64 west to I-25, then south through Raton, Springer, Wagon Mound, Las Vegas, San José, Rowe, Glorieta Pass, and Apache Canyon, Fr. Jon scripted and rehearsed his confrontation with his nemesis. The scenario, the more he worked at it, began to take on all the elements of an overwrought melodrama.

Enter Fr. Jon Armitage, stage left. The audience claps.

Enter Msgr. Amleto Montini, stage right. The audience hisses.

"Ah, Father Armitage. I see you are surviving the rigors of Nueve Niños."

"Yes, Monsignor. No thanks to you. But I come on another mission."

"That being?"

"The good people of Nueve Niños have charged me with

the duty of retrieving their San Eusebio, which you took under very suspicious circumstances."

The monsignor recoils. The audience gasps, then bursts into enthusiastic applause.

It was a Fr. Jon fortified by his imaginings who rang the chancery doorbell.

The smile of welcome from the young Fr. Tapia, in polo shirt and slacks, brought him immediately back to earth. "Father Jon. So good to see you. It's too bad no one's in."

So much for the script. "I had hoped to see Monsignor Montini."

"I'm afraid he's back in Italy."

"His uncle, I suppose."

"Yes, but this time the poor man has died. Monsignor was devastated."

"I'm sure there's more where that one came from."

"I'm sorry?"

"Skip it. I take it that the archbishop isn't in either," Jon said, pointing to Tapia's casual attire.

"Back east. He won't be in until the middle of the month."

"Your meals must be very quiet."

Fr. Tapia stammered a yes and blushed at his disloyalty. "I'm sorry you came all this way for nothing."

"Actually, what I have to do, I can do without them. I'd like to check the archives. I'm curious about one of the former pastors of Nueve Niños."

"Certainly. You can work in the conference room. I guess I don't have to show you where the coffeepot is."

From the baptismal records still at San Eusebio's, Fr. Jon learned that the pastor who had succeeded the Padre Juan and had been driven into the lake was Denis Archambault. The search through the archives would prove to be much more daunting. He did not expect to find the chronicles of Nueve Niños nicely bound and ready for his perusal, but a first scan of the shelves yielded nothing.

It figured. The village had never counted for much and were it not for its notoriety as a "pastor killer" and its reputation as a Devil's Island for recalcitrant priests, it would have counted for absolutely nothing at all.

For being so rich in history, the archdiocese had never devoted much effort to keeping its records in any usable order. Fr. Jon eventually dug up several accordion files jammed with papers from the first two decades of the century. He spread out his treasures on the long conference table and began a systematic review. It took considerable digging to come up with anything.

There was a letter from the bishop of Lyon introducing one Denis Albert Archambault to the then archbishop of Santa Fe, Peter Bourgade. In florid French, the letter cited the many virtues of Monsieur l'abbé Archambault, virtues that the priest had apparently never deigned to demonstrate to the people of Nueve Niños. There was a letter of assignment to San Eusebio. Apparently, either Archbishop Bourgade was not as sold on the sterling qualities of Père Denis as was the prelate from Lyon, or he counted on the priest's ignorance of the archdiocese to palm off one of its lesser pearls on him.

Fr. Tapia stuck his head in the doorway of the conference room. "Finding what you need?"

"I'm getting there. Half of these papers are ready to fall apart. Tell your boss to hire an archivist to work on this mess before it's too late. If you can ever get a word in edgewise, that is."

The young priest stammered another yes and blushed once more. "Do you mind being here alone? Don't worry about the phones or the doorbell. I've got to leave for a while."

Jon tilted his head. "When the cat's away . . . ?"

The too-earnest young priest half grimaced and half smiled and left.

The moment he heard the front door click shut, Fr. Jon was out of his chair. Actually, there was not that much snooping to do. He had hoped to find something in the vault among the tarnished reliquaries,

chalices, crucifixes, and monstrances that had outlived their useful-
ness. But there was nothing. His only other recourse was that Msgr.
Montini still had the santo in his office, but he knew this was a long
shot.

The chancellor's office was unlocked, a good thing but a bad sign.
Obviously the monsignor had felt that he had nothing to hide, specifically ill-gotten statuary. The credenza was bare except for a sizable
stack of manila folders ripe with papers. He flipped open the top one
and chuckled. A plea for annulment. It looked like it was business as
usual at the archdiocesan marriage tribunal.

The small satisfaction that Fr. Jon took from the lassitude of
his chancellor was not enough to overcome the disappointment in
the matter of the San Eusebio. It didn't take long to make a sweep
of the office. Nothing under the sofa. Nothing behind the drapes.
Nothing in the long drawers of the credenza. Nothing in plain sight
or hidden. Jon turned to the closet in one corner of the room. The
door was locked. After a moment's deflation, he remembered: he
was not *sin llaves*. In all the twaddle surrounding his departure, he
had not turned in his set of keys, a master set that fit every door in
the building.

The key turned in the lock with a satisfying click. The closet was
practically empty except for the miniature monsignorial robes hung
neatly on hangers from a rod. Partially hidden behind them was a
tall, narrow, wooden shipping crate.

Fr. Jon carried the crate into the office and laid it on the floor. The
front of the box had been pried open and repositioned loosely in its
nail holes. It was an easy thing to lift off the panel. Some of the excel-
sior fluffed out and spilled onto the carpet. When he brushed away
the rest of the wood batting, his fingers touched and traced the face
gash that identified San Eusebio. Jon had to smile. The scar made the
saint look like the survivor of a knife fight in a bar. What could be
more appropriate for the patron of Nueve Niños?

"Well, Eusebius of Rome, or whichever one you are, fancy meeting you here."

Someone had irreverently scotch-taped an envelope to the saint's
nose. Fr. Jon carefully peeled it off and removed a letter from inside.

Dear Monsignor Montini:

I am returning to you the santo designated SF32, which you left on consignment with us.

Unfortunately, the condition of the piece is such that I have been unable to generate any interest in it. As you may remember, we had discussed this possibility when we last talked, so I hope the news comes as no surprise to you.

On the bright side, all the other pieces you provided us are in wonderful condition and have created quite a stir among my clientele. You should be pleasantly surprised at the amount of the check I will be remitting to you.

Sorry again about SF32.

I do have some good news, however, regarding the Magi panels. I think we have a buyer. It is truly amazing how well the Italian works continue to do. I hope your sources never dry up.

> Sincerely,
> Julian N. Clairborne
> The Clairborne Gallery
> New York, NY

"Why, Amleto Montini, you little devil, you." Fr. Jon refolded the letter and returned it to its envelope. He was about to lay it on the corner of the chancellor's desk when he had second thoughts and slipped it instead into the inside pocket of his coat.

By the time Fr. Tapia was back from his errands, San Eusebio was stowed in the trunk of Fr. Jon's car, and he was back at work on the archival materials.

"Any luck?"

"A few things. I'm just about ready to wrap up. I'll make sure that everything gets back where I found it."

"You're leaving? I was hoping you'd have dinner with me. Maybe stay the night."

"You mean eat at the archbishop's table?"

Fr. Tapia shrugged.

"Thanks, but I think I'll pass. All that stale cigar smoke."

The night ride back to Nueve Niños was spectacular but lonely. Stars were bunched so thickly that it looked as if a giant geode had been split open and laid over the land like a dome. Such magic and no one to share it with.

Around Wagon Mound, the radio lost the signal delivering Mexican music from KFUN in Las Vegas. Just the other side of Springer it picked up the country-western offerings from KRTN, Raton. Jon hummed along and drummed the beat on the steering wheel.

The day had belonged to him. San Eusebio was stowed in the trunk, anchored in place by a gym bag and a carton of books that still needed unloading. Next to him on the passenger seat rested a spiral notebook. There wasn't much in it, a single page with a few cryptic notations.

Denis Albert Archambault

1904–1905: Nueve Niños, pastor
1905–1907: Los Lunas, parish administrator
1907–1910: Albuquerque (Sacred Heart), parish administrator
1910–1918: Pecos, pastor
1918: On list of four deceased priests (influenza epidemic)

So the caldera was a paper tiger after all. No priest haunted its depths. It had no watery secrets to hold over the parish. There was no legend, no curse to live down.

And there was even more good news. Jon had found the santo, and so the villagers could stage their procession. And he had an almost equally important trophy. He smiled and patted the breast of the coat where he had tucked the letter from the art gallery in New York.

It had been a good day all around.

Chapter Twenty-five

There was a general consensus among the people of Nueve Niños to make that year's celebration of the feast of San Eusebio the most spectacular ever. It was to be Christmas, Easter, and the Fourth of July all rolled into one.

Christmas.

Luminarias, small, square Lincoln log constructions of piñon and cedar kindling ready for firing, marked a path from the door of the church, down the lane, through the town, to the lake, and along the shoreline for at least a quarter mile. This was the same route taken every December by men carrying the statues of Mary and Joseph as they searched for a kind soul to take them in. Now the fires would light the triumphant parade of San Eusebio.

Easter.

The children dyed eggshells and then stuffed them with confetti from cut up Montgomery Ward catalogues, several pilfered from backyard outhouses. In fact, a few unwary citizens found themselves pawing desperately around their privies only to realize that they had been caught short in being able to complete their business. It was a small enough sacrifice. The children would sell the *cascarones* filled with the chopped up booty at five cents apiece for revelers to crack over the heads of the unsuspecting and leave them laughing in a shower of colored paper bits.

The Fourth of July.

The village square buzzed from early morning with the sounds of industry—sawing and hammering. In no time booths sprang up for the selling of *pastelitos* and cakes, tamales, and beef patties wrapped in flour tortillas and slathered with green chile. There were several gaming stands decorated with small American flags and red, white, and blue streamers of crepe paper—a fish pond for the children, a wheel of fortune for the adults, and tests of skill for everyone. There were large wooden rings to toss at pegs and rubber balls to knock over stacks of tin cans. Some of the men from the village drove the hundred miles into Texas and returned with as many fireworks as fifty dollars could buy. The pyrotechnics would be a grand finale to a grand day.

It was to be a great fiesta. Not only were they celebrating their santo's homecoming, but there was also cause for joy that their priest, whom they already accepted as a saint, was starting to show some signs of a few more earthly, human qualities. And to top it all, it would be the first time in the memory of any of the parishioners that the celebration would be held with but the merest wisp of the curse hanging over them.

Christmas, Easter, and the Fourth of July indeed. And, something that none among them had bargained for, a Final Judgment of sorts.

In the early hours of Saturday, August fourteenth, women scattered throughout the village to pluck blossoms from *varas de San José* and from bushes of *rosa de castilla*. By the end, hardly a hollyhock or a wild rose bush had a single bloom left.

The festivities began promptly at ten o'clock with a High Mass. The church was full by nine, and latecomers paid the price by having to stand in the churchyard and battle the August sun. Just about everyone was there except for two or three of the older boys who were strategically placed along the path to light the luminarias just before the procession through the village began. There were two men minding a spit over an open pit where a lamb and a pig turned and crackled while drops of grease caused mini explosions in the hot coals beneath. The men amused themselves by throwing rocks at the dogs that trotted in to check out the wonderful aromas. The cooks also devoted time to drinking much of the beer they claimed they needed to baste the carcasses with.

When it came time for the sermon, Fr. Jon stepped up into the pulpit.

"My dear people of Nueve Niños," he began, "this is the day the Lord has made. It is so good to see so many of you here. It shows that you understand how great are the blessings that our loving Father in heaven has bestowed on you. There are even more blessings than you realize, some of which I would like to tell you about today. But first let us welcome home our wandering patron. May he never leave us again."

Fr. Jon lifted an arm and at the signal Tobías began pealing the bell, a jubilant and uplifting sound so unlike the dolorous toll at the funeral of Danny García. How curious that one modest, tuneless bell could evoke such radically different sets of feelings to fit the occasion.

The people in the pews turned to the front door just as the crowd in the vestibule parted to allow the procession to pass through. First came a young acolyte holding high a cross and flanked by two candle bearers. After them, the flower girls in their First Communion dresses came up the aisle dropping flower petals in their wake. And finally there was the statue of San Eusebio. He was mounted on a wooden platform carried on the shoulders of four men. The women of the parish had dressed the santo in a long, white linen tunic, tied a blue velvet cape around his neck, and crowned him with a coronet of fresh flowers. He was wondrous except for the deformity on The right cheek that extended down to his neck. The parade made its way to the front of the church to a loud if uneven chorus of *"Bendito."*

> *Bendito, Bendito, Bendito sea Dios.*
> Blessed be God.
> *Los angeles cantan y alaban a Dios.*
> The angels sing in praise of God.

Fr. Jon stepped down from the pulpit and walked through the open gate of the communion rail to wait for the men to lower the santo onto two sawhorses decorated in pink and green crepe paper.

With great solemnity he circled the sacred image and sprinkled it with holy water. He layered a generous heaping of sweet-smelling incense over burning charcoal and censed the statue. Billows of smoke enveloped the santo before wafting up and moving over the congregation like an Old Testament cloud proclaiming the presence of the Almighty. It was pure theater, unapologetically orchestrated and unabashedly savored.

"*¡Viva Cristo Rey!*" someone shouted. "*¡Viva Cristo Rey!*" the congregation responded. "*¡Viva San Eusebio!*" the man continued. "*¡Viva San Eusebio!*" the people echoed.

Even Fr. Jon felt a swell of emotion from the sheer exuberance of the demonstration. By the time he returned to the pulpit, there was not a person in the church who was not ready to take in his every word.

"We must thank Señor Alcalde and the members of the council for this happy homecoming. They were the ones who set everything in motion. These men have shown that they are worthy of your trust and support."

"*¡Viva el alcalde!*"

"*¡Viva el concilio!*"

The alcalde beamed and Fr. Jon could not help but smile as he recalled the figure draped in shirt and crowned with fedora that had stumbled its way out of Cósima's house.

"I'd like to tell you something about your patron saint, but not much is known about his life or his death. We do know that he lived some fifteen hundred years ago, and that he was buried on one of the seven hills of Rome. We also know that he was a champion of truth and suffered greatly because of it. He even dared to challenge a pope. Something we can learn from.

"Why exactly this parish was dedicated to San Eusebio is lost in time. This statue came into being under the inspiration of your first pastor, a man who loved this place and its people very much. The santo was made by one of your own, a man who took a piece of cottonwood, carved it with great care, covered it in gesso, and painted it in whatever colors he could find. And by their devotion, the people of Nueve Niños breathed life into this image so that it could accurately represent their proud and courageous spirit."

Fr. Jon took a moment. It was time for the revelation, one that he hoped would mark a new beginning for the village.

"But then something happened that caused the people of Nueve Niños to doubt themselves. And in that doubt a seed of despair took root. Now San Eusebio has returned to you from Santa Fe, and he has brought something with him. The truth. For too many generations the people of this village have thought that a curse was laid on them because your ancestors drove a priest into the lake to drown. This is not true. The priest did not drown. I read it with my own eyes in letters and records written many years ago and now kept in the vaults of the archdiocese. The priest somehow escaped the lake. After he left Nueve Niños he became a pastor in other parishes in the archdiocese until he died fifteen years later. He was not swallowed up by the lake, but perished like so many others from the influenza.

"My good people, there is no curse." Jon looked across the congregation to catch some reaction to the momentous news he had just delivered. He was greeted by confused stares. "What happened to some of the priests sent to you," he continued, "happened because they were weak or because they were unwilling to serve you. Just as I was. I am no miracle priest who lifted a curse. When I came to Nueve Niños the first time, it was because of a foolish, careless accident. There was nothing miraculous about that. When I returned, it was as a pride-filled, resentful man who wanted nothing more than to be left alone. For this I am ashamed and beg your forgiveness. But I do not matter. What is important is that you remember your roots, that you stand up for the true and strong spirit of the people who first settled here. It is time to hold your heads up. There is no curse. There was no miracle. There is only God, the truth, and you."

There was absolute silence in the church. Even infants in their mothers' arms seemed to sense the moment and left off from their fussing. Then, an enfeebled, quavering voice of an old man broke through. "*¡Viva el padrecito!*" he said. The refrain was picked up by others in the congregation, not as a boisterous cheer but more like a mumbled prayer, one in which not everyone in the church joined.

❖

Fr. Jon's Emancipation Proclamation over the people of Nueve Niños showed both a genius in its timing and a gross miscalculation in its effect. The timing seemed right because the return of the santo was a positive milestone in the history of a village with such a checkered past. But the news of the supposed lifting of the curse was received with mixed results.

Many in the congregation welcomed the tidings and agreed with their pastor that this marked a new beginning, and for that they were happy.

Others tempered any possible enthusiasm with the disturbing thought that what had been would be no more. The legend of the caldera had been something to hold on to. It was the one constant in their lives. Without it they felt as if their moorings had been severed and they were adrift on the waters of uncertainty. It was one thing for the priest to tell them that they were now masters of their own fate, but quite another to actually make it so. And not only had their past been debunked, but the man whom they thought was the capstone to the legend was now telling them that he was, in effect, nothing more than a poseur, yet another in a long list of disappointing pastors for them to bear. To their minds, Fr. Jon had dispelled one curse only to impose another. Where once they had been bolstered by a legend, they were now saddled with cold reality.

A mixed and unsettling atmosphere colored the rest of the day.

The procession after Mass, with the santo carried on its pallet along a path lit by kindling fires that snapped and spit resin, was for some a triumphal parade. For others it was a slow, solemn march with funereal undertones. The music, played on fiddle and accordion, had its celebratory moments but also hinted at an ominous, dirgelike minor theme.

Those of a dour frame of mind nodded their heads in vindication. Had they not argued that luminarias should, by tradition, be reserved for use on the eve of a feast so that they could light the darkness? But they had been overruled in spite of their objections and warnings that no good could come from deviating from ritual. See now how things were in such an unsettled state?

Afterward, the fiesta in the village square, with its food and drink and its booths festooned in patriotic colors, bore at once the hilarity of a county fair and what could only be described as the dolor of a wake.

The people were about equally divided. Some surrounded Fr. Jon to pump his hand and slap him on the back, and the rest gathered to one side and refused to join in the celebration. These contented themselves to look on with sullen disapproval with an occasional cutting comment to reinforce their mood.

All the while Fr. Jon, still a neophyte in the ways of his parishioners, did not, could not appreciate the divisiveness that he had sown in spite of his good intentions.

The alcalde, however, recognized almost immediately what was going on. The glue that had held the community together for so many years was beginning to dissolve. Where once it had been Nueve Niños against the world, there was now a fast developing schism among the people—those who still felt that Fr. Jon could do no wrong and those who now felt betrayed, isolated, and abandoned.

For the entire afternoon the alcalde ran between the opposing camps, having a beer with one, sharing a plate of food with another, a smoke with a third.

"We are lucky to have a priest who cares so much for us."

"Nueve Niños is as good as Raton or Springer after all. They can't laugh at us now."

"*Ándale*. Don't spoil the day for yourselves and the rest of us."

He won no converts, but it was only his peripatetic diplomacy that kept a cap on the rising antagonism within one or two of the more disgruntled cliques.

Even at that, several arguments broke out that at least in two instances led to blows.

At dusk the congregation gathered around the statue according to their sentiments about the day's proceedings. Those still in thrall to their pastor crowded around San Eusebio. The others hung back with bowed heads.

"My good people," Fr. Jon proclaimed, "there is no better way to end the day than to reinstall our santo to his rightful place in his church. And may he never leave Nueve Niños again. This is a promise you must make to yourselves and to each other. Even if the archbishop himself declares otherwise, you must be brave and strong in your determination just as Eusebio of Rome stood up to the pope. Is it agreed?"

"*Sí*, Padre, *sí*!"

Even the garrulous had to concede that this was a good promise to make. If they no longer had their history, at least they would hold on to their santo.

The statue was raised on high once more and carried to the church behind the acolytes with cross and candles.

Some of the parishioners sang louder than ever to cover the fact that others were not singing at all.

After the ceremony of installation at a side altar in the church, the people retired to the plaza to resume the festivities that would climax with the fireworks display. Fr. Jon found himself alone in the sacristy with Tobías to put away the sacred vessels and vestments. The smell of incense still hung heavily.

"I think that went very well, don't you?"

"*Sí*, Padrecito."

"Thank you for all you did. It was a lot of work."

"*De nada*, Padrecito."

"Everyone seemed pleased to have San Eusebio back."

"*Sí*, Padrecito."

"And the news about the priest who did not drown. That went rather well, I thought."

Tobías was spared having to respond by the opening of the outside door to the sacristy.

Jon's friends from Santa Fe, the doctor, the lawyer, and the banker, filed in.

"Father Jon!"

It took a mental adjustment for Fr. Armitage even to recognize them. Was it only two months ago that he had come with them to the cabin on the caldera? They had been counted among his closest acquaintances, but now they seemed strangers, completely out of context in his present world. He could not say why, but the sight of them put him on immediate guard.

"Here for some more fishing?"

"Actually, no. We're driving back to Santa Fe tonight." The doctor eyed Tobías. "We'd like to discuss a certain matter with you. Business, you might say."

Tobías took a surplice from the priest and began to fold it. "I'll finish, Padrecito. You go with your friends."

Fr. Jon led the three men around the church to the rectory. The sun was touching the tops of the cones and fast dropping as they passed through the graveyard.

A woman with two children in tow passed them on the dusty road between the church and the rectory. *"Buenas noches,* Padre." She pulled the children to their knees beside her and waited for a blessing.

"Buenas noches, señora. Que Dios los bendiga." Fr. Jon made the sign of the cross over them.

"Looks like you're settling in," the doctor remarked when they resumed their walk.

"I think they're finally getting used to me."

"More than that, I'd say. Which is very good news for all of us, by the way."

"For all of us?"

"I mean it's good that the people have accepted you. That's always helpful."

"Why should that be helpful to you?"

"I'm talking in general, of course. We all want the best for you." The lawyer and the banker made acquiescent noises behind them.

Fr. Jon stopped and faced the doctor. "You mentioned something about business?"

"Big business. And we're plenty excited about it. In fact, we just came from a meeting with Monsignor Montini."

Montini. Jon speculated on how long it would be before the chancellor called to confront him with the absence of the San Eusebio and the letter from the art dealer. "The chancellor is back from Italy then?"

"Yesterday. We met with him as soon as we could. That's how important this thing is."

"Well, I'm always ready to hear about the good monsignor and his business dealings. He can be pretty slick."

Chapter Twenty-six

Was it Nueve Niños?

Fr. Jon couldn't really tell.

The surveyor's map was accurate enough in rendering the area. There was the eastern shoreline of the caldera and right of that a cluster of broken-line circles of varying sizes representing the nine cones. What sat between the lake and the cones and what stretched beyond brought him up short.

His guests had taken over the kitchen table to roll out a bundle of topographical and architectural drawings. At the bottom of each page, printed in a fine draftsman's hand was the legend, "Nueve Niños Fishing Resort and Golf Club."

The doctor was using a plastic ruler to point out the various aspects of their plan.

"Everything is, of course, preliminary," he explained, "but I'd say it comes pretty darn close to what we want. Here's the marina, which opens up to the main square. The hotel sits right in the middle, flanked by shops, all those high-priced boutiques the ladies love. The private cabins will run down the shoreline in both directions." The doctor stabbed at the area around the nine cones. "And you'll like this, Jon. This is where we'll put the golf course. Eighteen holes designed by Robert Trent Jones Jr. The fairways will wind between the cones. With an irrigation system from the lake, it will be the greenest course in the state."

"What about here?" Fr. Jon put his finger on a set of multiple rows of small oblongs about a mile beyond the cones, if the scale of the map were to be believed.

"That's the trailer park for relocating the villagers," said the doctor.

"All of them?" Jon could not hide his surprise.

"Those who choose to stay, of course," the lawyer added quickly. "There should be jobs for all your parishioners, and more."

"I was wondering when you'd get around to them. They do have a vested interest."

"And don't think we've forgotten that. We definitely want them to be part of this."

The priest put his hands behind his back. "It looks like you've thought of everything."

The lawyer beamed. "We've tried."

Now it was the banker's turn. "It could be big, Father Jon. Very big. And don't think we've forgotten about you. How does a bungalow overlooking the tenth hole sound? And the new church and rectory will sit between the golf course and the trailer park, along this connecting road. That makes it convenient for both guests at the resort and the local people."

"We already have a church."

"Which will have to come down, of course." The doctor pretended to care. "But from what I've seen of it, that should be no great loss."

"And the graveyard in front?"

There was a pause as the doctor, banker, and lawyer looked at each other.

The lawyer cleared his throat and spoke up. "Good question. Which is exactly why you can be so vital to the project, Father. There are a few, can I say, delicate details left to work out." He winked unpleasantly at Jon. "You could really do us *and* yourself a lot of good."

Jon ran a gentle hand over the area on the bluish paper where the church now stood with the graveyard where Danny García was buried. "So what does Monsignor Montini say about all of this?"

"He told us that it hangs on the archbishop's approval. Of course, we know that. The archdiocese owns the buildings and most of the land around the cones. We'd like to put the clubhouse where the church and rectory now stand."

"The monsignor feels he can get the approval for you." It was not a question.

"He was really enthusiastic. He sees it as a real boon for the area and for the parish."

"Where will you be building his bungalow? Next to mine?"

The doctor, unsure whether this was a joke, hesitated before he laughed. "Actually, he expressed an interest in securing some stock in the venture. I don't think he's much for fishing and golf."

It was Jon's turn to laugh, more of a snort actually. "Yes. I happen to know that his interests lie elsewhere."

The banker rubbed his hands together with great delight, as if he had just executed a particularly juicy foreclosure. "So, what do you think of our little plan?"

"Most impressive. What I wonder is what the people will think about it?"

The trio waited for the priest to elaborate, but he turned to the kitchen tap and pumped himself a drink of slightly sulfurous well water. "I'm sorry," he finally said. "Can I get you gentlemen something?"

The doctor waved the offer away. "What about it, Jon? Any comments? Surely you have some questions."

"Again, it's the villagers I'm thinking about."

"Which is exactly where you come in. You are in a unique, one might say most advantageous, position here. Look, Jon, we're not naïve about this. We expect a certain amount of resistance from the people around here. Perfectly understandable. This will be very radical, very new for them. Once we get started, the people here are going to have to get used to a new way of life. New town. New places to live. You can help to make the transition a smooth one."

Jon's eyes moved to the right side of the plat where the tiny oblongs represented neat rows of trailer homes. Why did it remind him so much of a cemetery? "Tell me more about that. About the places to live."

The banker was now in his element. "We'll buy out the existing homes—at fair market value, I might add, more than enough to cover a down payment on some brand-new mobile homes. And terms will be reasonable, certainly manageable with the salaries we'll be offering at the resort."

"So they end up paying you for the privilege of giving up their homes."

The banker, the whiner if Jon's memory from their weekend at the cabin served right, elevated the pitch of his voice. "That's negative thinking, Father. And shortsighted, if I may say so."

Jon took a slow drink of water and set the glass back in the sink. "But certainly something to explore."

The doctor jumped in. "OK. OK. So maybe there are still a few rough edges to smooth out. In the long run, Jon, it's a winning proposition for everyone. What do you say? If they know you're behind the project, these people will listen to you. They obviously trust you. What is it they call you? The miracle priest?"

"I'm working on that."

"Look around you, for crissakes. Nueve Niños will be a ghost town in ten years. It's close to that now. And then some land speculator from Texas will come in, pay the back taxes, and do exactly what we're proposing. Who's the winner then? Certainly not the people here."

"This is as good as they can expect," the lawyer said. "New homes. Jobs. New blood. Running water. Sewer lines. Paved streets. Dependable power. No reasonable person would turn this kind of opportunity down. You can show them that."

"I suppose I could." Jon thought of the sermon he had given that very day about how truth was liberating and they should meet it on their own terms. "Or maybe not."

The doctor thought he detected an opening. "Of course you can. These people practically adore you. That woman with her two kids. They went right down on their knees the minute they saw you."

Jon took a step backward from the table. "Gentlemen, it's late and you have a long drive ahead of you. There's a lot to chew on."

"Maybe we should have called first, but we just couldn't wait." The doctor began to roll up the plans. "You really had to see all of this for yourself to get the whole picture."

"So when is this whole thing supposed to happen?"

"The sooner the better," the lawyer said. "There's a lot to be done. Thank God the archdiocese is already in our corner."

"Which really makes this meeting somewhat moot, doesn't it?"

"What do you mean?"

"Well, since the monsignor has all but promised you the church and the property, it really doesn't matter what the people here decide."

The lawyer moved around the table to give the closing arguments. "I suppose we could work that angle but we really don't want to—not if we can get everyone to cooperate." He looked pointedly at Jon. "We're not the bad guys here. It's an opportunity for all of us. Oh sure, we could go about this whole thing piecemeal. Some would sell, some would try to hold out. But in the end it wouldn't matter. We have the inevitable on our side."

Jon ushered the men to the door and opened it. "Inevitable. What a sad word. Maybe I should give Monsignor Montini a call."

The doctor tapped Jon on the shoulder with the tight roll of plans. "Absolutely. Talk to him. Talk to your parishioners. Talk to as many people as you like."

"Oh, I'll certainly do that."

After the doctor, banker, and lawyer left, Jon sat in the kitchen for a very long time. He stared at the tabletop that had lately groaned beneath the weight of plans and plats and plots. Then he heard popping in the distance. Outside, he watched as the sky lit with the fireworks that the people of Nueve Niños had purchased in Texas to culminate their day of glory.

The last rocket burst and its sparks died well before they fell back to earth. He was left to stare at God's own pyrotechnics, the star-brilliant New Mexico night sky.

Where to start? He must talk to people, that was for sure. His parishioners. His chancellor.

But first on his list on Monday morning was a call to the Archdiocese of New York.

Chapter Twenty-seven

"Jon! How the hell are you? *Where* the hell are you?"

The next morning when Fr. Armitage dialed up the chancery office of the Archdiocese of New York, identified himself, and asked to speak with Fr. William Ferris, he did so with a certain hesitation. He was calling a classmate from Rome days, an assistant chancellor who was obviously in ascendance on the hierarchical ladder while he himself was barely clinging on to the bottom rung. Jon had severed all ties with his compatriot priests in the east, his ego too bruised to face them. Now he was ingesting whatever pride he had left to ask a friend for a favor.

"Long story." Jon made short work of it, bringing his friend up to speed on where he was and how he had gotten himself there.

"I heard something," Ferris said after the narrative was done, "but nobody was sure. Rough. I'm sorry. I wish I could do something."

Of course, he couldn't—nor did Jon expect anything. They were now on parallel tracks going in opposite directions.

"Don't worry about it. I'm really doing OK. Anyway, that's not why I called."

Jon could almost taste Ferris's sense of relief over the two thousand miles of phone lines. They both knew there was nothing to be done to ameliorate his present circumstances. There was no appeal process for the way bishops chose to deal with their priests. There was nothing anyone could do for Jon, and it was folly to think otherwise.

"Bill, I need a favor."

"Anything."

"Can you drop in on someone, an art dealer in Manhattan?"

"I can do that. Are you buying or selling?"

"Neither. I need you to do some digging on the quiet for me, and I'm not even sure what you'll turn up. Maybe nothing." Jon proceeded to sketch out what he knew about the ongoing dealings between one Julian N. Clairborne of the Clairborne Galleries, NYC, and Monsignor Amleto Montini, Chancellor of the Archdiocese of Santa Fe. There were Italian paintings and New Mexico carvings and only a hint that there might be something not quite right.

"The whole thing does sound a little strange. Still . . ." Ferris was obviously not convinced.

"I wish I had more. That's why I'm calling. Who knows what you'll find. I'm not even sure you can get the guy to talk to you."

The voice at the other end brightened with the challenge. "Are you kidding? He sees a priest from the archdiocese asking about the way he deals art and he'll be shitting in his britches. Nobody, and I mean nobody, wants to be crosswise with the Church in this town."

"Thanks, Bill. Anything you can do . . ."

"I'll stretch out my lunch hour. It's just around the corner from us. I should have something in a day or two."

The distance from the old archdiocesan offices on Madison and Fiftieth to the establishment of Julian N. Clairborne just off Park Avenue made for a pleasant walk that invigorated Fr. Ferris and had him primed as he entered the art gallery.

The door swished shut behind him, blocking out the noises and smells of the city. An almost indiscernible whisper of air told the priest that he was now in a climate-controlled environment, a cocoon to protect the pieces of art on walls, easels, and velvet-draped pedestals.

The priest was allowed only a moment to breathe in the scene before a figure emerged from somewhere in the back of the establishment.

The man smiled and offered his hand. "Yes, Father, can I help you? I'm Julian Clairborne."

He was not what Ferris had expected. Not at all. He was young. He was slim but broad and muscular and well-fitted out in his dark blue suit. Squash or tennis, the priest surmised. Somehow he had pictured someone more disreputable looking, perhaps a weasel of a man with a comb-over, nervous twitches, and wrinkled, sagging clothes. He hoped that this initial miscalculation did not bode ill for the rest of the encounter.

"I'm Father William Ferris, from the archdiocesan offices."

Clairborne pursed his mouth and bobbed his head, suddenly submissive. "Oh, yes, Father. The gallery has had a most amiable relationship with the Church going back to my father who started the business. The cardinal was particularly pleased with the tenth-century reliquary from Damascus that we were able to negotiate for him. Very pleased. Very pleased."

Ferris relaxed. Clairborne might not look like a weasel, but he certainly had the soul of one. "Actually, Mr. Clairborne, I'm here on official business of a sort. I was hoping you could help me with some peculiar inquiries."

No sale today. Clairborne the Salesman gave way and left Clairborne the Proprietor to handle the priest.

"Inquiries?"

"They deal with a certain Monsignor Montini, from Santa Fe, New Mexico. You are familiar with the name?"

Clairborne blinked and his response came out more studied than the question seemed to warrant. "Why, of course. Monsignor Montini. What a delightful man. So refined and knowledgeable. We've built a nice little rapport over the past couple of years."

"How has the monsignor represented himself?"

Clairborne adjusted a drape on a pedestal. "I'm not sure what you mean?"

Keep away from the specifics, Ferris. Let the guy think that you know more than you're letting on. "Let me approach the question in a different way. What has Montini told you about the art he's been bringing to you?"

Clairborne spread his hands. "Again, Father, I'm afraid I'm a little dense today."

Or stalling.

"The archdiocese has learned that the monsignor might be involved with some artwork of questionable ownership."

Clairborne turned ashy. "Perhaps my office would allow us a bit more privacy."

The art dealer led the way through a narrow hallway that opened up into a workshop. "Clarise, could you watch the front please?"

A severe-looking older woman stopped unwrapping a canvas and slipped by the men, careful not to look up at them.

The office proved to be nothing more than a storeroom with empty frames stacked against its walls. A scratched and nicked fossil of a desk, its surface heaped high with messy stacks of paper, nudged for space in a corner. The smell of boiled coffee mixed with the odor of stale cigarette butts and Clairborne's cologne.

Clairborne dropped some art books on the floor and scraped a chair in Ferris's direction. "Please, Father, and forgive the mess."

Ego te absolve, Ferris thought, but only for the untidiness.

Clairborne then made for a swivel chair behind the desk. He did not relax even then. He kept a stiff back while his hands twitched involuntarily in his lap, a preppy called to the dean's office. "I usually don't bring visitors into this part of the gallery." He made a half-hearted gesture at a percolator behind him. "Perhaps some coffee?"

"I'm fine, thank you. Now, about Monsignor Montini?"

"Yes, yes. I can tell you that he offered me complete assurance that he was fully authorized to consign the folk art on behalf of the Archdiocese of Santa Fe. I had no reason to doubt him." Clairborne attempted a smile. "I mean, he's a priest just like you."

"You're telling me that he just walked in off the street one day and gave you some religious carvings to sell?"

"Well, yes and no. I mean he did come in unannounced one day with some art that he wanted an opinion on, but it was not the New Mexico pieces. They were canvases from Italy. Some lovely little items from various Renaissance schools. He showed me an introductory letter from the Diocese of Padua. He's Italian, you know."

"And you questioned none of this?"

"Surely, you understand. He was dressed just like you." Clairborne tried to show a little backbone now. "I didn't ask you for your credentials, did I?"

"And I'm not here to sell you any art. That being said, believe me, I am who I claim to be."

"Exactly my point. I mean, after all, if you can't trust a man of the cloth . . ."

"Tell me more about the Italian art."

"Minor masters. Students of Raphael, Titian, and the like, but still very fine. Small oils on canvas, mainly. One or two triptychs on wood. He's come in at least a dozen times over the past three years."

"What were the financial arrangements?"

"I can tell you that the money was for hospitals and orphanages in Italy. I'm happy to say that the pieces have done quite well. I send him a check every month or so. He even talked me into cutting my commission fee in half. A very persuasive man."

"Orphans, was it? Did he have any supporting documents? Authorizations?"

"Father, as I said, he's a . . ."

"A priest. Yes, I know. You've kept a file, I presume."

"Of course. But you do understand that it is strictly confidential. I wouldn't think of showing it to you without the monsignor's consent."

"Mr. Clairborne, let's cut through the crap. The Archdiocese of New York has no interest in how you conduct your business. This is not a legal matter." Ferris raised his brow. "Unless, of course, you choose to make it one."

"Oh, heavens no."

"Our only concern is with the ethical behavior of one Catholic priest."

Clairborne now decided to take his stand. "Surely you can understand my position, Father. My clients expect my utmost discretion. I rely on their trust to stay in business."

Ferris lifted his glasses and rubbed the indentations on his nose. How long could he keep up the bluff? "As I said, we are not interested in the least about you and your gallery. However, that might just change. And then what would your clients think? We're trying to control a possible public scandal here, and we can be as discreet as you."

Clairborne's shoulders slumped. "Well," he finally said, "since it's a Church matter and since you've assured me of your discretion . . ."

Ferris nodded solemnly.

The art dealer stood and turned to a metal file cabinet behind him. "I can certainly show you what I have."

What he had was a manila folder stuffed with bills of sale, artless descriptions of the art, and correspondence between himself and Montini.

"Is this all?"

"It's everything, I promise you."

"No customs declarations? No letters of transfer from the Diocese of Padua? Nothing from the Italian Ministry of the Arts? What a trusting man you are, Mr. Clairborne. It's a wonder that more of your clients don't take advantage of you."

Clairborne slumped down in his chair and actually pouted, the prep schooler to the end. "But he's a priest."

William Ferris was back on the phone to Jon by that evening. "This was just too good to wait. Your monsignor has a nice little racket going."

"That's what I thought. But can we prove it?"

"You want proof, I got proof. Montini is up to his neck in some high-flying art traffic. He brings in Renaissance paintings from Italy. God knows how he gets ahold of them. He leaves them on consignment with Clairborne, goes back to Santa Fe, and on his return trip brings a couple of suitcases full of New Mexico carvings."

"And Clairborne didn't ask any questions?"

"Montini claimed he had authorization both from Padua and Santa Fe. Flash a Roman collar and you can sell honey to a beehive."

"Still. Clairborne should have smelled something fishy."

"I'm sure he did. The man's been in the business for almost fifteen years, both with his father and now on his own. He knows the law. I asked to see all the paperwork on Montini. There wasn't much there. After that he caved in like an eggshell. I told him I asked for a signed statement for the archdiocese to notarize. I told him to spell out all the details including the money going to Montini. Wanna guess?"

"I have no clue."

"How does $623,478 sound to you?"

If Ferris wanted Armitage to be impressed, he succeeded beyond expectation.

"My, my, my," Jon whispered.

"He told Clairborne that the money was going to orphanages and hospitals back in Italy. Swallow that and I've got the deed to the Brooklyn Bridge to offer you."

Jon had a sudden picture of Montini, fastidious, glossed, perfumed, manicured, tailored. No, there was nothing there to suggest philanthropy.

"I'd laugh if the whole thing weren't so damned pathetic. Do you think he'll come through with the statement?"

"I'm holding it in my hand. He had it over by courier before we closed the doors."

"And he probably was on the phone to Montini right after you left."

"Give me some credit, Jon. I told him to put a lid on it until he heard from us. He knows the score. You should have seen his eyes."

"You're a genius. I think you missed your calling. You should be in criminal law."

There was a pause on the other end before a suddenly subdued Fr. Ferris essayed an answer. "Yeah. Some days it's a real temptation."

Chapter Twenty-eight

When Jon called Montini the next day, the monsignor was the model of circumspection. No mention was made about the missing santo or the suspicious letter from the art gallery. Perhaps he had not missed them yet.

"How are you getting along in your new parish, Jon? I know that the archbishop will be anxious to know."

"Well enough, Monsignor. Thank you for asking. And your trip to Italy? I understand that your uncle finally passed away. My condolences."

"*Tante grazie.* It was a blessing after all, although the family was reluctant to let him go. But I'm sure that's not why you called."

"Actually, there are a couple of pieces of business that I'd like to discuss with you. Best done in person, I feel."

"Parish matters?"

"Among other things."

"You are being very Roman right now, Jon."

"I'm sorry. I don't mean to sound so evasive, but I would prefer to meet with you."

"Well, as you can imagine, things have piled up here in my absence."

Yeah, Jon thought, how many more marriage cases are you stacking up? "I understand, and I wouldn't ask unless I thought the matters were of some urgency."

"Can you at least give me a feel for what we might be discussing?"

"I had some visitors a few of evenings ago. Dr. Wright, Frank Hill, and Norman Velasco. It seems they have some big plans for Nueve Niños."

For the first time in their conversation, Montini's voice lost some of its wariness. "Ah, yes. They were here to see me the day I got back. Very interesting. Of course, I told them that I would have to speak to the archbishop before we could pursue any further discussions."

"They said that you seemed quite enthusiastic about their plans."

"There is certainly some merit to them. And you never want to discourage people who have been such strong supporters of the archdiocese."

"About our meeting?"

"Would Friday be soon enough?"

"Fine."

"I'd hate for you to make the trip to Santa Fe, especially with the weekend coming up. I know how busy that time is for a pastor. Suppose I meet you in Las Vegas?"

"That's most considerate of you."

"There's a restaurant, the Hillcrest, just off the highway. Do you know it?"

"I'm sure I can find it."

"Shall we say noon?"

"Friday. I'll buy your lunch."

That Friday morning, as Jon climbed into his car, white clouds of delectable texture, roundish, plump, and inviting, were beginning to gather east of the caldera. But it was mid-August and the landscape was seared brown. The voluptuous clouds would once again turn out to be nothing more than come-ons, pure white whores who seldom delivered on their promise of wet, titillating gratification.

On the hundred-mile drive from Nueve Niños to Las Vegas, New Mexico, the older, more storied community having little of the glitz of its Nevada namesake, Jon Armitage had time to think about many things, all related to his upcoming meeting with Monsignor Amleto Montini.

Was the old adage true? That the lingering taste of revenge is ashes? He reminded himself that this trip was not about him, that it had to do with the lives of the people in his charge. No, not in his charge. He had made that abundantly clear to the parishioners of San Eusebio. He was their servant. For this he had been ordained and for this he had been assigned to them. But if there were some collateral vindication for himself, he could live with that.

He was not nervous about the meeting, but he was on edge as any challenger might be as he enters the arena. Montini had had three days to prepare for their face-to-face and Jon, even with right on his side, had every reason to be wary of the Italian. No doubt, Montini had already conjured up with a rationale for the San Eusebio and the letter from Clairborne. Jon, however, could think of no explanation from Montini that could adequately dismiss the art dealer's admissions in writing.

How about it, Monsignor? What say you now? But he mustn't get too cocky.

In this frame of mind he pulled into the half-filled parking lot of the restaurant.

Inside, Fr. Jon inventoried the clientele at the various tables and booths—ranchers, teamsters, families on the move. Montini was not among them. This brought a thin smile to his lips. So the game was on. How long would the monsignor permit him to wait and perhaps to stew?

The hostess offered him a table in the middle of the room but Jon declined.

"I'll wait for that booth over in the corner," he said and pointed across the restaurant. There, a reed-thin truck driver had just wadded up his napkin, tossed it on an empty plate, and was preparing to light up a cigarette.

"I'm meeting someone and he's not here yet."

Ten minutes later, the former occupant of the booth was at the cashier register. The hostess handed him his change, invited him back, grabbed a pair of menus, and motioned Jon to follow her.

"Can I get you something while you're waiting?" she asked as she piled up the dirty dishes and wiped off the tabletop. Her smile was inviting. He wore nothing to identify him as a priest, and so she offered her coquettishness unabashedly.

"Water will be fine."

The hostess had topped off Jon's water glass twice before Montini came through the door. Jon lifted himself halfway up from the bench and waved. Montini waved back and began to weave his way between tables to the corner booth.

It was the first time that Jon had seen the chancellor without his clericals. He still wore black trousers and a white French-cuffed shirt, but instead of a Roman collar and suit coat he had on a dark green Windbreaker. He did not wear the mufti well. His obvious discomfort made him seem innocent and even vulnerable, a little boy whose mother had slicked down his hair with a wet comb and dressed him for an outing.

No time to go soft now.

When the monsignor reached the table, he spread out his arms. *"Ciao caro.* How good to see you. You are looking well. Nueve Niños seems to be agreeing with you."

No apology for being late and a pointed comment on Jon's present exile. So the good monsignor had decided to take the immediate offensive.

Jon smiled. "I'm surviving."

The waitress was over quickly to take their orders—a hamburger for Jon, dry toast and tea for Montini.

"I'm afraid I overindulged on my trip." Montini patted his belly. "Who can turn down *carciofi alla Giudea* and *cannelloni al vitello*?"

They chatted amiably enough, mostly about Italy, until the harried waitress served them and moved on to a table full of teenagers tossing ice chips at each other.

Montini concentrated on dipping the tea bag several times into a cup of steaming water before he finally looked at Jon. *"Allora, ci siamo."*

"Yes, here we are."

"You said on the phone that you were interested in discussing the plans for Nueve Niños. As for the archdiocese, nothing has been decided."

"Really? I had the impression that you had shown quite a bit of enthusiasm for the project. They talked as if it were all but consummated."

"*Americani*. You like to push, don't you? Everything must be done today. It is at once your source of weakness and a strength. But no, things are still very much in flux, regardless of what they told you."

"Does that include the sale of the Nueve Niños church and property?"

Montini squeezed the last drop of amber liquid from the tea bag and dropped the soggy mass onto his saucer. "Of course that is our only concern. Still, you must admit, it is a very attractive offer. A new church. A new rectory. Room to expand."

He took his time wiping off his thumb and index finger with a paper napkin. "Who knows? If things go well, San Eusebio might even have its own parochial school one day." The chancellor held his gaze steady, daring rebuttal.

Jon did not blink.

"Of course, there's another way to look at this. The old church razed. The graveyard dug up. The dead moved. Homesteads leveled. People displaced. Traditions destroyed."

"Jon, Jon. You and I both know there is little artistic or architectural worth to the church. And as for the people, once they see what they are getting in return for so little, they'll appreciate what is being done for them."

"You might be right, Monsignor. But you know what? It should be their decision. You cannot present them with a fait accompli and expect them to uproot with no real choice. Without the church, there is no Nueve Niños. It's been the one constant from the beginning, good priests and bad. You can't sell it from under them."

The monsignor broke off a crust of toast and dipped it in his tea. "The archdiocese must do what it must do. We are not dealing with a democracy. There is a broader good to consider. Everything and everyone is answerable to the archbishop and the archbishop is answerable to no one but Rome." Montini smiled except for the eyes. "But you know that."

"I also know, Monsignor, that in this as in most things the archbishop will follow your advice."

"You give me too much credit."

"I've seen you operate."

The monsignor gave a slight shrug and smiled wryly in concession.

"Be that as it may, the final decision on San Eusebio is not now and never will be in the hands of its parishioners . . . or its priest."

Jon pushed his untouched plate aside. "*Basta*. In language as plain as I can make it, Monsignor Montini, you will butt out of this affair and keep your counsel to yourself."

The chancellor tilted his head to one side and shook it slowly. "Jon, *Giovannino* . . . why are you doing this to yourself? You are in no position to alienate your superiors. Surely you are not ready to look for another diocese to take you in."

"That will happen only by your fiat. I don't think you'll want to do that."

Montini pursed his lips as if the tea he was drinking had suddenly turned bitter. One small hand came up and presented its palm to Jon. "All it will take is a little push, Father. The archbishop is not your ally." Up went an eyebrow. "Or didn't you know that? Were he to hear that you were showing signs of insubordination . . . And we won't even get into your theft of a santo and a personal letter from my office." He made a kissing sound with his lips and dropped his hand. "Well, why dwell on unpleasantries?"

It was all Jon could do to stop himself from laughing out loud. The monsignor had misanalyzed the very situation he had engineered. Thanks to him, Jon had no options, and so he had nothing to lose. There were no personal stakes here, at least not for him.

The monsignor stretched out a hand. "Do you have the letter with you? I'd like to have it back, if you don't mind."

"Ah, yes, I was wondering when we'd get to that. The letter. And the santo you took from my parish."

Montini's tone became pedantic. "With the former pastor's permission. And I left a fine statue of *la madonna* in its place. Such an ugly San Eusebio. That disfigurement. The parish is well rid of it."

"Not so ugly that you didn't try to sell it."

Montini raised his shoulders ever so slightly. "What good was it to us? If some collector wanted to pay good money for it, *meglio così.*"

"So there is absolutely no collusion of any sort between you and the Clairborne Galleries?"

Montini took one last sip of tea and began to stand. "This is all getting very tiresome. I'm going back to Santa Fe now. If you have a change of attitude by Monday, give me a call. If not, you might start looking for another diocese and for that I can only wish you *buona fortuna.* Are we quite clear? *E tutto chiaro?*"

"Clear as glass. One last thing."

Montini was peeling a bill from a money clip. "Please, Jon, don't make it any worse on yourself."

"It's about your friend, Clairborne."

"What about Mr. Clairborne? He's a respected art dealer with an impeccable reputation."

"Perhaps so, but a little sloppy, don't you think?"

"What do you mean?"

"The fact that he received art objects from you without verifying their ownership or even requesting some basic documentation."

Montini fingered the five-dollar bill, replaced it in his pocket, and sat down. "I acted on behalf of the archbishop. I am authorized, you know."

"And for whom were you acting when you brought in the artwork from Italy? Where is the proof of ownership? Customs declarations? Letters of transfer? Something from the Italian Ministry of Culture? And we won't even get into the finances. I don't pretend to be a businessman, but even I have some questions. Where did the money go? Are all parties justly compensated? And what about the taxes?"

For a moment, while Montini processed Jon's words, he stood perfectly still. Then he waved his hand. *"Ma, non e niente.* You make too much of it."

"I don't care. Your comings and goings are for someone else to sort out. That day will come. A complete account of your dealings, spelled out and signed by Mr. Clairborne, now sits in the chancery files in New York. *Adesso é rimasta sola una cosa chiara.* What is clear is that you will cede approval of any transaction regarding the church property in Nueve Niños to the parishioners of San Eusebio. *Capisce?*"

Jon stood, pulled a ten-dollar bill from his wallet, and dropped it on the table. "Lunch is on me, remember? Now *I* will return to my parish and *you* can call me should you have a change of attitude."

Jon couldn't resist a wink at the hostess as he walked out of the restaurant. She melted on the spot.

Like hell it wasn't at least a little bit about revenge.

Chapter Twenty-nine

Dear Sally—

I'm up to my neck again! This time, though, it's for a good cause. My parishioners asked for a favor, and I'm having to tweak the chancellor's nose. I'd like to think that I'm being completely altruistic, but I'm having too darn much fun.

Does the monastery need a handyman?

Jon

Dear Jonny:

So your parishioners finally got to you. Did it hurt? I know I'm out of touch behind these walls, but isn't it time that the clergy started listening instead of talking? I think that's what Vatican Council II is all about.

We can always use a strong back and a weak mind on the farm. Do you qualify?

Sally

Chapter Thirty

It was one of those rarest of Friday evenings. Monsignor Amleto Montini had actually deigned to grace the table of the archbishop. He showed up because the meeting with Jon Armitage had left him without the wit to come up with a plausible excuse to absent himself. He also needed to reassure himself of his position in the grand scheme of things. If he could not control a lowly pastor in the lowliest of parishes, he could at least take his rightful place in the halls of power.

The archbishop crushed a handful of saltines and dropped the crumbly mess into his soup. "Glad you're back, Monsignor."

"No more than I, Excellency. It's home."

"You had us wondering for a while. Your place is here."

"Absolutely."

"Those trips of yours put a real burden on those of us left behind to man the trenches." The archbishop turned his attention to his secretary. "Isn't that right, Father Tapia?"

The young priest, head bent to meet a spoonful of soup, looked over his rimless glasses and managed the weakest of smiles. The trenches for him had been sitting at the table alone with the archbishop for two tortuous weeks.

Montini shook his head and sighed. "Well, Excellency, now that my dear uncle has passed away, I will not be obligated to make so many trips."

The sigh was genuine, although it had nothing to do with the purported death of an uncle who was at this moment up, taking solids, and making a general nuisance of himself. The monsignor's stress came from more pressing matters. What was he to do now about his partially gutted, completely uninhabitable villa? What lay in store for him were he to set foot back in his beloved Italy? Why had he put off applying for U.S. citizenship? Perhaps it was not too late to begin the process. What were the laws covering extradition should it come to that? The Italian courts were not very tolerant when it came to the looting of the country's national treasures.

The archbishop rang the silver bell at his elbow. A nun came in from the kitchen to clear the first course from the table.

"We need you here."

"Thank you, Your Excellency," the nun said.

"Not you, Sister, although of course we need you also. I'm talking about our wandering chancellor here."

It wasn't that the archbishop took on more duties or worked harder in the absence of the chancellor. He just wanted to be sure that he never had to.

"Yes, Excellency. By the way, should you receive a call from Dr. Wright in the next few days, it has to do with some business that I can easily handle."

The archbishop bristled at the mention of the name of one of the golf partners who had displaced him without so much as a by-your-leave. "Just as well." He harrumphed and speared a boiled potato with such violence that the fork tines shrieked against the china platter.

Thoughts of the doctor's treachery put the archbishop in the foulest of moods, and wonder of wonders, this led to a nearly silent meal.

Grazie a Dio, thought the monsignor. There's no ill wind that doesn't blow some good.

Fr. Tapia, at least, savored both the meal and the quietude.

Jon didn't have to wait long before hearing of the monsignor's decision on the matter of San Eusebio. He received a call on Monday, but not from the chancery.

"Father Armitage, what the hell are you trying to pull?"

"Dr. Wright. How are things?"

"You know damned well how they are. I just got off the phone with Montini. Apparently you had a meeting with him behind our backs. He told me everything."

No, not *everything*. "Yes, we had a very productive conversation. And, if you recall, you're the one who encouraged me to talk to him."

"He tells me that the archdiocese is bowing out of the picture. They're leaving the decision on the church and the property to the parishioners. Some bullshit about tradition and respect for the will of the people. When's the last time the chancery office gave a rat's ass about the will of the people?"

"High time, don't you think?"

"Bullshit. And you're at the bottom of it. I thought we were friends."

Jon tightened his grip on the telephone. "You know, Doctor, you've presumed an awful lot. A few games of golf and some cards don't make us bosom buddies. You can't buy me off, bungalow on the tenth hole or not."

"You want more? You should have said something the other night."

"What I want is exactly what the monsignor told you. The people of Nueve Niños have a right to decide their own fate."

"Our offer is more than generous. If you don't see that, the hell with you. We're willing to approach the people one house at a time. We are prepared to divide and conquer. All I have to say to you, Jon, is don't cross us."

"It has nothing to do with me. You are proposing to destroy a village, to turn its inhabitants into peons in a company town. Why not give them a say?"

With no success as a browbeater, the doctor now went down a more conciliatory path. "OK, OK. Let's not get carried away here. No sense in looking for trouble. The way I see it, it's the same game only with different players. There's no reason we can't adjust to that. What are you suggesting?"

"That the plans be presented to the village council. That you answer all their questions as completely and truthfully as you can.

That any changes they might suggest be considered with the weight they deserve. That you live with the final decision."

"You mean it will come down to a vote?"

"Probably."

"And you will have a vote?"

"If they give me one."

"And which way will you go? That's all that most of them will care about."

"That could be. We'll just have to see, won't we?"

So involved had Jon become in his dealings with Monsignor Montini and the doctor, lawyer, and banker, that he failed to notice a change of climate outside his front door—a certain coolness in the air. For the last two Sundays there had been a drop in the collection—just twenty dollars or so, but significant in a parish that still struggled to reach the eighty-dollar mark. People must have overspent at the fiesta and income from the harvest and roundup was still more than a month away, Jon thought, and let it pass. The pews also seemed to be a little emptier. It's the end of summer and people are probably getting a bit of leisure time in, Jon thought, and let this pass too.

Tobías, the sacristan, could have set him straight on both accounts.

The women were talking of nothing else nowadays but the hornet's nest that el padrecito had swatted at with his sermon on the feast day of San Eusebio. For the most part they steered clear of the controversy. They needed a priest to bless, baptize, marry, and bury their families. They needed someone who didn't berate them in the confessional and who didn't beg for money all the time. At least Fr. Jon was better than most. Anyway, it was their husbands, not they, who were embroiled in the controversy. If some of the men decided to pare down their contributions and boycott Sunday Mass, it was on their own heads. Let them stand on their principles and meet their maker. The women had to consider the day-to-day.

When Tobías tried to defend Fr. Jon, the women proved to be resigned or indifferent. *"Que sea lo que sea,"* was their stoic response.

It was not until Jon approached the alcalde after Sunday Mass to suggest a special meeting of the village council that he was informed that things were less than copasetic.

"Señor Alcalde, there is something very important I would like to discuss with the council."

The alcalde thought immediately of the seven men who would attend such a meeting. Three of them at least were among those who had taken the news of the curse quite badly.

"Perhaps it is something I can take care of for you, Padrecito."

"Ordinarily I would agree. However, there is so much to consider that I feel it would be best for me to deal directly with the council."

"Does it have to do with the curse, Padrecito?"

"The what?" The alcalde's question seemed so disengaged from their conversation that Jon struggled to register its meaning.

"The curse. Your sermon about the curse."

"No, no. Of course not. Why would you think that?"

"Padrecito, forgive me for saying this, but there are some people in Nueve Niños who are not happy with you right now."

"Not happy with me?"

"What you said. Some of the people think they've been made fools of for so many years for believing that something was true when it wasn't."

"I certainly did not intend that."

"Sí, Padrecito, but now they don't know what to do. They blame you."

"What about el alcalde? What do you think?"

"I think that what you said had to be said, and that it was good to put the past behind us. But you know how some people can be. *Siempre buscan pleito.* They are not happy unless they have something to complain about."

"Well, I'm not sure what I can do. I can't unsay what I've already said. I can't make something true when it isn't. I can only hope that they eventually come around."

"*Sepa Dios*, Padrecito. And again, forgive me, but there are men on the council who also think this way. Maybe it would be best if I met with them. Just tell me what you want me to say."

"Thank you, Señor Alcalde, for your concern. But no. It has to be done by me. Just let them know that it has nothing to do with the curse. Tell them that I want to talk to them about the future of Nueve Niños."

"Sí, Padrecito. I will tell them if that is what you wish."

The night before the meeting with the village council, the winds came up from the caldera. They were strong enough to rip up panels of corrugated tin from some of the low-slung roofs of homes and sheds close to the shoreline. Sand and grit pelted and pitted the windows of long-dead pickup trucks sitting up on gray cinder blocks in a number of side yards. Trash and debris tumbled across roads and pinned up against rusting barbed wire strung loosely between swaying fence posts.

Had Jon been able to sleep he would have been constantly awakened by the rattle of the rectory's windows and doors. As it was, he lay awake in his bed and fretted, mainly about how the council would take his news. What would they think of the plan to sell Nueve Niños? Would they bristle at the idea that outsiders were trying to cheat them out of their birthright? Or would they welcome the opportunity for a new beginning? He cringed at his words from the pulpit that encouraged such bold independence. Had he known the repercussions, he might not have been so high-minded in his determination to set history right. What possessed him, an outsider himself, to disturb the status quo? What perverseness made him think that he could hold himself up as the beacon of truth? In his need, yes *his* need, to serve, had he forgotten the recipients of this service? He would be gone from Nueve Niños in a year or so, either by will of the archbishop or because he could no longer survive in this alien place. And what would he leave behind? What was to be the legacy of Fr. Jon Armitage to the people of San Eusebio? All he knew now is that he had broken something they valued, something he did not understand, and he did not know how to fix it.

When his heart could no longer endure such ruthless self-scrutiny, he allowed the wind to take him elsewhere. To the cabin across the lake where he had gathered with his friends not long ago to drink, play cards, and forget the world. To the boat on the calm lake where his pride overcame his respect for the elements. To the darkness beneath the waters. To his fear and despair. To the bed of Cósima. To her gentle nursing. To her touch. To the only friendship he had managed to cultivate in Nueve Niños, which he had destroyed in an orgasm of self-pity.

Then he stopped thinking altogether and listened to the wind, an ill one that seemed to blow no good.

When Jon approached the home of the alcalde the next evening, he could count six men gathered in the shade of a large elm tree. They were talking and smoking and sometimes laughing, oblivious of him and obvious in their enjoyment of the moment. When they spied the priest walking toward them, they went silent. Several of them dropped their cigarettes, ground them underneath their boots, and removed their hats. Two did not. Instead, they set their jaws, puffed furiously on their smokes, and looked away.

The alcalde advanced to greet the priest. "*Buenas tardes*, Padre. It is so hot and my sala de recibir is so small that I thought we could meet under the tree. *¿Está bien?*"

"Yes, that's fine."

"Tito Chacón is in Mora for a funeral."

"As long as most of you are here."

"*Sí*, Padrecito. But Tito was one of your supporters. Now there are only two, maybe three of us."

"It doesn't matter. This has nothing to do with who agrees with me or not."

A couple of the men leaned against the tree while the rest hunkered down and pushed their hats back, ready to listen.

"*Señores del concilio*," Jon began, "thank you for meeting with me. I know you would rather be in the cool of your homes with your families right now. However, what I have to tell you is important and it can't wait. I'm sure most of you are acquainted with Dr. Wright. He owns the cabin across the lake. He and some of his friends have come to me with a proposition that would affect all of you. In fact, it would change Nueve Niños forever. They want to meet with you to discuss their ideas. Tonight I would like to spell out some of these plans so you can decide whether you want to hear what these men have to say."

The council listened without interruption as Jon described the scheme for a new Nueve Niños. When he was finished, there was much shuffling and exchanges of glances before one of the men finally spoke. His words could not have taken Jon any more by surprise had he hauled off and slapped him in the face.

"Padre, priest or no priest, I must say this to you in front of these men. We have put up with bad tempers, drunkards, womanizers, thieves, cripples, and crazies. Even someone who wanted us to dig holes to save us from the Russians. *¿No es verdad?*" A couple of the men laughed while the others nodded solemnly. "But of all the priests who have been sent to us, you are the worst. Of all of them you are the first who ever tried to betray us."

The alcalde started to protest, but Jon cut him off. "No, no, let him speak. Say what you must, señor."

The man, one who was leaning against the tree, took off his hat and fiddled with its brim. "First you rob us of our history and claim that it is for our own good. Then after you leave us with nothing, you bring in your gringo friends to rob us of our homes, our village. We've put up with a lot from you priests over the years. But this . . ."

The man, left with no more words, replaced his hat, stuffed his hands in his pants pockets, and stared at the dusky sky. There were tears of anger in his eyes.

"I am sorry you feel this way," Jon said. "I won't even try to defend myself. I have come here simply to tell you what these men have in mind. I leave the rest to you."

One of the men who was hunkered down shifted his feet to redistribute his haunches as he weighed his words. "Maybe we should listen to them. At least hear what they have to offer."

Another of the squatting council members stood up and brushed some dust from his trousers. "Benjie is right. What do we have to lose? Things are not going to get any better around here. How many of you are already thinking about moving out? We owe it to ourselves and to our families."

The alcalde spoke up. "And you, Padrecito, what do you think? These friends of yours, can we trust them?"

Jon swiped his hand through his hair. "I have already said enough. Can you trust them? They are businessmen and businessmen always look after their own business. Will they lie to you or try to cheat you? I think they are more honest than most. You may see some good coming from all of this. That is for you to decide."

When the doctor received the news from Jon that the council had agreed to meet with them, he was delighted but also apprehensive.

"How did they take it?"

"They listened, made a few comments, and went home."

"That doesn't tell me much."

"They don't trust you, if that helps."

"I hope you didn't have anything to do with that."

Jon's laugh was hollow. "If it will make you feel any better, they don't trust me much, either."

Chapter Thirty-one

Although Fr. Jon wanted to distance himself from the proceedings as much as possible, he could hardly refuse when the alcalde asked to use the rectory for the meeting with the men from Santa Fe. To better accommodate the participants, the priest arranged with the mayordomo to bring over two of the back pews from the church.

The doctor, lawyer, and banker arrived long before the scheduled four o'clock and went about arranging the props for their presentation. They came prepared to overwhelm. In addition to the architectural drawings that Jon had already seen, they set up a watercolor rendering of the resort, a beautiful and most impressive piece of work. It was as if by some magic the Emerald City had been deposited on the shores of the caldera that was, by the artist's whimsy, fringed with pine trees and looking very much the placid blue alpine lake. Another easel held a stiff placard covered with photos supplied by a manufacturer of mobile homes. The trailers in the pictures were spanking new and set in a landscape of lush lawns and flora that would never experience much less survive the rigors of New Mexico's high and dry eastern plateau. Interiors boasted of simulated wood-grain walls, sparkling kitchens and bathrooms, floral-patterned carpeting, and, by clever manipulation of a wide-angle lens, spacious living areas.

When the three men were finished with their preparations, they sat and waited. The hour of the meeting came and went. They began to check their watches. They fidgeted and spoke in whispers to each other. The banker rose to rearrange the pictures and the doctor barked at him to sit down. Through all this, Jon parked himself in the back pew and buried his nose in his breviary. It was a posture calculated to let his guests know, should there be any lingering doubts, that they must not consider him a part of their cabal.

The members of the council began to drift in. It was anyone's guess whether their tardiness was tactical or according to the practice of people who lived more by the sun and the seasons than by the clock.

Two of the villagers approached the easels but were scared away by the too eager banker who tried to engage them in conversation about the wonders of trailer living.

From the back, Jon counted the house. All seven council members were present, together with an eighth man in a dark suit carrying a briefcase. He reminded Jon of Fr. Tapia from the chancery office— young and resolute. He even wore the same kind of rimless glasses. But the resemblance ended there. This young man seemed in his element, comfortable, self-possessed, even a bit cocky.

Jon caught the doctor's eye. "I think we can start." He walked to one side where he could address the council. "Señores, these are the men from Santa Fe, Dr. Wright, Mr. Hill, and Mr. Velasco. They can tell you more about themselves. As you can see by all these displays, they are prepared to talk to you about their plans for Nueve Niños and to answer any questions you might have."

Jon introduced each of the council members. Even the announcement of their names did not stir them. They sat rigid and stone-faced in the pews as if half listening to a Sunday sermon. "And as for this gentleman," he said and nodded toward the man with the briefcase, "I'm afraid he will have to introduce himself."

The young man stood. "My name is Ernest Esquibel. I was born in Nueve Niños. My father lived here until he died. He is buried in the camposanto across the road from here. My mother still lives in their house near the lake. I am an attorney now practicing in Pueblo, Colorado. The council has asked me to attend this meeting and to be of whatever service I can."

Jon had to smile as he caught the nervous glances that the three men in front exchanged. So. The "sad inevitable" had taken a sudden turn.

The doctor recovered quickly. "Yes, yes, a good idea. We certainly want everything laid out to everyone's satisfaction. You're more than welcome, Mr. Esquibel. Our intention is to give every person here a fair and open hearing. So let's begin. Father Jon, would you care to join us in front and perhaps lead us in a prayer?"

Jon shook his head. "I'll just stay in the back out of everyone's way."

"Suit yourself then," the doctor said, none too graciously.

The men from Santa Fe had rehearsed their roles. The doctor began with an overview of the project. How he had enjoyed his cabin across the lake. How so many of his guests had expressed an interest in owning property there. How it was a shame that the natural beauty and resources of the place should lie fallow when they could be put to such good use.

When his turn came, the lawyer described the details of the project. He constantly referred to the watercolor drawing to show what a wondrous thing was in store for the new Nueve Niños. The money that would be rolling in. The jobs that would be available. The Eden that was soon to throw its gates open to all of them.

It was left to the banker to address the key issues: money and relocation. He talked about property values, the arrangements for moving the villagers, and the financial support that his bank would extend to them. To underline his points he passed out a stack of photos of mobile homes similar to the ones tacked on the easel.

"Every unit with electricity and running water."

He started to his chair and then remembered one last thing. "There are many investors lined up for this project, including several banks in Chicago and Kansas City. All they need is the word." He beamed over the audience and finally sat.

The doctor took the floor once again. "That's our story. As you can see, we do not intend to destroy Nueve Niños. We want to rebuild it. To make it something that all of us can enjoy for many years to come. Thank you for listening so patiently. Now then, it's your turn. Tell us what you think."

The alcalde stood up and cleared his throat. "Thank you very much, señores. *Muy interesante.* But there is one thing you must understand here and now."

The doctor leaned forward in his chair. "And that would be . . . ?"

"The church. It must stay where it is. If you do not agree to this, then this meeting has been for nothing."

The banker, cranking up his whine, bolted from his chair. "But that's not possible. Surely you can see that." He crossed to the easel with the watercolor. "You do understand that we will be building you another church, much closer to your new homes. A better church. Roomier. More comfortable for your families, something you can be truly proud of. Besides, our investors expect us to do other things with that property."

The young lawyer spoke from where he sat. "I'm afraid you'll have to inform your investors that there's been a change in plans. The church and the graveyard will remain where they are. Now if you will oblige us, there are some other provisions the council would like to put on the table."

The council had done some preparing of its own. It was clear that just as the men from Santa Fe had been given time without interruption to make their case, a reciprocal courtesy was now required. They were to sit and listen.

Esquibel pulled a single sheet of paper from his briefcase and handed it to the alcalde, who made a ceremony of putting on a pair of glasses before he began to read. His voice was halting at first, but steadied itself and grew strong as it gained momentum.

The points he read from the paper were succinct: the council would be supplied with a complete set of plans and drawings to be updated as necessary; the council would be given a timetable that, if approved, would be strictly adhered to except by mutual agreement; all houses and property would be appraised not at their present value but according to their projected worth to the project; the mobile homes would be purchased together at a bulk price discount that would be passed on to the occupants; and the relocation of the villagers would be given top priority, to occur in toto before any major construction began.

There were other demands, corollaries really, having mainly to do with living conditions at the trailer park—paved roads, fully maintained green belts, a community/recreation center.

The alcalde finally put down the paper. "These are the things we would like you to consider, señores. When we have reached an agreement on these matters, we can put it to the people for a vote. After that, *¿quién sabe?*"

The council had nothing more to say, and the men from Santa Fe did not know what to say. The excruciating hush over the room was mercifully broken by the honking of a flock of geese flying in the evening sky toward the caldera. Then a dog barked somewhere outside and another answered.

The doctor, by default, was left to fill the silence. "If we could have a copy of your proposal to take with us, please." Of all the bombast and bullying he might have employed, the best he could then come up with was to wish everyone a good evening. "We'll be in touch," he concluded.

After the council and its attorney had left, the doctor, the lawyer, and the banker gathered up their pictures, collapsed their easels, and rolled up their plans. When they were walking out the door, the doctor uttered his first words to Jon since the beginning of the meeting.

"You could have warned us."

"Believe me, I had no idea."

"Bullshit. You set us up."

"Believe what you like, but I had nothing to do with any of this. Interesting though. I mean how things can sometimes turn and bite you square in the ass."

Chapter Thirty-two

Dear Sally—
Nueve Niños has suddenly developed a bad case of politics.
This time I intend to stay out of it. It's those investors I told
you about who want to buy the village for a golf resort. You'd
think I'd be jumping for joy. I'm not sure what's best, so I'd
best leave it up to the people who are most involved.

I'm beginning to have a good feeling about my stay here.
Maybe you were right about God's will. And, no, you are not
a better theologian than me. The only thing you ever beat me
at was cussing.

Jon

Dear Jonny:
Finally a note (and I emphasize note) of hope from you. I
know it's been tough going but everything has its purpose.
(Wow, do I sound like Mom!) I've got to get out more.

Sally

Chapter Thirty-three

The debate among the villagers over the fate of Nueve Niños claimed center stage and Jon became the unwitting beneficiary. The controversy surrounding him was set aside. At least it was no longer talked about.

Negotiations flew furiously between the council and the consortium of the three men from Santa Fe. Tempers flared. Deliberations broke down. Major issues were sidetracked while disagreements on lesser points were blown out of proportion and took inordinate amounts of time to resolve. Small victories, small defeats. The council went to Santa Fe. The triumvirate came to Nueve Niños. The young lawyer, Ernest Esquibel, put in many billable hours between Pueblo and wherever he was summoned. This in particular stuck in the craw of the builders. They had agreed to pay his retainer since the village couldn't. Of course, he worked against his benefactors at every turn. At last, miracle of miracles, the parties agreed on a date for the election.

Jon was not privy to any of this. The doctor and his group had long since stopped thinking of the priest as an ally, and the council simply did not need him.

Only at random times did the pastor of San Eusebio find himself involved on the edges of the proceedings.

It happened, for instance, when the alcalde approached him with an inquiry. It was really more a courtesy call than a consultation.

"Padrecito, since we are not going to build a new church, we have decided to ask for some improvements to the old one. It needs a new roof and the adobe on the south side is beginning to crack and crumble. We also want to build an addition to the sacristy, a hall to meet and to hold social events in. Catechism classes for the children too. Maybe we'll even ask for a fence around the graveyard, one made of iron with a gate that has the name of the church over it. Can you think of anything else?"

"If you think you can get it, a heating and cooling system would be nice."

The alcalde smiled and winked. "Oh yes, Padrecito. I think we can get it. Look at all the money they will be saving since they don't have to build a new church."

The second time that Jon found the occasion to discuss the project came from the west, west Texas, that is.

There was this oilman from Amarillo.

He was on the prowl for investment opportunities to round out his considerable petroleum portfolio. When he got wind of the possible renaissance of Nueve Niños, his nose for financial gain began sniffing the air. At the land office in Santa Fe he found that most of the area around the caldera was part of a Spanish land grant from the days of viceroys and kings. He knew that such entities were routinely treated with suspicion in U.S. courts and that property lines and title rights were murky at best. A quick review of tax records told him that many of the assessments on Nueve Niños properties were either out-of-date or in arrears. He began to feel that certain raw hunger in his stomach that only predators can appreciate. Perhaps it was time to drop in on Nueve Niños. Let them know that there was a new player in town.

To see Jimmy Jerome's pickup truck as it pulled up to the San Eusebio rectory, one would be hard-pressed to imagine that he was one of the richest men in west Texas. Jimmy J was good ol' boy to the core. The truck was a 1952 Chevy with a bashed-in front grill and a pushed-in cab roof to match. Its dull green had long since disappeared under the dust and dirt of countless drives through the Panhandle's vast crop of oil rigs. Three large tires were stacked in the truck bed, secured in place by a sturdy chain and padlock.

The man and his truck paired well in the looks department. He wore a three-day growth of stubble on his face, a straw hat with a cracked brim, a faded checkered shirt with a torn pocket, soiled jeans that were cinched up under his overhanging belly with a wide, tarnished silver buckle, and a pair of scruffy, steel-toed work shoes. His tongue played constant games with the wad of tobacco in his mouth.

He knocked at the rectory door, and when there was no answer, he strolled along the side of the house to the back.

Fr. Jon was shoveling clods of dirt into a hole, that once-upon-a bomb shelter abutting his house. It was a job that Tobías always seemed to be working on but never with much progress.

Jimmy J touched the brim of his hat. "Howdy."

"Hello."

"You wouldn't be able to tell me where the parson is, now would you?"

"I'm the pastor of the Catholic church, if you mean me."

"Yessir, I guess I do."

Jon laid down the shovel, peeled off his work gloves, and extended his hand. "I'm Father Jon Armitage."

Jimmy Jerome still had the rough, punishing grip of his wild-catting days. "Glad to meetcha. Jimmy Jerome from Amarillo way. People call me Jimmy J. A real purty spot you got here."

"It can be."

"Get a lot of people from outside?"

"Not many. There are a couple of cabins on the other side and a few campers, but that's about it."

"Sure seems like a shame to waste it. Like I said, real purty."

With the conversation at full circle, Fr. Jon started to put his gloves back on.

Jimmy J wasn't quite done though.

"I hear all of it might be in for a few changes."

"That depends on who's talking."

"The word's out that people are coming in to redevelop the area."

Jon nodded. "There's some discussion about that."

"Well, you can't have a race with just one horse, can you?"

"I suppose not. If you have a race, that is."

"Reverend, let me lay my hand down so you can see what I'm holding. The name Jimmy J might not mean much out here, but back home it carries a little bit of weight. Oil. Lots of it. Not braggin', just sayin'. Now I'm looking to branch out. Real estate. Building. Development. Things like that."

"If you're thinking Nueve Niños, you might just be a little late."

"Or maybe just in time."

"I couldn't tell you."

"Let me ask you this. A reverend hears a lot from his flock. Don't you think they might want to hear from somebody with some different ideas?"

"I'll tell you what, Mr. Jerome . . ."

"Jimmy J, please, Reverend."

"OK, Jimmy J. You don't want to talk to me. There are other people who can help you out a lot more than I can."

"Just who might they be?"

"There's the village council. You can ask down at the general store, and they should be able to direct you to the alcalde."

"He a kind of mayor?"

"Something like that."

"And you think this al-whatchamacallit fella might be interested in hearing me out?"

"That's something you'll have to take up with him."

"Much obliged. I won't keep you from your work." He spat a dark brown effluence into the hole and wiped his chin with the bandanna that dangled from his hip pocket. "Kind of hot for this kind of digging."

"It keeps me in shape."

Jimmy J thrust out his hand. "Maybe we'll meet up again sometime. If you're ever in Amarillo, Reverend, just ask for Jimmy J."

Jon watched the oilman disappear around the side of the house. In the time it took him to slip on his gloves, pick up the shovel, and pitch another load of dirt into the hole, Jimmy J was back. This time it was not the ambling, agreeable Texan who came barreling around the corner. His red face had turned purple and his arms were beating at the air around his head as if he were fending off a swarm of yellow jackets. His mouth spewed forth a torrent of both words and tobacco juice.

"Goddammit. Goddammit to hell. Sonsabitches don't know who they're messin' with. Some Mexican's gonna end up with a butt full of buckshot."

The best that Jon could figure out from Jimmy J's ranting was that while they were having their congenial confab around the dirt pile, someone had been busy in front having their way with the truck.

It was not a pretty sight. The truck listed badly to one side where two of its wheels had been removed. The hood was up—always a gut-wrenching sight to come upon—to expose the gaping maw that had once housed a battery. The chain with its padlock was snipped neatly in two and the tires in the bed were gone. The crowning insult was the absence of the Texan's shotgun, the one with which he had just been threatening all and sundry with harm to their posteriors.

It took three hours for a service truck to come in from Clayton with two tires plus a battery. It took another hour for the pickup to be road worthy. It took ten seconds for Jimmy J to jump behind the wheel, slam the door, screech the engine to life, grind the gears, squeal his brand-new tires in a precipitous U-turn, and rumble down the road in a massive cloud of dust.

He spoke not a word, but Jon heard him declare as he drove out of sight: "Goddamn Mexican sonsabitches!"

Jon's next peripheral involvement with the proposed resort project came from yet another unexpected origination—not Texas, but somewhere just outside of the village.

One morning as usual, a line of women waited at the rectory for their rations of Jon's services and holy wares. Last in the queue to reach the pastor's desk was Dr. Ridley Ashford Fell.

The archaeologist/would-be suicide/lotus eater did not look any better or, for that matter, any worse than the last time Fr. Jon had seen him. And it appeared that he had left his brace of butcher knives at home.

"Dr. Fell. How nice to see you up and around. Interested in some candles?"

"Not today, Father, thank you, but I will keep you in mind. I am compelled to bring you news of impending calamity for the people of Nueve Niños."

"And what would that be?"

"All this talk about tearing down and rebuilding. The spirits are not happy. Sacred ground will be violated. Ancient taboos will be stirred up. The people of this godforsaken village will live to regret their actions."

"You're talking to the wrong man. Any issues concerning the resort should be taken up with the village council and the people backing the project."

"Ignoramuses, one and all. It takes men of spiritual vision like you and me to understand these things. It's up to us to put a stop to this insanity."

"Again, Doctor, you'll have better luck with the council. As much as I might appreciate your concerns over the ancient burial grounds, there's not much I can do about it. Your quarrel is with the council and the resort consortium."

"They won't listen. They never do." Fell began to pace as if he were working himself up to something.

Jon was on instant alert.

Finally the archaeologist stopped in front of the desk and pounded a fist into his open hand. "So, it appears that I'm in this alone. Very well. I see clearly now the only avenue that is open to me."

Jon's memory flashed back to gas cans, magic mushrooms, and newscasts of immolations in downtown Saigon. "Let's not go off the deep end here, Doctor. Anything you do, especially of a drastic nature, may not have the expected result. Then where will you be?"

Fell stared at the priest as if he had just been addressed in a for-eign language. "What you don't seem to appreciate, Father, is my unique position in all of this. You see, I have a special bond with the spirit world. Not only am I a scientist, but I am also a shaman, a holy man just like you. Since these desecrators will not listen to reason, I am left with but one course of action."

"Please, Doctor . . ."

"A blessing."

"Pardon me?"

"I have it in my powers to say a great prayer and make a great cleansing, one that will appease the spirits and deflect some very dire consequences that will surely overtake this land and its people if they persist in their blasphemy. It's the only way." For a split second Fell wandered off into his own little universe. "Yes, yes," he said to himself and rubbed his chin. He snapped back and continued to converse quite matter-of-factly with Jon. "And, of course, I would be willing to do so for a most reasonable fee. What would you charge for something like that? I'm thinking that five hundred dollars would not be out of line."

The last words came from Tobías.

One morning after Mass, when the two were going through their routine of folding and storing, the sacristan spoke up.

"Ay, Padrecito, *qué males piensan hacer.*"

"Who's making trouble now, Tobías?" By now Jon was used to these daily recountings by his sacristan of the foibles of the parishioners of San Eusebio.

"The people who want to change things. All this talk about selling Nueve Niños to strangers."

"It's their right if they want to. It's up to them. That's the reason for the election. Next week by this time it will be over and then we'll see."

"*Es demás.* Too much. *Es una desgracia.* All they can think about is money."

"You never know. Maybe enough people will see it your way."

"I don't think so. *Ya no tiene la gente respeto.*"

"Things change, Tobías."

"Not here. *Nunca.*"

Chapter Thirty-four

Dear Sally—
I hate it when you're right. I am learning something from my parishioners. And it doesn't hurt a bit.

Three months ago I would have sold my soul to get out of here. Now I'm not so sure. It's not what I want to do for the rest of my life, but then again, I don't know what I want to do for the rest of my life.

All that praying you've done seems to be paying off. Don't stop now!

Jon

Dear Jonny:
The praying is easy. The hard part is biting my tongue whenever I hear you falling into your old habits. You sound happy for the first time in a long, long while, including Fall River. I won't even nag you for a letter. Your little scribblings say it all.

Go somewhere with a friend and treat yourself to one of those steaks you keep bragging about. Buy me a hamburger while you're at it. All those cows back in the barn and all we get is cheese! And remember, NO ONIONS!

Sally

Chapter Thirty-five

Election day had arrived.

Weeks of negotiation had dragged on through the end of summer and well into fall until both sides hammered out an agreement that could be presented to the citizens of Nueve Niños for a vote.

When it came, the campaign for the hearts and minds of the villagers rivaled anything contrived by a Chicago ward heeler.

The consortium made sure that every voter was supplied with photos of idyllic trailer park living. They supplied every household with a list of the job opportunities that would be available as soon as the project got underway. They tacked up campaign posters with the single word *¡SÍ!* in blazing red.

Those in opposition lacked for resources, but not creativity. They circulated rumors of kickbacks that the alcalde and his supporters were receiving. They played on people's sense of ancestral pride. They vandalized the posters by painting over them with a large *¡NO!* in black.

It was impossible to divine which way many of the villagers were leaning. For the most part they held their counsel while seeming to agree with whoever last solicited their votes.

"Sí, sí, *es una cosa muy buena*," they would say, or "No, no, *es mala idea*," and walk away, satisfied that they had hurt no one's feelings. Meanwhile the campaigner was equally satisfied that another vote had been secured.

Lawyers on both sides of the issue formulated a ballot question that they presented to the state election commission. The commission declared the referendum legal and binding on all parties and set a date for the balloting. A reluctant and very minor election official was dispatched to Nueve Niños to serve as poll judge.

There was one polling station, the back room of the general store. There, a bedsheet was stretched across one corner for a voting booth. A slotted box sat on a table by the door to receive the votes. This table was to be manned by the state official to take down names, pass out ballots, direct voters to the bedsheet, and monitor the proper folding of the paper and its insertion into the slot on the top of the box.

The day took on many of the trappings of the fiesta of San Eusebio. Women commandeered the booths that were still standing in the square and began to prepare grills so they could cook green chile burgers. They would soon be joined by others who would serve up tamales steaming in their husks from pots covered with hot towels.

People milled about. There were some last-minute arm twistings that still did not offer up a clear trend on how the voting would go.

The doctor, lawyer, and banker set up a command post in the doctor's cabin. From there they drove back and forth to Nueve Niños to consult with their supporters and to try to come up with strategies to sway the last of the undecideds.

Fr. Jon sequestered himself in the rectory.

Tobías sat at the lake's edge about a half mile out of town. He was ready to launch his plan.

The sacristan had a secret, one he had never divulged to anyone, not even Fr. Jon. He had never known why he had kept the information to himself. It just seemed the thing to do. But now it was perfectly clear to him. San Eusebio had guided him to keep his secret for just the right moment.

And what was this secret? It was locked up in a small room just off the vestibule of the church. The room, not much more than a large closet, contained a ladder that led up to a trapdoor that opened onto the belfry. Tobías kept the room locked and there were no extra keys. Tobías was the bell ringer and no one must usurp the privilege. Not the priest, not the mayordomo, and God forbid, not any young mischief maker who might find the ringing of the bell in the dead of night too tempting a shenanigan to resist.

And Tobías's secret, even more of a sacred trust than the guarding of the bell? There, propped next to the ladder, was the small, flat-bottomed boat that the first pastor of San Eusebio, Father Jean Baptiste L'Cote, had built and used to gather fish for his flock.

The boat had seen better days. Its leather fittings had cracked and shredded. Many of the wooden pegs that held it together had rotted or wobbled in their holes to the touch. There were seams where boards separated. But all in all and with a little work, Tobías felt he could make the boat lake-worthy again.

His plan for the boat had hatched the very morning he spoke to Fr. Jon in the sacristy to vent his feelings about the resort. When *el padrecito* dismissed his concerns, it became obvious that it would be up to him alone to put a halt to the foolishness. After the priest returned to the rectory for his morning coffee, Tobías lit a candle at the side altar and knelt to pray at the statue of San Eusebio. Something had to be done. But what? Please help me, San Eusebio. I am so slow. I am not clever. Give me some help. Then the inspiration came. There was only one way to keep things as they were, and that was to make things as they had been. What was it that had started everything? El padrecito's sermon, of course. He meant good, Tobías reasoned, but it had turned bad. This made it clear to the sacristan that he would have to reinstitute the curse.

Late that same night, when Nueve Niños had bedded down and the only sounds were the barking of dogs and the occasional squawk from a water fowl on the lake, Tobías drove his mother's 1949 Studebaker to the side of the church. There, in the darkness and amid many struggles, he managed to haul Padre Juan's boat out of its hiding place and lash it to the roof of the car. At his mother's house he reversed the process, again with many struggles, and dragged the boat into the front room. It was not a large boat, but then again it was not a large room. Until the day of reckoning, Tobías had to step into the boat every time he moved from his kitchen to his bedroom.

The next day he drove into Clayton and purchased of spool of 20-gauge wire, two square yards of canvas, a pound of nails, a jar of wood filler, and a can of paint.

For the next two weeks Tobías was nowhere to be seen except at morning Mass and to ring the Angelus at 12:00 noon and 6:00 p.m. The women who were so used to his company over coffee and gossip wondered where he was keeping himself. At least they knew from his sightings at the church that he was neither sick nor dead, so they let it pass and in a few days stopped missing him.

Tobías worked steadily on the renovation of the boat. He gouged out the pegs and filled in the holes with the putty. He wrapped split boards tightly with the wire and hammered them back in place with shiny new nails. He cut strips of canvas and stuffed them into the gaps where the planking had separated. He brought home a bucket filled with discarded pieces of candle from the church, melted down the stubs on his stove, and caulked every seam with fragrant bees-wax. Finally, when the work of restoration was done, he painted the entire boat a pale blue, the color of Our Lady's mantle.

Satisfied with the job he had done, Tobías sat in the boat by the hour and worked out the finer details of his plan.

Early in the morning of election day when nothing was yet stirring, Tobías once again tied the boat to the roof of his mother's car and drove out of the village on the lake road. After a few hundred yards he left the road and pulled up behind a sand hill. The mound was not very high but sufficient to hide his activities from the prying eyes of any villager.

He undid the ropes and pulled the boat carefully off the top of the car. He pushed it and pulled on it and lamented his stupidity for not having parked closer to the water. Finally he reached the lake's edge, sat on the ground behind the boat, planted his feet on the prow, and with one last mighty push launched the vessel. It slid into the water, rocked back and forth for a moment, and then, wonder of wonders, floated and rocked gently on the ripples that were wash-ing on to the shore.

Tobías put his hands to his chubby cheeks and laughed with delight. Then he stood up and began to prance around in an awk-ward little dance. He splashed into the lake to his ankles and ran back to shore, shouting, crying, giggling, cheering.

When he was done with his celebrations, he played out a long piece of rope tied to one of the cross boards and tied the other end securely to a half-buried piece of driftwood. A closer inspection showed him that the boat displayed no signs of taking on water. The beeswaxed seams were holding and Padre Juan's boat was back once more where it belonged. What better sign of the righteousness of his mission could he ask for?

Tobías checked the knot on the mooring rope one last time before he climbed into the Studebaker and drove back into the village. It was almost time to ring the first bell for morning Mass.

Only two people were lined up at the rectory in need of Fr. Jon's services that morning. Since he had no intention of showing his face anywhere near the polling place, he would have the rest of the day to himself. It was a good time to take advantage of the solitude for some quiet reading. He thumbed through the tables of contents of several theological journals. "The Impact of the Parousia on the Evangelization of Asia Minor," he read. Yeah, that would really help him be a better pastor. He finally decided to indulge in a romp through a novel he had purchased before he left Santa Fe. Ten pages in, he was interrupted by a banging and shouting at his front door. He opened it to two breathless boys standing on the stoop, jabbering at him. Something about the lake, a boat, Tobías, and San Eusebio.

"Slow down. Catch your breaths."

The boys obeyed and stood there panting like little dogs that had just been taken for a very long run on very short legs.

"Now, tell me slowly. What about Tobías and a boat?"

The older of the two boys took the lead.

"Tobías is out on the lake and he's got the santo of San Eusebio.

He's shouting a lot of things but I don't know what. The alcalde told us to come and get you."

❖

The excitement of the election was about to take a backseat to the spectacle now unfolding on the caldera. Practically everyone in the village had gathered on the shore.

The crowd parted to let their priest pass through. At the water's edge the alcalde joined him. They both stood for a moment taking in the sight of Tobías sitting in the ancient craft about a hundred yards out.

"What's this all about?" Jon asked.

"*¿Quién sabe*, Padre? Someone came to tell me that Tobías was rowing a boat on the lake. They saw him coming from the other side of that little hill over there. By the time I got here he had stopped where you see him. He's been shouting *tonterías* ever since. Then he stands up and holds up the santo and waves it at us. *Está bien loco.*"

"What's he saying?"

"He's talking about the curse and how we're going to be more cursed than before. Crazy things like that."

"What does he want?"

The alcalde stuck out his lower lip and shrugged. "I don't know. He keeps saying that we want to change things and that God will punish us."

"Oh, great." Fr. Jon made a megaphone of his hands and shouted, "Tobías! Tobías!" There was no response. "Tobías. It's Father Jon. Talk to me."

Tobías raised his head, which had been bowed, and his words, faint but distinct, came over the water. "Padrecito. You tell them."

"Tell them what?"

"Tell them they are evil."

"Why?"

"They want to change things."

"Maybe yes. Maybe no."

"*Ya no creen en la maldición.*"

"Tobías, that's over with."

"I will make another one."

"Don't be foolish, Tobías. You can't make a curse."

"I can if San Eusebio helps me." The sacristan raised the wooden statue high above his head.

Jon was getting hoarse from all the yelling. "Row in, Tobías. Then we can talk."

"No! *El santo y yo.* We will go to the bottom of the lake together."

Just as Jon was about to respond, Dr. Wright elbowed his way to the priest's side.

"What the devil are you trying to pull here?"

"What?"

"What cheap trick have you come up with?"

"What do you mean?"

"These people are supposed to be getting ready for an election. This isn't going to stop us, you know."

"You think I staged this?"

"That's your man out there, isn't it?"

Jon leaned in so only the doctor could hear him. "Doctor, for once in your life, shut the hell up."

"Padre, Padre, *mira, mira,*" someone from the crowd called out.

Tobías was standing up and raising and dropping the statue in front of him like a priest presenting a chalice during the Eucharist. The boat began to list side to side, making it harder and harder for the sacristan to maintain his balance.

"Sit down, Tobías, sit down!" Jon shouted.

Tobías started to squat, lurched sideways, made a futile effort to grab the side of the boat, and went over into the water. The statue flew in a high arc and kerplunked in on top of him. For a moment Jon could see nothing out there but the rocking boat, then the statue bobbed to the surface, immediately followed by Tobías's head. The sacristan hooked one arm over the boat's side and wrapped the statue in the other. He made several attempts to hoist himself up, but fell back each time. Finally he stopped trying and simply hung there.

"Tobías, let go of the statue," Jon called to him.

Whether the sacristan heard or not, he kept his stranglehold on the santo.

Jon turned to the alcalde. "Does anyone in the village own a boat of any kind?"

The alcalde seemed momentarily thrown by the question. Did the priest not realize that these were people of the land? They had nothing to do with the lake, even though it was the most looming presence in their lives. "No. No one here," he finally answered. "We never needed one."

Jon turned his attention to the doctor. "You still have that aluminum canoe at your cabin?"

The doctor nodded. "We found it beached the day we were looking for you."

"Go get it. And hurry. He can't hold on out there very long."

By this time several women were weeping. A few of them dropped to their knees and began to pray.

The priest returned his attention to the lake. "Hold on, Tobías. Help is coming."

Jon could see a dust cloud rising on the caldera road. The doctor was on his way. The priest did some calculating. Ten minutes to get to the cabin. Another ten or fifteen to load up the canoe. Ten minutes back. Ten minutes to unload, launch, and row to Tobías. More than half an hour of precious time. It wasn't going to work. Tobías could not hold on that long, not in his condition. And who knew what the cumulative effect of being in the water was having on him?

Fr. Jon began to strip.

"¿Qué haces, Padre?" the alcalde asked.

"There's no time," Jon responded as he kicked off his shoes.

Some of the more modest in the crowd averted their eyes or turned their children away. Most, however, gaped to see their priest down to his skivvies and wading out into the lake.

When Jon was waist-deep, he stretched out and began his kick and stroke. The water was colder than he remembered it. He could feel the familiar undertow, but now it was working with him and he glided across the surface with surprising ease. Sixty yards. Forty yards. Thirty. He was soon close enough to the sacristan to hear his labored breath and the chattering of his teeth. The chill of the water was beginning to take its toll.

"Steady, Tobías," Jon said. "I'm almost to you."

When Jon touched the side of the boat, he heard distant cheers from the shore. He reached one arm around Tobías to support him, buried his head in the crook of the sacristan's neck, and worked the air back into his lungs.

"You OK?" he finally managed.

Tobías nodded.

"Let's just relax here for a minute, and then we'll see what we can do to get you back in the boat."

"I'm sorry, Padrecito. I have caused you so much trouble."

"Don't talk. Just rest."

The two men hung there for several minutes until Jon felt his reserves kick in.

"The first thing we have to do is get rid of the statue. Give it to me and I'll put it back in the boat."

Tobías tightened his arm around the santo and shook his head.

"You have to do this. Otherwise I can't help you."

"San Eusebio tiene negocios conmigo."

Jon put a hand on the statue. "Tobías, you have no business to do with the santo. He is not yours. You stole him. And that's a sin."

During all his plotting with San Eusebio, Tobías had not considered the moral implications of his plan. His only concern was the final outcome. Now the priest had posed an entirely new set of problems for him. Stealing was a sin. He was no thief; nor did he ever intend to become one. Slowly he released the statue. Jon took it and slipped it up and over into the boat where it landed with a leaden thump.

"Now, Tobías, listen carefully to me. I'm going to let go of you. Then I'm going to duck into the water and swim up under you to push you back up into the boat. But I can't do it without you. You've got to help lift yourself. You think you can manage that?"

"Oh, Padrecito." Tobías started to cry.

"Not now, Tobías. Save your energy. You have to concentrate. I'm going to count to three and go under. Be ready. The instant you feel me pushing at you, try to pull yourself up. Understand?"

The sacristan sniffled and nodded. "Sí, Padre."

"Good. Ready? Here we go. One . . . two . . . three."

Jon took a final breath, lifted his arms to the sky, and sank from view. Now completely submerged, the priest maneuvered himself directly beneath Tobías. Please be ready, he prayed. He kicked furiously and came shooting up so that one shoulder caught the sacristan in the rear and lifted him. Suddenly Tobías's weight was off him and he could see the sacristan's legs dangling comically in the air. By the time Jon surfaced, Tobías was hauling the last of himself into the boat. Then he sat in a heap with his lips puckered to suck in air like a fish netted and pulled in by Padre Juan.

Jon grabbed the edge of the boat and rested. "Tobías?" he finally called.

The face of the sacristan peered over the edge. His hair was pasted to his skull and his eyes were swollen and red.

Jon smiled at him. "Good job. That was the hard part. Now, let's get back to land."

"No, Padrecito. I must finish what I started."

"After all this? You can't be serious."

"You are right, Padrecito. The San Eusebio cannot go with me. He is not mine. But I can still do what I have to do."

"And what is it that you have to do?"

"I am going to the middle of the lake to jump in. I will give them a new curse to think about."

"It's over, Tobías. The curse is no more. It never was. Most of the people never believed in it anyway. It was just something to hold on to, to talk about."

Tobías grew angry. "No, no, no. I will make it like it was. I will offer my life for the people."

"You already did that once. You even have the medals to prove it. That's enough sacrifice for any man. And don't forget about Danny García. You buried him. Only you, of everyone in Nueve Niños, know what he went through. But if you die, Danny dies twice. Is that any way to treat a fellow marine?"

Tobías's eyes grew sad even as he managed a smile. "Danny was a good boy. I taught him how to serve Mass. He never made fun of me."

"Besides, Tobías, you forget that taking your own life would be a sin too. You can return the santo and be forgiven. But if you kill yourself, who can you confess to? San Eusebio will be very angry with you. And God will turn his face from you and never look at you again."

Tobías slumped so that his head rested on the back of Jon's hand. "*Ay, Dios, ay Dios*," he cried. Finally he looked at Jon. "Will you give me the forgiveness, Padrecito?"

The water was getting uncomfortable and Jon was beginning to lose patience. "Yes, Tobías, I will give you the forgiveness. But you have to promise. No more talk about jumping in the lake."

Tobías nodded and tried with little success to brush away the tears with his sodden sleeve.

Jon reached out and made the sign of the cross over the sacristan's bent head. "*Ego te absolve ab omnibus peccatis tuis, in nomine Patris, et Filii, et Spiritus Sancti.*"

When the formula was done, Tobías signed himself and bowed to kiss Jon's hand. "Amen," he said. "Amen."

The irony of the moment was not lost on Fr. Armitage. He suddenly realized that this was the first time in his entire priesthood, with all his training, with all his posturings, with all his grand ambitions, that he had ever really touched a soul.

"Good, then," he said. "What say you we get back on shore and into some warm clothes?"

"Sí, Padrecito."

"The boat is too small for both of us. Here's what we do. You paddle, and I'll push from the back."

"*Lo que usted dice*, Padrecito."

"The current is against us and the wind is starting to pick up. We're going to have to work a little bit. But don't worry. We can stop and rest whenever you say."

"Sí, Padre. *Está bien. Vámonos a la casa.*"

And so the two began their voyage home across the caldera.

Jon soon realized how right he had been to warn Tobías about how hard the going might be. Every yard won was hard fought, and he now had cause to recall how relentless and grasping the undertow could be.

The priest began to tire and the muscles in his arms and legs tightened. He wanted to stop, but Tobías seemed so invigorated and attacked the water with his paddle with such savagery, bent on showing that he could pull his own weight.

Only a few more stokes, then he'd have to ask Tobías to stop. How heavy his legs were beginning to feel. And the water was getting so cold, cold. He closed his eyes and the darkness brought it all back to him. The greed of the water. The isolation. The loss of self. He thought he heard a voice, but discounted it as the slapping of the waves against the boat or perhaps the growing sound of the wind in his ears.

"Let's stop for a minute, Tobías," he called out, but the sacristan could not hear him over the splashing of the paddle and the accelerating groan of the wind.

Try as he might, Jon could no longer hold on. His hands slipped from the boat and he was suspended in the infinity of the caldera. A small wave swept over him and he came up coughing. Tobías and the boat were now out of reach. He felt a touch to his thigh, gentle like Cósima's. But this time he was no surrogate for a dead and buried husband. This time, the touch was meant for him. He tried to kick at the water and move his arms to catch up, but his arms had nothing left in them.

He felt his toes contracting before the pain traveled up his calves to his thighs and torso until his back arched involuntarily and his entire body began to convulse in an indescribable wave of cramping muscle. Just as suddenly the pain passed and he was calm. Calm enough to hear the voice, for this time he knew it really was a voice. It was his own.

"Oh, Sweet Jesus . . ."

And then it was joined by another voice coming from deep within the watery womb of the caldera.

"Jon."

Chapter Thirty-six

There was no question but that the election would be canceled for that day. Even the resort consortium agreed that things should be held up until the authorities had an opportunity to try to recover the body. It was seemly, not to mention good politics.

There was also an additional consideration. No sooner had the villagers pulled Tobías to shore than the wind started up with such a fury that even the oldest citizens of Nueve Niños could recall nothing like it. It was merciless, and the worst was the sand and grit. They began their dance as nervous, ground-churning swells that snapped and bit into anything that offered resistance. Soon they formed a massive column that rose higher and higher to dull the sun to a pumpkin orange, and eventually settled back to earth, a dry, itchy blanket that gave neither warmth nor comfort. Not only that, but the blowing continued for a full seven days, another phenomenon that was new even to the old ones.

People stayed indoors except when the *basines* were filled and someone had to carry them out to empty. Those who preferred the privy to the chamber pot paid dearly for their fastidiousness. They stumbled out into a brown wall of swirling dirt, fought for every inch of headway, and struggled even to open the rustic cubicle. More than once a door was ripped clean off its hinges and cartwheeled out of sight.

Any kind of dragging effort on the lake was unthinkable. The Union County Sheriff's Department and the state patrol remained on call.

The doctor and his friends made a near hostage of the election official for three days.

"I'll call the secretary of state to explain the situation. She's a good friend. And don't worry," he added. "I've been through lots of these. They usually blow out overnight."

But cabin fever finally took its toll.

"Let us know when you're ready," the official said and stumbled to his car for a quick getaway.

The winds were terrifying enough to send old women to their windows where, in expiation, they placed saucerfuls of smoldering pine needles blessed on Palm Sunday. Others turned their statues of St. Anthony to the wall. "And there you will stay," they said, "until you rid us of this storm."

Then one old crone said the word, *maldición*, and it spread through the village, through sealed windows, under doors, and into houses, like a biblical plague.

"The curse. The lake has taken another of our priests."

On the eighth day, the wind blew itself out. On the ninth, tenth, and eleventh days recovery teams took to their boats, tossed their grappling hooks overboard, and plowed the caldera's bottom. By this time, given the contrary nature of the caldera's currents, they knew that their task was hopeless. On the twelfth day they gave up the search.

A week later Nueve Niños had its election.

Those in opposition made political hay with their pastor's demise.

"He was against it," they said. "Why do you think that he never spoke in favor of it?"

"He caused the wind storm," they said. "Why else did it start at the very instant he drowned?"

But even the invocation of the priest's name and memory could not win the day. By a narrow vote, the referendum passed. Nueve Niños was open for business.

Chapter Thirty-seven

Dear Jonny:
Where are you? Even a postcard would be better than
nothing.

Forget what I said about your picture in my brain and
your memory in my heart. I need to hear from you.

And yes, I miss you too. A lot.

Sally

Chapter Thirty-eight

Dr. Wright never lived to see his dream come to fruition. Six months into the project he suffered a massive heart attack while inspecting the construction site. By the time the ambulance arrived from Raton, there was nothing for the medics to do but strap him to a gurney, throw a blanket over him, and take him away.

Dr. Ridley Fell was unable to convince anyone of his powers over the ancient spirits, so his shamanic services were never enlisted. He cut his price several times, but even that didn't work. So he would come daily and rain imprecations on the workers. Most ignored him. Some felt sorry for him or were amused by his ranting and invited him to share from their lunch pails and to have a beer or two with them. He was never without a story and paid for his food and drink by regaling his hosts with accounts of spirits, both the benevolent ones and those dedicated to mischief making.

One night a patron approached Cósima's door only to find it wide open. When he entered, it was apparent that she no longer lived there. No one ever found out where Cósima had gone. But now women lay restless next to their husbands wondering who their men would seek out on their trips to Clayton, Springer, and Raton.

❖

Mother Providenza was considered a saint to her nuns and to the townspeople who lived around the convent of San Giacomo della Valle on the outskirts of Verona. Not that she had ever performed any healings or claimed any visions. It was just that she was so kind and helpful that how could she not be a saint?

Silvio Tuffone, from the Italian Ministry of Culture, found her to be exactly as advertised when he visited the convent.

Tuffone was making a tour of the area to inventory all the artwork he could find. Such a catalog was long in coming. It had been estimated that Italy held a disproportionate percentage of the Western world's cultural treasures. Perhaps, the authorities opined, it would be a good idea to find out exactly what and where these treasures were.

Mother Providenza was as kindly and helpful as ever. She personally took Tuffone through the convent to show him what they had.

When they came to a wall, blank except for two squarish discolorations, Tuffone inquired as to what had hung there to create these shapes.

The Reverend Mother eagerly recounted the philanthropy of a monsignor from America, even though he was Italian, who had purchased a new stove for them and how they had pressed on him two small oil paintings that he had admired.

He visited other places around here too, she volunteered, and was always so generous. *Che regali!* One would have thought it was the feast of the Three Kings. A refrigerator for the convent of Santa Giuliana. Desks for a school. A water heater for an orphanage.

Tuffone was scribbling furiously. "And did they give him paintings too?"

"I certainly hope so. There are so many of them around these parts. We hardly miss them."

"Madre, mi dica. Questo monsignore. Do you have a name? An address?"

Mother Providenza blushed. "My memory is not what it used to be. But I think I have a letter from him. Would that be useful?"

Five minutes later, Signore Tuffone was holding in his hands a typewritten letter with the coat of arms of the Archdiocese of Santa Fe emblazoned on top. At the bottom was the name, address, and telephone number of one Amleto Montini.

As it turned out, the Nueve Niños project was badly underfunded, especially when a major investor bowed out, soon to be followed by others. Plans had to be scaled back and eventually scuttled. The trailer park was up and running, of course, since it was the first thing to be built. And there was a marina, a bait and fishing supply store, and a few bungalows along the lake. Construction on the main building never progressed beyond the pouring of its massive foundation. The golf course never got beyond the surveyor's stakes.

Some of the villagers took the money they made from their properties and hightailed it out of town. Others took up residence in their mobile homes that never met the promise of those beautiful photographs. At least, the people consoled themselves, living on the far side of the nine cones gave them some protection from the winds.

After a ten-month hiatus the new pastor of San Eusebio arrived. It was Father Tapia, lately the archbishop's secretary. It seems that in his twilight as chancellor, Monsignor Montini had become so paranoid that almost all of the chancery staff was replaced. Fr. Tapia was doubly suspect because he had the run of the office and who knew what possibly damaging information he had squirreled away.

Fr. Tapia was the last pastor of Nueve Niños. The archbishop reluctantly decided that using the parish as a penal institution for recalcitrant or damaged clergy was no longer practical. There were too many other holes to fill and, as he was still fond of saying about his priests, "If they can breathe . . ."

Archbishop Duggan informed the bishop of Fall River of the death of Fr. Armitage.

"Too bad," the prelate said. "A good man. Just a little too full of himself."

When the Mother Abbess broke the news to Sally, she bowed her head, put her hands underneath her scapular, and excused herself. "Oh, Jonny," she repeated to herself over and over at Vespers that evening. And finally she said, "Give Mom and Dad a big hug for me."

Tobías stayed on as sacristan of San Eusebio. He rang the bell every day and kept the sacristy in perfect order. He cared for the grave of Danny García and the five priests who had been buried there. He found a smooth piece of flagstone on which he painted the name *Padre Jon* in the blue color of the Virgin Mary's mantle and set it upright next to the church entrance. Every six months or so he had to retouch the markings since the sun and wind seemed determined to erase the words.

There was no more talk of curses and miracles.

Everything had changed.

Epilogue

Yahweh had arranged that a great fish should be there to
swallow Jonah: and Jonah remained in the belly of
the fish for three days and three nights. From the
belly of the fish he prayed to Yahweh, his God:

"Out of my distress I cried to Yahweh
and he answered me;
from the belly of Sheol I cried,
and you have heard my voice.
You cast me into the abyss, into the heart of the sea,
and the flood surrounded me.
And your waves, your billows
washed over me.
And I said: I am cast out
from your sight.
How shall I ever look again
at your holy Temple?
The waters surrounded me right to my throat,
the abyss was all around me.
The seaweed was wrapped round my head
at the roots of the mountains.
I went down into the countries beneath the earth,
to the peoples of the past.
But you lifted my life from the pit,

Yahweh, my God.
While my soul was fainting within me,
I remembered Yahweh,
and my prayer came before you
into your holy Temple.
Those who serve worthless idols
forfeit the grace that was theirs.
But I, with a song of praise,
will sacrifice to you.
The vow I have made, I will fulfill."

And Yahweh spoke to the fish, which then vomited
Jonah onto the shore.

—The Book of Jonah 2:1–11